THE LAST DAY
OF TERM

THE LAST DAY OF TERM

FRANCIS GILBERT

First published in 2011 by

Short Books
3A Exmouth House
Pine Street
EC1R 0JH

10 9 8 7 6 5 4 3 2 1

A CIP catalogue record for this book is available from the British Library.

ISBN 978-1-906021-51-1

Printed in Great Britain by Clays

Cover illustration: Mark Ecob

To all the
Heroic teachers I've
Ever met and the students who've been
On the ball

To-morrow, and to-morrow, and to-morrow,
Creeps in this petty pace from day to day,
To the last syllable of recorded time;
And all our yesterdays have lighted fools
The way to dusty death. Out, out, brief candle!
Life's but a walking shadow, a poor player,
That struts and frets his hour upon the stage,
And then is heard no more. It is a tale
Told by an idiot, full of sound and fury,
Signifying nothing.

Macbeth by William Shakespeare, Act 5, Scene 5

The truth is rarely pure and never simple.

The Importance of Being Earnest by Oscar Wilde.

Hickory dickory dock
The mouse ran up the clock
The clock struck one
The mouse ran down
Hickory dickory dock

20th July

12.01am

To: *helen.hick@cityhealthtrust.gov.uk*
From: *m.hick@gildaballacademy.co.uk*

Dear Helen,
  It feels weird writing this when you're upstairs probably pretending to sleep and I'm sitting here at my desk, but it's so hard saying the right words to your face.
  Helen, Helen, let's not fight anymore. Let's not...
  Do you remember how it was when we were young? Do you remember how in love we were, driving around Scotland in my Beetle, swimming in the sea at Uist, running about on those empty beaches, cooking fish in the sand dunes? Do you remember that time I swam out to sea and the seal's head popped up next to me, and the seal and I looked at each other and I thought he was another human being, and he thought I was another seal and then both of us realised that we were different species and we screamed at each other, diving away?

Do you remember how fearless you were? How we kissed, your breasts pressed up against my chest?

My head is full of the sunshine of that windy summer.

I'm sorry, I just can't do what you ask. The school needs me more than ever. I won't end up like Jack. I'll be fine. And we'll be fine.

Let's go to Scotland again when you get back from your conference this summer. Let's leave the kids with your mum for a few days and head north. Let's make things better. I love you, Helen. I adore you.

I'm sorry for the things I said. You're a good person and I love you.

Please forgive me,

I love you, Helen!
Martin

I click 'Send', switch off the computer and sit thinking for a moment. The lights of the city ripple over the ceiling, but everything else is shrouded in darkness. There's no way I'm going to be able to sleep.

12.05am

Top 5 things to do before I die

1. Wear a disguise that will fool Ma.
2. Become a great detective.
3. FIND OUT MY HEADTEACHER'S PASSWORD!

4. Fuck a fair maiden, well, any maiden…
5. Compose a concerto for harp, guitar and castanets.

"Béla!, Béla! You must come here now!"

"Yes, Ma, I'll be right there, I promise."

I am crouching over my old laptop. The password quivers in the tips of my fingers. I type it quickly: "Arsenal1989".

Oh-My-God, I cannot begin to express the joy I feel when I see the screen change to white and the lozenge start to fill with blue.

I'm in! Finally, after so much trying, I've done it!

"Béla! I need you right now!" Ma's voice is hoarse with impatience in the kitchen. In a minute, she'll come into the room and haul me away from the screen by the ear.

"Yes, Ma, I'm coming. I promise."

I stand up, transfixed by the unfurling screen. This email account is a personal one, a very personal one. My eyes widen. It's full of emails to one Mrs Helen Hick.

Fuck. Not what I expected at all.

I open a thread.

Helen, I'd really like to talk to you about the autopsy. Just between you and me. Sam.

Then an email dated a few days later:

Helen, I had to say it. I am not going to apologise for my feelings. I had to. Sam.

A day later:

> You are the only one I've thought of. You are. Let's meet
> in Daquise, the Polish restaurant by the Royal Albert Hall.
> It's well away from everyone and we can walk in Hyde Park
> afterwards. Looks like it's going to be a nice evening.
> Sam x☺.

Three days later:

> I love you. You give meaning to this nightmare. You do. I can
> carry on now that you've given me the right medicine. I love
> you! Sam xxx.

One day later:

> You've made me the happiest man in the universe. Happy to
> have an examination any day. xxxx

I open another:

> I need you to strangle me with your stethoscope.

Another:

> Champers, M&S sarnies, usual place? I'll text you.

Although the earlier emails are comprehensible,
the later ones confuse and alarm me. Why would my
headteacher want Mrs Hick to give him an examination

– is he ill? I know Mrs Hick is a doctor but she's a hospital doctor as far as I know – is Ndlova really her patient? And to be strangled by a stethoscope, that's just *random*.

Plus, what is "champers"? And what's so great about M&S sarnies?

It's just weird, plain fucking weird that my old headteacher would be talking to her like that.

"Béla János Pongrácz! This is an order, you must come now!" Ma screeches from the kitchen. I can hear her wheelchair scuffling over the carpet. I slam down the lid of the laptop and make my way towards the kitchen, my head full of sticks and sarnies and Mrs Hick.

12.15am

I head out of the house, trying my best to shut the front door quietly. But evidently not quietly enough because once I'm at the top of our street, I see my son, rushing towards me in his leather jacket and pyjama bottoms, shouting out in his broken voice: "Dad, Dad! Come back!"

He reaches me quickly, emitting the pungent odour of marijuana smoke and anxiety.

I hesitate for a moment, deciding whether I should snap – or smile. I decide upon the latter option.

"Have you been smoking dope, Josh?" I ask.

He sighs, flicks his long fringe out of his face and says: "Dad, where are you going?"

I look down at his bare, hairy feet planted before

me on the littered pavement.

"You didn't answer my question. Have you been smoking?"

"It doesn't matter, Dad. It really doesn't. What matters is where the fuck you're going."

His pupils are pinpricks and his cheeks are sweaty. His leather jacket is covered in badges that are either angels or harps. He looks a real mess.

"Josh, you've got no shoes on! There's dog shit everywhere!"

There's a breeze blowing. Even though he's sweating, he's shivering; his flesh goose-pimples making the black hairs on his feet prickle as if they have a life of their own. He folds his arms. He says: "Dad, you mustn't go. You mustn't."

Ignoring the strong smell of dope, I put my arm around him and pull his bony frame into my belly. I feel the top of his shoulders poke into my ribcage, as I nuzzle his brown hair with my nose and whisper as calmly as I can: "Joshy, I'm not going anywhere. I'm just going for a walk."

"At midnight?"

"I need some air."

"Dad, you can't go. You can't." His upper row of teeth digs into his lower lip.

"Josh, you have to go to bed now. You've got school tomorrow."

"So have you."

"Yes, but it's different."

"Just come back home, Dad, please!" he insists.

I sigh but I don't flip. I'm sober enough to know I'm drunk; I manage to enunciate my words slowly and clearly: "Josh, I'm not going to argue. You need to turn around and let me get some air."

"Dad, you've got to come back and say you're sorry."

I tighten my hands into fists and bury them in the pockets of my chinos.

"Josh, could you please just let me have a walk by myself?"

"It's not safe at this time, Dad."

"It's not safe for you, walking in bare feet and stoned out of your head!"

Before he can say any more, I take my boy in my arms and lift him up in much the same way I used to when he was younger. Although he's tall and big and hairy now, he's surprisingly light for a fifteen-year-old.

"Upsy-daisy!" I exclaim.

"Dad, let me down!" he says, kicking his feet a little.

The advantage of having a large paunch is that I can rest a good part of him on my stomach.

"Here we go!" I say, laughing.

"Dad, you'll break your back!" he says, but it's clear he's enjoying the ride.

"No! I won't because I am SUPER-DAD!"

Josh laughs again. This time louder. The bristles on his chin tickle my cheek as I hoik him back to our house and plonk him down on the mat. The door to the house is still open. Although I'm out of breath, I walk off at a fair clip, leaving him there in the lighted threshold.

Ahead of me, I can see the lights of Hackney Road; girls in tiny black dresses and high heels are tottering towards the clubs; cab drivers are hovering around their bust-up cars, smoking; meaty arms are taking large knives to kebab-meat on the spit roast and slicing off the processed flesh.

12.30am

"Ma, what is champers?"

Ma twirls a cigarette in my direction and chortles a little. "Béla, it's not time to break it open yet."

"Yes, but what is it?"

"It's Champagne, you ignoramus."

I bow my head in shame. I am sixteen – legally an adult – and yet I am very ignorant.

"The boy is not living in a cultured environment," my great-uncle says in his customary sarcastic way.

"But why are we talking about champers, when you are not changed for your audition!" Ma barks before puffing again on her cigarette. "Why do you never listen?"

"Is this a proper audition?" I gulp.

Ma always holds "auditions" when there's something important about to happen. Well, she calls them "auditions" because it makes her feel like a dreadfully prestigious impresario, but they are more like what Mr Hick would call "speaking and listening assessments". My top "auditions" so far are:

1. Playing an "English boy" on the night before we

moved to London for good from Budapest.

2. Reassuring her that I will get A*s in all my GCSEs.

3. Proving to her that I never threw that firework.

Tonight's audition is perhaps one of the most important I've ever taken: I need to prove that I can help her with her disability benefit claim.

"I'm on the case!" I say. I jump up and return to the bedroom.

But once I'm there I can't help getting distracted by my laptop. I glance at the emails again. Why would Mrs Hick talk to Mr Ndlova like that? Why? Are they having an affair? I find the whole thing so distracting that I'm just standing in the middle of the room staring at the computer rather than getting changed.

Then I hear Ma's wheelchair moving towards the bedroom. She's going to check on me in a minute. I shut down the laptop and start rooting around my "disguises" drawer.

I have to concentrate! I have to be on top form if I am going to pass one of Ma's auditions. I replace my freshly pressed magenta corduroys with bum-revealing jeans, my polo-necked jumper with a faded Cheryl Cole T-shirt, and my Converses with a pair of plastic sandals. Then I drop my mobile, my MP3 player, my Oyster card and my wallet with all my fake ID cards into the huge pockets of the trousers. That's one benefit of being a dork with big trouser pockets: you can fit all your gadgets and gizmos into them. I have to carry around a man-bag when I wear my magenta cords.

I mess up my hair and return to the kitchen.

"Do you think I should spatter my clothes with bits of food?" I ask Ma.

She pushes towards me in her wheelchair and says: "Right now, you must show us how your disguise will work – we can fine-tune the details in the morning. Let's not mess with food now."

"But won't it look more convincing if I'm encrusted with *old* food?" I suggest.

My great-uncle, the Count, who is now sitting at the table in his purple dressing gown, drinking *palinka* and smiling, advises: "Old and odoriferous food detritus should greatly improve the effect."

Ma agrees. I dip a spoon into our huge pot of Magyar apricot jam and flick a dollop onto Cheryl Cole's face. Then I smear it across her nose with the back of the spoon. To make things even more real, I press in a few Rice Krispies and Cornflakes. This I do without getting a single finger sticky; that's how skilful I am at jam-spreading.

I turn triumphantly to Ma and the Count and give them my best audition yet. I jut out my jaw and lips, hunch up my shoulders, let my arms dangle, fiddle stupidly with my fingers and make grunting noises through my nose.

"I do feel the characterisation lacks, shall we say, a degree of subtlety?" the Count says.

"I think it's very convincing," I protest.

"Yes, but you look far too like a person imitating an imbecile rather than a real imbecile."

"I reckon anyone who didn't know me would be

convinced," I say, looking in Ma's direction.

She muses for a moment. Then she puts up a finger. "Mmmn… I think I have it. Do what you are doing but speak Hungarian at the same time: that way we tell them you are an idiot and you're struggling to speak English as well. That will be very good."

I repeat my performance, but this time add even more spice by yelling out random swear words in Hungarian.

The Count shakes his head again. "The boy is a monstrous caricature! It needs to be toned down."

But his views don't matter because Ma says: "Well done, Béla! This is excellent! Now let's just run through the points again."

I stick out my tongue at the Count when Ma isn't looking. He waves me away with his long, thin fingers.

"I'm going to tell them that I've been kicked out from school because no one understood that I'm Special Needs," I say.

"But what happens when they learn from the school that you're not Special Needs?" Ma says, still looking puzzled.

"You tell them that the school didn't diagnose me. It happens all the time. I mean, Jakaria is the stupidest person in the universe and he isn't Special Needs," I reply. I'm lying here, but how's Ma going to find out?

Ma harrumphs. "I suppose we could say you threw the firework because you've got some attention deficiency disorder or something."

"I didn't throw the firework, Ma. I don't think we should

bring the firework into it at all."

"And next I suppose you're going to tell me you haven't been excluded from school for ever?"

"Ma," I say mournfully. We've had this argument too many times.

Ma blows a smoke ring from her wheelchair as she thinks about this. Then she says: "I'll think about it."

"Do you think we should say more about my disabilities?" I ask.

Ma shakes her head. "No, I think we should say you've Special Needs and can't care for me. We must not exaggerate too much. It sounds bad as it is."

She climbs out of the wheelchair, grabs her fags from the table and returns to the chair, where she lights up. There is a moment of silence. She looks over the letter from the benefits office again, puffing smoke into the air.

"So you don't think they suspect anything?"

"No, Ma. It's a routine letter. They assess everyone who's getting disability benefit, I'm sure."

Ma puts the letter down and then fiddles nervously with her fag packet. The Count drinks more of his *palinka*.

"So when the doctor lifts my leg, the sciatica must get worse?" Ma asks.

I repeat what we have been saying all evening. "If in doubt about anything, yell. Make noise. Show you are in the maximum amount of pain. They won't want to touch you. The slightest movement should be agony."

"This is good. This is good. I think this will all be good," Ma says.

It's great the way I can reassure her.

Then she gets up from the wheelchair and claps her hands together. "I think it is now time for us all to go to bed. After all, we mustn't be late! We do need some discipline here if we're going to be successful."

"Does that mean I've passed the audition?" I ask with a growing sense of hope.

"I don't know yet. I'll make my decision in the morning."

Well, at least I've got a "recall". This probably means I will get a starring role.

Unfortunately, just at that moment, my mobile vibrates in the huge pockets of my trousers, massaging against my cards and wallet, making it look like I've got an animal wriggling around my groin.

The Count gives me one of his worst Transylvanian stares. "Béla, my dear boy, what is going on in your trousers?" he asks in his most august Hungarian.

"I'm sorry, Your Excellency. I thought I had it switched off."

"Béla, you know you must switch that off when we have an important family conference like this!" Ma admonishes me.

"I didn't expect anyone to call this late," I say apologetically. I pull the offending object out of my pocket and see that Josh has called.

Ma gives me a knowing look. "Béla, you are not going to be talking with that boy all night! You need your beauty sleep for tomorrow."

"My Special Needs sleep."

"Yes," Ma says without amusement. She's not a great

one for joking in moments of stress.

I help the Count up from his chair and guide him to the bedroom we share. Although I don't – thank fuck – have to help him go to the toilet, I do have to help him take off his dressing gown. This is chiefly because it makes him feel important and not because he can't do it by himself. In his early life, before the Communists arrived in Hungary, he had his own butler.

Once he's in bed, I switch on Radio 3 for him. He can't go to sleep otherwise. The noise of the sirens and the city outside drive him mad so he likes to block it all out with his precious classical music.

My great-uncle has four main occupations:

1. Drinking beetroot medicine and moaning about his "deteriorating health".
2. Reading Thomas Hardy, Charles Dickens, George Eliot. "The reason why I came to this forlorn country Béla!"
3. Playing the piano: he is a composer and loves to play Bartók, Kodály and Debussy.
4. Listening to Radio 3. "The reason I stay in England!"

I used to mind the classical music, but now I've got so used to the music that I even secretly like it.

"Oh lovely! It's Schubert's *Winterreise*! My favourite song cycle. And this, very appropriately, is 'Gute Nacht'!" he expostulates.

I switch off his light and sit on the edge of my bed, waiting in the darkness, listening to the song.

Yellow streetlight filters through the blinds and flickers over the old man's closed eyelids. The *palinka* has sent the Count off to nod straight away. I listen for a moment to the song. My German is good enough (I'm predicted an A* in my GCSE) to understand quite a bit of it: it's all about snowy roads and saying goodbye to your loved one. It would be good to have one of those.

12.40am

I am standing outside a block of flats near Old Street, thinking about whether to enter. C. is expecting me. It's very late and I have an interview tomorrow. An important one. What am I doing here?

At the top of the road, a few clubbers are drunkenly wending their way down the street.

Oh, it'll be all right! I won't be long. Besides, it might relax me. I ascend the stairs, make my way along the concrete walkway and look at all the dark windows. Everyone else is asleep. Except for number 43. The lights are on.

I hesitate. No. I can't. There's still a chance Helen and I will patch things up. We will. I will have sex with her again. I'll sort everything out.

I edge away, and then turn and run. My stomach joggles up and down as I puff along. Once I'm back on the street, a car races by, honking its horn, scaring me. I jump back from the kerb, feeling disturbed. My heart is racing. But I feel like I have done the right thing. I'll go home and go to sleep.

There are a lot of people on Old Street, mostly much younger than me, scarcely a few years older than Josh if truth be told, probably students. They're laughing and joking about, milling in and out of the kebab shops, the bus stops, the thresholds of various clubs and bars. Everything is very end-of-termish. Their terms probably finished months ago. Schools always go on much later than universities.

Normally, I find their gregarious energy quite reassuring, but tonight it frightens me. The sudden guffaws pounce upon me, making me flinch as I pass by. When a boy in a long trench coat shrieks "You cunt!" at his mate, I jump away. It takes me a while to work out that he isn't addressing me, but my nerves don't really recover. Their ejaculations – this is what they feel like, great orgasms of sound – unnerve and awe me. I feel so desperately lonely. And old.

Jack, I need you. I need to talk to you. How am I going to get my life back on track – make things right with Helen?

I pass by the club, 333, the Shoreditch Electricity Showrooms, the derelict Courts of Justice, head under the East London Line bridge and dash across Kingsland Road, away from a troop of youths hanging about by the traffic lights, smoking, away from Browns, the strip joint, and cut through the graveyard of Shoreditch Church. I'll be home quite soon.

12.45am

Once the Count is properly asleep, I fetch my laptop and three tangerines. I bite into the succulent segments, feeling the juices run down my throat as I look over the emails between Mr Ndlova and Mrs Hick again. All great detectives investigate things thoroughly. You see, I am, above all, a serious investigator, a great detective in the making. Like my dad was.

As I scan through the emails, I think: Mr Ndlova sure doesn't come across as the respectable headteacher of an academy with all his "fucking" this and that. Two phrases stick out: "I'm fucking sick of all the moaning teachers at this bloody place." "Why do they always fucking blame me?"

And Mrs Hick! Blimey! She's supposed to be a top doctor, a consultant or something, but her language is even worse. She writes: "Don't let the cunts grind you down, love and xxx Helen."

Still, for all their swearing and kissy-stuff, I don't find anything in the emails that proves they're bonking each other. As her husband, Mr Hick, my former English teacher, used to say: "Always find hard evidence to back up your assertions."

Still, I'm gathering quite a bit of circumstantial evidence. Ndlova does have form: he's not known as "Loverman" for nothing. I've seen him chatting up the younger female teachers at school on a few occasions.

**Mr Loverman's top 5 chat-up lines to
female staff (as observed by DCI Pongrácz)**

1. "That was a wonderful learning objective you wrote
   there."
2. "Your displays are marvellous."
3. "I wish I was a pupil in your class."
4. "You're getting me all pumped up about Thomas
   Hardy now."
5. "Your lessons are nang, as they would say in the
   street vernacular here."

I do a search for my name but I find nothing connected
with me except one email to Mrs Hick – which is very
brief.

"Béla has to go. He threw the firework."

It all needs thinking about. Now that I have the
password, I can think about it at my leisure in the coming
days. I log off and meet Josh on Facebook chat. Josh
is my best friend, but sometimes our relationship can
be very awkward because his dad was my old English
teacher, and he got me excluded from school. And now I
know his mum is shagging Loverman.

Me: Wot's up?
Josh: Cant u cum out?
Me: Wot's happened now?
Josh: You have to get yr arse over here rite now!
Me: U no I can't
Josh: Cant u sneak out?
Me: Ma's up, she'll see

Josh: U mong
Me: Wot do u want to c me 4 anyways?
Josh: I need u 2 help me find my dad
Me: Ur Dad?
Josh: He jst walked out
Me: He did?

I pause and eat another tangerine segment. I think: fuck, maybe he found out about his mum and Ndlova? Should I say anything? It all feels very awkward. I really want to tell Josh I've been reading their emails, but I know this would be a really bad idea.

Josh: I think I no where he is
Me: Where is he?
Josh: It dont matter since u aint cuming out anyway.
Me: How cum he walked out?
Josh: Same ole shit

Yes, all the rows that Mr and Mrs Hick are having are making sense to me now. Perhaps Josh deserves to know that his mum's having an affair with his dad's boss. I decide to change the subject instead.

Me: Hey why don't we take our band up to this harp symposium these holidays. I found it on the internet: http://www.harpsymposium.co.uk

I'm always thinking of ways me and Josh could promote our band. He's a great musician: he can play the harp and guitar and keyboards and everything. I play guitar and I'm brilliant on the castanets, but my main role is motivational; I'm Simon Cowell to his Cheryl Cole, Keith Richards to his Mick Jagger, George Sand to his Frederic Chopin. I wait for a minute while Josh checks out the link.

> **Josh:** It looks really gay man. And it's in Cardiff, and it's tomorrow!
> **Me:** On Saturday
> **Josh:** Yeah, tomorrow in case u hadn't noticed
> **Me:** It may be gay, but it will be a great place to showcase our new songs
> **Josh:** It'll be really gay. We'll get touched up by old men flashing their dicks at us
> **Me:** Don't be stupid
> **Josh:** My parents wld never let me go anyway
> **Me:** There mite b girlz there with long flowing hair and big boobies playing the harp just wanting to suck our dicks
> **Josh:** In yer dreams
> **Me:** We won't do it then
> **Josh:** U shld cum around n practise now then u mong

Someone who didn't know Josh would think he hated the whole harp symposium thing, but I can tell he's interested. I'm good like that: I don't get put off by people's cruelty. Where there's abuse, there's also passion that can be turned to your advantage.

Me: I can't m8. But we'll hook up tomorrow
Josh: It dont matter
Me: I'm sorry but I've got 2 get up early tomorrow n go to the clinic. I gotta sleep now
Josh: Wot's the matter?
Me: Mum's not very well
Josh: Im sorry m8
Me: Yeah, weve got 2 c the dr
Josh: Wot about?

I hesitate for a moment. Josh is my best mate in the whole world, but I know I can't tell him the truth about a few things. Besides, I'd quite like his sympathy.

Me: She mite have cancer
Josh: Fuck man thats shit m8
Me: Yeah. It's real shit. It cld b lung cancer. All the smoking
Josh: My mum's a dr. She mite b able to help u. She nos how to get the best treatment for things
Me: Have u got her mobile no?
Josh: Ill txt it 2 u
Me: U r a real m8
Josh: Hey, maybe u wanna play COD?
Me: Ive got to go m8

I'm determined not to let Josh drag me into yet another *Call of Duty* all-nighter. And I have willpower, real willpower. I will go to sleep.

2am

Mercifully, no one seems to be up when I let myself in. Standing in the tidy hallway, with the streetlight filtering through the fanlight, I look at the family photographs hanging on the wall and smell the clean, fresh smell of the house. Everything around me feels so neat and tidy – but I don't. I feel grimy and guilty and tired. But, at least, I'll sleep.

3am

The great thing about having a long, pointy nose is that you can use it as an extra finger when you're simultaneously playing *COD*, tweeting and having a Facebook chat with your mate. I stab my nozzle down on the "Enter" button in order to retweet a link to a great-looking "Babes and Harps" website I found via Twitter while sharing some whacko FB photos with Josh.

But there can be problems when your fringe gets caught between the screen and the keyboard and you lift your head up and it feels like your hair is being pulled out by the roots and you yelp and the bloody computer springs out of your lap and onto the floor.

When I pick up the laptop again, I see the accident has opened a new Twitter page: Countess Feckula's – whoever that is. It's a tweeter I've never stumbled upon before. I must have clicked through from Jakaria's page. The top tweet screams at me as I crane closer to the screen:

It's the last day of term, the last day of Martin Hick's term on earth. (1.03am)

There's a link to an image on another tweet which says:

This is what is going to happen to Hick.

Fuck.

It's a photoshopped pic of Hicky's head on top of the Terminator's muscly chest, and a great bullet wound in his breast, leaking blood.

Jesus fucking shite.

Even though I know it might upset him I stop playing COD, and chuck the offending tweet Joshy's way. He has a right to know this shit.

We resume our Facebook chat.

Me: U cn this?
Josh: Who the fuck is Countess Feckula?
Me: No idea
Josh: Its bad man. BAD. Its been fucking retweeted x 150! The whole fucking year group have got hold of it…
Me: Do u fink they mean it?
Josh: I dont no
Me: This is the weirdest fing Ive cn in ages. Who could it be?
Josh: Ur mum's a countess, ain't she?
Me: Wot's that got 2 do with it?
Josh: Just saying…

Me: You saying my mum is Feckula?! U IS MAD!
Josh: Just saying that's all. Keep ur wig on
Me: It mite b Jakaria. I found the link on his page
Josh: Hes too thick
Me: It mite b…

I get up from the laptop and run my fingers through my sticky fringe. All great detectives check every angle. Even dumb angles.

Emergencies like this bring out the best in me. I am, above all, a serious investigator.

Grabbing my magnifying glass and torch, I leave the cramped bedroom, go to the kitchen, fetch the biggest, shiniest spoon in the drawer and examine Ma's shut bedroom door. I know she's awake because I can smell fresh ciggie smoke.

So I dig the spoon into the carpet underneath her door, hunker down low, shine the torch on the spoon at an acute angle and then look at it through the magnifying glass. The spoon catches the light in her bedroom and with the magnifying glass I can magnify the reflection and work out what's going on there. Or not.

All I can see is a shadow sitting on a chair at a desk. The shine of a computer screen shimmering on a shadow.

I lie on the floor for a minute and think: *Ma deserves her privacy.*

I return to Facebook but see Joshy's logged off. So I text him: "No way its my mum itz got 2 b Jackaria or Mercy or one of them lot…"

But he doesn't reply.

I have to go to sleep: it's so late that it's almost time to get up.

But just before I log off, I check Countess Feckula's Twitter stream and see a new tweet with another image attached: it's been retweeted by Jakaria.

Wanna know wot Béla Pongyboy jerks off to in his spare time? Here's a pic I found on his USB.

Even though I don't want to see it, I click on the link.

Oh lordy, lordy fuck. It's the photoshopped image of me fucking Mercy, except of course it ain't me, it's just my head and porn stars' bodies.

To make matters even worse, there's another tweet after this one:

Hicky likes to play puppets with his pupils penises.

God, it feels like I'm being set up! Yet again! Fuck, fuck, fuck.

I Facebook chat Jakaria. As per normal, he's up.

Me: Why did you RT the Countess Feckula?
Jakaria: WOT?
Me: R u the Countess?
Jakaria: WOT?
Me: Do you say anything else but wot?
Jakaria: U R BAD BÉLA
Me: You are the Countess Feckula, ain't you?
Jakaria: WOT IF I AM

Me: U fat twat
Jakaria: U GAY FUCK
Me: Bet u cant find ur knob amongst all the folds of fat
Jakaria: GAY FUCK
Me: Oh fuck off
Jakaria: FUCK OFF
Me: I can't believe I'm even talking to someone as stupid as you
Jakaria: LICK UR MUM CUNT
Me: Don't you know how to use the apostrophe, you moron?

The conversation finishes there. To think he used to be my best friend.

Checking my Facebook page, I see most of the Year 11 night-tweeters have got wind of the Countess. Mercy has put a link to it on her page and done a status update:

Béla just cant stop spunking over me, can he? Im gonna SORT him out.

I put up my own status update:

I am not the Countess Feckula. Jakaria is.

God, I need to sleep. But I know now I won't get a wink. There's far too much going on online. Far too much.

Best things about Facebook and Twitter	Worst things
Gives you the feeling that you've got loads of friends when you've only got one	When all your "friends" gang up on you and send you abuse
Something to do when you can't sleep	Means you never sleep
You can see loads of photos of your friends having fun	You learn about all the parties you've never been invited to but the rest of the world is at
You can become lots of other people by using aliases and fake photos	You get loads of abuse when people find out you're a troll

Oh God, everyone think I'm the Countess Feckula, everyone thinks I'm a pervy paedo troll, oh fuck, fuck, fuck.

6.00am

Think positive: that's what I say to myself as soon as I wake in my office chair. Sure, I may have woken up with a nasty crick in my neck, I may have a pretty bad hangover, but it's important not to let these things get you down.

I tighten my hands into fists, lift myself off the swivelling chair and repeat to myself: *think positive*! This is the day things are going to go right! I'm going to do it!

The most important point is this: the Power-Point is now firmly entrenched on the memory stick! Retrieving it from the USB port, I wend my way two flights of stairs down to the kitchen. Once I've gobbled a couple of ibuprofen and co-codamol pills and swished them down with a can of Diet Coke, I'm raring to go.

I feel the sunlight falling through the slats and shut my eyes, enjoying its warmth for a moment.

I open my eyes and think: *life will be good*.

As I go back up the stairs, I start singing "I've Got You Babe". Such is my optimism.

"Oh, Daddy! It's so early!" I hear Martha shout from the double bed. This is good. It gives me an excuse to enter my bedroom. I stand before my eight-year-old daughter and look at her twinkly eyes staring up at me from behind the covers. Although I can't see her mouth, I know she's smiling.

"Dad, you're being very noisy and Mum's still asleep," she whispers at me.

I gaze at the form of my wife lying beside her, her brown hair spread against the pillow, her snub nose turned towards the slatted window, her sensual mouth pouting like it always does when she's sleeping, and I think: *God, do you know how much I love you?*

"Sorry!" I whisper back, making funny eyes in the

way that Martha likes. "But you, Martha, my dear, are going to need to get up. Why don't you go to your room and get dressed?"

"But Daddy, I don't need to get up for another hour and ten minutes."

"Martha, Martha, you haven't heard the news, have you?"

"What news?"

"I am going to make bacon and eggs for breakfast!" I say.

"Sunny side up?"

"Yes, sunny side up for my sunny girl! Sunny and runny!"

"Sunny and runny!" Martha giggles.

"The show's starting at six thirty exactly, so I will need you dressed by then!"

"And I can have ketchup on them?"

"Yes, you can have as much ketchup as you want!"

"Thanks, Daddy! I love you!"

Martha reaches up for me and wraps her arms around my neck. I smell her young, fresh skin and kiss her cheek. For some reason, I feel a bit of a twinge in my throat. *Think positive, Martin. Think positive!*

"Daddy, can I say something?" Martha asks as she scuttles towards her room in her Harry Potter pyjamas. "You really need to have a shave! And perhaps brush your teeth? And perhaps have a shower?"

"So you're telling me I'm an unshaven, dirty, smelly monster with bad breath, is that it?"

Martha chuckles as she disappears into her room.

I had been intending to use this window of time – which I estimate to be about fifteen minutes – to sit down on the bed beside Helen, but I realise it might be a better idea if I got cleaned up first. Particularly before Josh gets into the bathroom.

Locking the door behind me, I chuck off my T-shirt and boxer shorts and climb into the shower. The warm water against my face feels good. Shutting my eyes, I'm back on that Scottish beach with Helen and I find myself tossing off. My headachy brain thuds against my skull as I explode into that naked body on the beach, into that moment.

At which point I hear a banging on the door. "Martin, I need to get in here!"

I clean up hastily and open the door with a towel wrapped around my considerable middle. Helen's tousled hair jostles past me, brushing against my upper chest. She doesn't say anything but goes straight to the mirror, leaning close to it, examining her face. It's not a bad face for a forty-year-old, a little worn and tired-looking this morning, but she still looks younger than her years.

"Would you like a cup of tea?" I ask, standing by the door.

Helen turns away from the mirror and looks down at the bath as she says: "Yes, that would be nice."

She pokes her finger into a bead of water on the edge of the bath. To my horror, I see that it's a sticky bead of white water, which extends between her forefinger and thumb. Realising what it is, she washes her hand, commenting bitterly as she does, "Martin, you could at least clean up properly in here. Josh is bad enough, but having you too!"

I shut the bathroom door behind me, and say in a mincing, sheepish voice: "I just had a quick wank."

Helen looks at me with her hard hazel eyes. "It's nice to clean up afterwards!"

"Don't worry, I was thinking about you."

"You were?" she says, seeming quite surprised and a little guilty. A smile flickers on her lips. A smile that reminds me of the old, fun Helen who loved to talk dirty with me.

"I'm sorry about last night," I say.

"Let's not talk about that now," she replies, wrinkling her lips.

Her tone is neutral; I imagine it's the tone she takes with her most trying patients. I think for a moment about searching for more reassurance – I want to ask her again whether she loves me – but neediness is never appealing. No. I need to think positive. As she's brushing her teeth, looking at her in the mirror, I say: "When I get the promotion, we'll have quite a bit more cash. I want to spend it on you. I thought we could go up to Scotland again. We'll leave the kids with your mum and really splash out on a nice hotel. You know, one with a spa where you can get pampered, and we'll go for walks on those deserted beaches, and drink whiskey in the evenings by a nice fire, and just…"

I trail away, thinking that perhaps I should have

said this in the email rather than remembering her stripping off naked. Helen swills and spits out into the sink.

"I thought perhaps we could go in a couple of weeks. You're due some leave, aren't you?" I venture.

"That's when I'm at my conference, Martin," she says, running the shower now. "Look, let's talk about this later."

"I think it would be good for us to get away. Just the two of us."

She disrobes before me in that easy way that a wife does before her long-standing husband. I reach out and massage her back. She flinches a tiny bit but, realising that my hands aren't going to stray, she lets me knead her knotted back. It is very tense.

"Oooh, that is nice. You've got very strong hands, Martin."

"Do you remember when I used to do this for you every night?"

"You speak like it was centuries ago," she says.

"I haven't at all since…" I am just about to say since Jack died, but I resist. I don't want to bring him into it.

"You know what, let me buy the new series of *Brothers and Sisters* and we'll watch it together and I'll rub your back. Let's do that next week. I can order it on Amazon. It'll come tomorrow if I order it this morning."

Helen laughs one of her old easy laughs. "But you hate *Brothers and Sisters* and all that mushy lady

American soap opera stuff. And it'll be very expensive. And we'll only watch it once."

"You won't. You've watched the last series loads of
times."

Helen turns around, thrusting her naked breasts
before me. They're much bigger than they used to be;
two children and some extra pounds have made her
quite voluptuous. "Look, Martin, perhaps we should
have a chat."

She looks up at me.

"Yes, let's have one tonight," I say, feeling pleased
that she's obviously thinking we need to repair our
relationship with a bit of TLC. "I'll get your tea."

The shower steams and sizzles. Clouds of steam are
beginning to engulf her, shrouding her bare form.

7am

There's no messing around with Ma on days like this.
Whereas normally she's pretty slow about getting up,
and frequently expects me to bring her breakfast in bed,
today, as with all major operation days, she's up way
before us.

She bends over me with a lighted fag hanging out of
her mouth. I sit up in my bed and rub my eyes, feeling the
smoke in my nostrils.

"Béla, it's time to get up. We need to go now!"

"But Ma, we'll be years early."

"Our appointment is at 8.45am, Béla."

"But it'll only take twenty minutes to get there."

"Not with me in a wheelchair, it won't."

She puffs some more smoke in my face, making me feel quite breathless. I reach for my inhaler and take a puff. That's better. She must have been up for ages: she's washed her hair and put on some make-up. As she's leaving the bedroom, I comment: "Do you think it might be better if you were scruffier? I mean, it might look more realistic, like you've really struggled to get everything together."

"Béla, a countess must be decent – even at the benefits office!" she says.

I swing my legs off the bed, go into the kitchen and make coffee for the Count. Once I've brought him his cup, I chuck some Rice Krispies and milk down my gullet, munch a pear and then change into my Special Needs outfit. (I also pack a rucksack of my "real" Béla Pongrácz clothes so that I can change on my way back from the health centre and see Josh without having to return home again.)

I check myself out in the mirror. When I hang my head forward and hunch my shoulders, I look very convincing indeed. I practise my Tourette's Hungarian swear words: *fasz* (fuck), *szar* (shit), *picsa* (cunt).

"Please beware of crude characterisations!" the Count warns me as he reaches for his ancient gold fob watch on the bedside table, watching me.

"It's not crude. Ma thought it was good," I say.

"I don't think she did; I think she has her grave doubts, very grave doubts."

Though he criticises me all the time, he still expects

me to get him dressed. Ma enters before I've even started and persuades him that he must forego his normal powder-blue suit and tie, and look imbecilic like me. If I'd suggested this, he'd have refused, but he doesn't argue with Ma.

From my drawer of disguises, I pick out a ripped shirt, some old brown trousers and then, my masterstroke, some string to hold it all up with. By the time I'm finished with him, he looks like a real tramp.

He isn't too pleased about this when he surveys the wreckage in the mirror. "Béla, I look like a character from a John Steinbeck novel," he complains.

I chuckle. "You're Candy, the old swamper, and I'm Lennie!" I say, adding in a Lennie Small voice: "Can I play with the rabbits. I like to stroke soft things."

The Count tuts. "Oh, don't remind me of that ghastly novel. No wonder English children are totally illiterate if that's the only book they read at school! Béla, I insist that you find a more suitable outfit. I simply won't be Candy the old swamper!"

Ma agrees with him. "We must have our dignitas, Béla. Dignitas."

I can't help grinning at this because she pronounces it "dignit-arse".

"It's dignity, Ma," I say.

"It is whatever I say it is! But we really have to go."

"You mean there's no time to change?" the Count asks mournfully.

"Come on, chop-chop!"

The Count looks crushed, but he knows better than to

argue with a countess. At the door, Ma checks we've got everything: passports, citizenship naturalisation forms, birth certificates, utility bills.

Pushing Ma around in the wheelchair is always very awkward. Firstly, there's loads of litter along the walkway, which the wheels of the chair find very hard to go over, and then secondly, the lift is out of order — yet again.

"You'd better get out," I say, staring down at the dark, smelly stairwell.

"I can't get out, I'm disabled," Ma replies.

"Yes, but how are we going to get you down otherwise?"

"You'll have to carry me!" Ma insists.

"But Ma, you're not disabled."

"Keep your voice down," Ma hisses. "From now onwards, I am disabled."

"What, I've got to do this every day?"

"You might do," she says, fixing me with her gimlet eyes.

I look at Ma in wild alarm. Fuck. That prospect seems quite terrifying. Then it occurs to me that this is what the carers of really disabled people have to do. Jesus. What a life!

I decide to take Ma down first. She wraps her arms around my shoulders and breathes her smoky breath on me as I hurry down the stairs with her. She is pretty light: after all, she lives mostly on a diet of cigarettes, coffee and sauerkraut, so she's pretty thin. When she dresses up properly in one of her real countess dresses, she looks knock-out.

As I carry her down, she smiles at my grunting sweating face. "This reminds me of when you we and I used to carry you everywhere in Budapest."

"Didn't Dad carry me around?" I ask.

"Sometimes. But he was at work a lot of the time so it was me mostly."

Once I've put Ma down on the bench outside the block of flats and she's lit up another fag, I go back for the wheelchair, the bag and the Count. He needs a bit of genuine guidance coming down stairs because he's quite unsteady on his pins.

Eventually, we are all ready to go to the bus stop. I keep my head low on Vallance Road and Bethnal Green High Street, which is near where Jakaria lives. I certainly don't want that fat fool to think that I'm trying to imitate him.

Getting on the number 8 is quite fun because the driver gets out a ramp for the wheelchair to go up on and then we have a whole section of it to ourselves. Once I know I'm safe from prying eyes, I start getting prepared for my Special Needs role, by loping around and grunting. Ma tells me to stop it, but she's laughing so I carry on for a bit until she shouts at me.

7.03am

As I'm getting dressed in the bedroom, I look at Jack's tweed suit at the end of my row of shirts and trousers. Since no one is in the room with me, I touch his sleeve after I've buttoned up my shirt. "Don't worry,

37

Jack, I'm going to do it," I say. And then I put my hand over my mouth. God, what am I doing? Why am I talking to a suit?

But I can't help it; that suit *was* Jack. Without really thinking about what I'm doing, I take off my trousers and try and put on Jack's. They are a tight fit – Jack was much thinner than me – but they look pretty good. Wow! Now, wouldn't that be something, if I wore Jack's suit for the interview?

"Martin, what are you doing?"

I turn around quickly and face Helen with my belly spilling over the rim of the trousers. She's in a bath-robe, has a towel wrapped around her head and is looking at me as if I'm a mental patient.

I grin at her.

Helen puts her hand over her mouth. "Oh my God, you're wearing his trousers."

"They fit – well, just," I say, moving stiffly around the room.

"Martin, get them off this moment!" Helen says, her eyes now quite wide.

I don't want to get into an argument, so I take off the trousers. "I just thought it would tell people that I'm doing this for him."

"I thought you were doing it so we could go on holiday together?" Helen retorts as quick as a scalpel incision.

I hang the trousers back in the cupboard.

"I'll go and see how the kids are getting on," I say.

At the top of the house, I find Josh still in his pot-scented bed but I'm not going to let it worry me. I pull back his curtains and see that his windowsill is covered in ash and roach ends.

Another positive thought pops into my head: *England are going to win the Test match today*. As a result, I saunter into my son's room and exclaim: "Hey, Joshy boy, the Aussies are 315 for five! Do you think we'll bowl them out today?"

Josh remains dead on top of his bunk.

I shake the duvet. Then he opens one eye; it's such a strategic opening of an eye that I realise he's been awake for a while.

"And it's the last day of term! Holidays tomorrow! And I'm making bacon and eggs in ten minutes – and counting – so what about shifting your arse out of bed!"

"OK, Dad, I get the message, now just give me two more minutes!"

I always make breakfast for the children. Every morning for the last ten years. Without fail. Normally, it's a healthy breakfast – cereal, yoghurt, OJ – but today I'm going to indulge them a little. I heat the pan and slap on a few rashers of bacon, get the bread toasting and bring out the eggs. It smells lovely.

I decide today that instead of nit-picking about my children's table manners, their inability to hold a knife and fork properly, the way they drop bits of food on the floor, I'll not only accept the way they eat their food, but I'll love it. Having a hangover has actually helped me because it's forced me to take a positive attitude towards my pain on every level: the pain in my head, the pain in my job and the pain in my family.

I feel good about what Martha can do with a knife and fork instead of what she can't. First and foremost, she can cut her food – she may do so by screeching the cutlery across her plate in a rather clumsy fashion, but she is at least able to cut the bacon into little sections. And the majority of the food does get into her mouth; a significant minority finds its way onto her school uniform, but it is only a minority.

Josh's manners are not that bad. He cuts up his bacon and eggs very nicely and doesn't get even the slightest bit on his uniform.

"Martin, why are you giving them this greasy food?" Helen says, as soon as she enters the kitchen. Being the super-efficient person she is, she is already packed and ready for work, with her consultant's photo ID flapping outside the breast pocket of her tweedy skirt suit.

"I don't do it every morning, do I, Martha?"

"You do! We always have lovely, lovely bacon and eggs and lots of ketchup!" Martha says a little too brightly.

"Martha, you know that's not true!"

"It is!" Josh says, burping loudly.

Helen shakes her head. "I'm going to have to sort this out, Martin. From now on, I'll write down the breakfast menu and Martha will make sure my instructions are followed to the letter."

She indicates with her eyes that we should have a private conference in the hallway. Our children's gazes follow us as we leave the kitchen. Helen stops by the coat rack.

"Martin, I think we really need to talk sometime."

"But we've agreed, haven't we? I thought we agreed to have a chat tonight?"

Helen looks down at her fingernails. "Last night was very bad, Martin. Very bad."

"Let's not go over that again. I said I was sorry. Let's make tonight a positive experience instead of raking over the past."

"Tonight might be a bit tricky."

"Well, tomorrow night then?"

Helen seems grateful that I'm not insisting on talking tonight. "Did you really say sorry?" she asks gently.

"Yes, I sent you an email."

Her face brightens at this news. She always likes my emails. In the early days of our relationship when we were at college and we would go back to our families for the holidays, we would write to each other. She always said how much she loved my letters. Has she kept them?

"OK, I'll look at it," she says.

I accompany her to the door and out onto the porch.

"Anyway, good luck with today. It's obvious it's what you want to do – and you're not going to listen," she says. Helen steps out into the street. A shaft of sunlight burnishes her tweed jacket, making her look like a duchess about to go for a constitutional around the family estate. I smile at the contrast between this image and the reality of her life, immersed as it is in the nitty-gritty of the most urban hospital in the UK.

"Look, I'm just worried that it'll all be a bit much," she continues. "Martha and Josh need one of us around."

"Helen, I'm forty-three years old, not a hundred and three. I've still got some life in me yet."

I follow her onto the pavement and try my best to look relaxed.

"What have you got today?" I ask, putting my hands to my forehead to shield my eyes from the sun.

"There's a liver transplant."

"Has a liver come in?"

"Got a text at three in the morning that it has."

Suddenly, I tense up, wiping my hands against my apron. My belly wobbles as I do so. "But who's going to pick up Martha?"

"We discussed this last night. You're going to have to!"

"We didn't talk about it. I can't recall…" I say, stunned by this comment. It's something Helen has been doing to me quite a lot recently: saying that I've agreed to do things I have absolutely no recollection of.

"Martin, you were very drunk last night."

"But I've got my interview in the afternoon. I can't possibly."

"Can't you sort something out? Please?" she pleads,

pulling a rare winning smile out of the bag. I stand before her, open-mouthed.

She clicks on her car keys and her Mini Cooper's lights blink in the street. She's virtually in the car before I can come up with a good reply: "I'll get Josh to pick her up."

She bashes her hands against the steering wheel. "You can't be serious."

"I have no choice. I'll miss my interview otherwise," I say, leaning close to her. So close that the strap of my apron touches her shoulder.

"Can't Sam change the time?"

"No, he can't. This is a proper job interview, Helen. It isn't a joke."

Helen starts up the car. "Martin, the job is a poisoned chalice. Take the day off, recuperate, pick up Martha at noon and then we'll talk everything through."

"OK, OK, I'll pick Martha up," I say, without really thinking how or when.

"Thank you," she replies grudgingly, and drives off.

Back in the kitchen, both my children gratifyingly want more bacon and eggs. I make more, wolfing down a few rashers and a fried egg myself on the counter. I know I shouldn't, but my hangover has weakened my resistance. As it always does.

"Dad, have you ever heard of someone called Countess Feckula?"

I flip the bacon over and catch my thumb on the

hot pan, burning it. Shit.

"Josh! Watch your language! Martha's here!" I say, dashing to the tap and running cold water over my digit.

"Feckula, not Fuckula!"

"Josh!"

Martha giggles. "Countess Feckula? Who's she, Josh?"

"Martha, please could you learn not to use that kind of language? I don't want to get hauled into your school again."

"Oh, just someone," Josh says, more or less ignoring his sister. "But seriously, Dad, have you heard of her, or do you know someone who might have used a name like that?"

"No, I don't! Josh, do I look like someone who has associates like that? Do I seriously?"

I spread out my arms and indicate in a wordless gesture that lurking underneath my England cricket apron there's a rather expensive shirt and a top-of-the-range pair of trousers.

Josh mutters sulkily: "Well, you might. I was only trying to help."

"Only trying to help? What are you talking about?"

"Well, you might have heard of her, and that might help."

"Help who?"

"You."

"Me, how would it help me if I knew this Countess of dubious repute?" I'm trying to be light-hearted, but Josh doesn't smile.

"It just might, that's all. But it doesn't matter. I'll sort it out myself."

I dish out some more rashers and determine not to discuss the Countess Feckula anymore. Just then the front door opens again. Helen comes into the house.

"Helen, what is it?" I ask.

She is holding my memory stick in her hand.

"I believe you might have dropped this!" she says, looking at me with surprisingly indulgent good humour.

My eyes widen as I pat the top pocket of my shirt and find that it's empty. "Oh my God, that's the one with my presentation on it!"

"I thought it might be." She throws the memory stick at me and I catch it.

"Good luck with today," she shouts in the hallway.

"Thanks, Helen, you're a star! I love you," I shout after her.

Then she disappears again.

"It's lucky you've got Mum otherwise you'd have lost your memory!" Martha says with a big grin.

"It is indeed," I agree. "It is indeed."

7.45am

I have that tingly sensation I get when I feel in touch with my Hungarian past as I push Ma towards the health centre, because the air has the same summery scent of

45

my Budapest childhood.

Top 5 things that remind me of Hungary
1. Dark underpasses after it has rained.
2. The smell of buttery pastry.
3. The cubes of blubbery meat.
4. Any wobble under my feet, reminding me of walking across the Chain Bridge with Dad.
5. The fresh scent of a summer morning.

Ma's voice, of course, sounds exactly the same as it did then. She says: "Are you sure this is normal, Béla? I have been claiming for two years and they've never done this before. You don't think one of our neighbours reported us, do you?"

Ma wriggles in her wheelchair as I try and reassure her. "No, Ma. Just relax. It's just new procedures. Jakaria's mum had to go recently as well. They're assessing everyone."

That's one thing I never had to do in Hungary: reassure Ma. Dad always did that. Sometimes I feel a bit angry with him for leaving me to do his job now, but mostly reassuring Ma makes me feel very grown-up.

"Yes, but Jakaria's mum is disabled."

"Exactly! They're checking everyone out."

We pass the Stepping Stones City Farm and some sheep baa at us. Then we cross the road and enter a pretty grotty shopping precinct: there's a launderette, an Afro-Caribbean café, a pound shop and an Asian supermarket, and then, shining amidst this dross, the health centre.

"Look, they've got to have something to do at the health centre. Just remember to yell in pain at everything and you'll be fine."

"Keep your voice down!" Ma hisses at me.

"Ma, there's no one here. We're miles early!"

"Miles early?" the Count nit-picks in his cotton-picking tramp's dress. I stick my tongue out at him when I know Ma's not looking.

I look down the street, and stare at the tall glass buildings of the City in the far distance and the deep blue air beyond them and think that the sky looks infinite today. These blue mornings make me think of Dad and being in Budapest. When I was very young, he would take me down to the promenade by the Danube and we would stare up at the amazing buildings that lined the river. I feel the sunlight on my face and remember those times. Happy days! The cherry tobacco smell of his pipe, the rough texture of his tweed jacket, his big hairy hands, and his voice saying: "That's where we fought the Nazis, Béla, up there, in the beautiful Buda Castle, yes, you wouldn't believe it to see it now, would you? And that building there, that's where the Gestapo tortured the Hungarians, but you wouldn't think it now, would you? It just looks like an innocent building, doesn't it? That's why you should find out everything, Béla, leave no stone unturned, and trust no one, no one until you find the truth!"

It's remembering these words that makes me crouch down by the wheelchair and ask: "Ma, you don't happen to know anything about someone who goes under the name of Countess Feckula, do you? I mean, obviously it's a fake name, but it doesn't ring any bells, does it?"

Ma sucks on the cig and exhales a cloud of smoke in my direction.

"Do I know about who?"

"Countess Feckula."

"Who says I ever known such a people in my stinking life!" she cackles, rattling the wheelchair in amusement.

"So you haven't?" I persist.

"Countess Feckula, you say, who is this? A lady of the night? Béla, you are too young to know these kinds of women!"

I try to laugh but I feel a bit wheezy so I take a puff on my inhaler and then, feeling my passageways unclog, I cough a little. Even though it's summer, I still haven't got rid of this cough.

Just at that moment, Josh texts me: Can u meet me this am?

I text right back: Where?

Josh: Outside school fence 8.15am?
Me: Nah. Wont till later on. Got a drs appoint
Josh: Oh yeah. Gud luck m8. Hope ur ma is OK
Me: She's bad. VERY BAD
Josh: When do the test results come thru?
Me: Dunno, but she's bad

"What are you doing, Béla?" Ma asks, pedalling the wheelchair towards me.

I hastily put the phone away.

"You know it's very rude to text while I'm talking to you."

"But we'd finished talking," I protest.

"We have not! We are talking about a countess," the Count interjects, leaning on his walking stick.

"I wasn't talking to you," I argue, thinking that one of these days I'll kick his stick away.

"Yes, exactly, *we* are talking about her," Ma says. "Béla, you need to be Hungarian in your manners. No more British thug stuff."

"But…" I say and then stop. I know it's useless to argue with Ma. She is always right in matters of decorum.

"Now tell me, what is your interest in this lady?" Ma asks.

I decide to impress her with a blunt exaggeration of the truth. "Apparently, she wants to kill Mr Hick."

Ma thrums her fingers on the armrest of her wheelchair and then says: "She does? Hmm, have you told Mr Hick this?"

"Why would I do that?" I say, putting on my best Duh!-face.

"He was once your best teacher. And he is father of your only friend."

"He got me booted out, Ma. I don't owe him anything. He, he…"

I change the subject. "But it was just Twitter stuff. It's not real stuff. The kind of stuff that happens now."

"It does? What is the world coming up to, Zoltán?" Ma says, wheeling towards the bleak concrete statue in the middle of the shopping arcade. "When children pass notes around the internet about killing their teachers?"

"Nearly as bad as doing benefit fraud," I chuckle.

The moment after this joke has popped out of my mouth I know I have made a terrible mistake. You see, my mum has five states of being:

1. Orange alert. This is more or less her permanent state: constant anxiety. Béla remedy: live with it.
2. Red alert. Heightened anxiety. This is when I forget to do something she's asked me to do: quite common. Béla remedy: soothe her.
3. State of national emergency – only happens maybe once or twice a week. Panic. Béla remedy: give her Valium.
4. State of global emergency. Very rare. Once a month. Béla remedy: time to hide in the bunker – or run.
5. Armageddon. Only major events like Dad's death and me getting excluded from school make this happen. Béla remedy: there isn't one.

Ma lights another fag. I can tell immediately she's on number 4. As with all global emergencies, there's a moment of calm before the tsunami strikes.

She glances at the health centre, its silver balconies shining in the sunlight.

Then she lets the smoke filter in between her gritted teeth.

I glance nervously at the Count. Lurking behind his solemn expression is a sly grin.

"Béla, you do not say that. You do not speak like that,"

Ma says. "If you hadn't been expelled we wouldn't be in this terrorising mess."

"What has that got to do with it?"

Ma laughs hollowly. "You think you're going to get good jobs, now? Do you? You throw fireworks at your teachers, you do nothing but addict yourself to computers, you spend money, and now you want me to be locked up. Locked up. You are a bad boy. Very, very bad boy."

"But Ma, I didn't throw the firework!"

"You think I trust your lies?"

"Ma, it was only a joke," I say in my most apologetic voice.

Ma jabs a cigarette in my direction. And then wheels her chair right up to me. The wheel scrunches over my foot. I don't complain but slowly take my foot away, feeling the pain in my toes. If this carries on, I really will be disabled.

"Béla, I think you should go now," she says.

"But Ma…"

"No, you go now. We don't need you. Your idea is a bad idea. I must show the doctor I am very disabled, and you must go away and leave us alone."

"Situations like this need finesse and nuance, not pranksters playing the clown," the Count adds.

"But Ma, we'll get more money if we show them I'm Special Needs. I mean, it ties in with me being excluded. We could say that I was Special Needs and didn't know what I was doing," I protest.

"But think, Béla, what happens when they go to the

school and ask them, and they say you are not a dum-
dum? It don't fit, Béla."

"We say the school didn't assess me properly. They
didn't assess Jakaria properly, and he really is a dum-dum."

"Why this Jakaria all the time? Shut up your face about
him!"

"But Ma…"

"Go! Go! Go!" she says, stabbing the air three times
with the lighted end of her cigarette and adding her most
vicious order: "Get the fuck out of my face."

"But how will you get home without me?"

"I need you no more. No more!"

"Oh Ma, please. I could be really good. I'll do it,
seriously, I promise."

"Go!"

Ma gets out a Parcel-Force card from her gilt-edged
handbag – a handbag I bought for her in Petticoat Lane
Market – and hands it to me. "You can go to the post
office and get my ciggies. Do something useful."

"Please, Ma. I'll be very good. I'll save the day!"

"Béla, go and get the ciggies. Now!"

I turn away with my shoulders sagging, feeling like
Lennie after he's been told he can't tend the rabbits.

8.ooam

Pleasingly, Josh has opted to come along while I drive
Martha to her private school; before Béla left, he usually walked to school with him.

On this fine, sunny morning, he listens to his iPod

and gazes out the window, looking at the great glittering towers, the churches, the commuters. After I've dropped Martha off at the school entrance and given her a kiss goodbye, plucking out his earphones, Josh taps me on the shoulder. He's sitting in the back seat but I don't turn around to face him.

"Dad, is it true you've never heard of Countess Feckula?"

"Like I said before, I've never heard of her or him or it! Josh, what were you thinking, talking like that in front of Martha?"

"Dad, this is serious. According to this person, today is going to be your last day of term."

I laugh hollowly. The bloody internet!

"Josh, if I believed everything I read on the web, I'd be in a mental hospital right now."

"I just have a feeling this is serious, Dad. I just don't think you should go in today."

"What do you know?" I ask him, twisting around and looking hard at his long, black fringe, the thin film of hair on his upper lip and his dark brown eyes. I'm reluctant to drive off until I get some answers.

Josh says: "Béla thinks it's Jakaria."

"Ah, Jakaria. That makes sense."

Pleasingly, the car starts first go. For some reason, it nearly always stalls in front of the private school; it's as if all the fancy vehicles that drop off the other children make it nervous. There's no pulling on the choke, no great revs with the accelerator, no pushing down the street, just a lovely puttering away into the full glory of the morning on Cheapside.

"It's a miracle the Beetle didn't fail me this morning! Must be a good omen," I exclaim and then, looking in the rear-view mirror at Josh, comment, "I'll deal with Jakaria when I get into school. He's a ridiculous boy. I'll make sure he gets excluded for this."

"You should, he's a stupid fat fuck."

"Josh! Please don't speak like that. Please!"

As I leave the City, passing underneath the East London Line bridge, and steer past the shuttered strip joints, the newsagents and the forlorn billboards, I feel the sunlight once again on my face. My hangover has nearly gone and I'm on my way. I flip open the glove compartment, reach for the sweet packet that I always make sure is there and pop a few fruit pastilles in my mouth. The sugar gives me an extra lift.

At the traffic lights before Hoxton Street, I even feel a little bit cheeky. I turn around and pull an earphone out of Josh's ear. Exaggerating about everything as normal, he yells out: "What did you do that for?"

"I just wanted to have a conversation, that's all – but not one about the bloody Countess Feckula!" I rev up the car as the traffic lights change. "I mean, last night was rather difficult."

"Oh that."

"Nothing happened to me, you know. I was fine," I reassure him as the VW Beetle goes over a speed-bump by Hackney College.

"Yeah."

"You seemed very worried."

"It's all right. I'm not worried any more," Josh mutters in a somewhat aggrieved tone.

"That's good."

Josh rubs his ear as we pass the old Hoxton Music Hall and head towards De Beauvoir Town. It's time to inject a little joy into the conversation. A little hope.

"Josh, I thought you and me might do something together in the holidays. Just you and me."

"You did?"

Josh sits up in the passenger's seat, fiddling with his mobile phone as he does so.

"I've got my ideas, of course. But perhaps you could give me some ideas."

Josh puts his mobile phone in his pocket. "Well, I was just wondering if I could go to the European Harp Symposium. I think it's just the kind of place for me and Béla to get some publicity for our band."

"Hmm," I say. "What's the European Harp Symposium?"

"It's a place where all the harpists in Europe get together and play, share ideas. You can pitch up and sell your stuff. There are competitions too."

"Where is it?"

"It's only in Cardiff, that's not far."

"When is it?"

"Tomorrow."

"Tomorrow! You haven't given me much notice!

We can't just suddenly up sticks and leave at the drop of a hat."

"You shouldn't mix your metaphors, Dad. It's not what English teachers do," Josh says.

"Why didn't you ask me about it earlier?"

"I didn't know about it," Josh replies. "I only found out at the weekend. They're very keen for me to go, though. And Béla wants to come."

"Béla?"

"Yes, Dad. Béla."

"I really don't think you should be hanging around with him any more. He's a very bad influence. He's encouraging you to smoke, for one thing."

"Béla doesn't smoke; he's got asthma. How can he encourage me to do it?"

"He's very messed up."

"He's my only friend, Dad."

His words cut into me like a knife, making me feel even guiltier than I do.

"I'll think about it," I say.

Josh falls silent. He sticks the stupid plugs back in his ears, winds down the window and lets the wind stream over his face. "You won't think about it," he says. "It won't happen."

"It might. It's just that I was hoping we might do something that we can all join in, Martha and Mum included. Like go camping, you know, do some out-doors stuff. Go up to the Peak District and do a bit of climbing together. I need some fresh air."

"So you're not going to take me?"

"I didn't say that."

Another silence. Then he says: "Now that Béla's gone, it hardly feels like there's any point going to school any more."

I've heard this one so many times before that I've stopped replying to it. Just before the canal, I stop the car and dash out to the florist's on the high street, where I buy a bouquet of carnations. I give them to Josh to hold in his lap and start the car up again.

"What are these for?" he asks.

"For Jack," I say.

"Oh."

That brings back the silence. It's not a silence I want, but I can't see a way out of it. I just feel it's so hard to talk to Josh. But then, to my surprise, he says: "Dad, when you first met Mum, did you ask her out?"

I blink. God, I have to start dusting off the cobwebs from the old memory to remember that one.

"Yes, I did," I say.

"How did you do it?"

"It was at university. I remember I met her in the refectory one lunchtime. She was sitting with Sam."

"She was?"

"Yes, I thought she was going out with him, but then I found out he had someone else, so that gave me the courage to ask her to a movie. I remember it very well now. It was called *Betty Blue*. It was at the Duke of York's in Brighton. We sat in the back and I slipped my hand into hers."

Josh twitches in his seat.

"Why do you ask? Are you thinking of asking someone out?"

"Well… I don't know…" he mumbles.

"Josh," I say with a growing insouciance in my voice, "have you got your eye on anyone? You know you can always talk to me about that!"

"Dad! Don't be embarrassing!"

"No. No. I'm just curious, that's all."

When we reach the Gilda Ball Academy, I notice some very familiar faces standing outside the school gates: it's my old GCSE English group, looking like they've been far longer on this earth than their sixteen years. For some reason I can't quite fathom, they've decided to turn up today.

"Bloody hell, what are they doing here?" I mutter.

"Dad, it's like I told you, this Countess Feckula has got all around school."

"But they left in May. They got kicked out," I say, wrinkling my forehead. "They've got nothing to do with this."

But I feel nauseous; if anyone has anything to do with wishing me dead, it's this lot.

I try my best and smile at them as I putter past. They grin back. *Think positive, Martin. Think positive.*

To my surprise, in the car mirror, I see Béla emerging from the end of the street and making his way in his inimitable loping way towards them. What is going on?

Just after I've swiped my card at the entrance gate

and the huge steel door is opening, Josh says: "Dad, you know I love you, don't you?"

I shift the Beetle into the wrong gear and we stall. I start the engine up again.

"Of course I do," I say, glancing at him out of the corner of my eye while also looking for a parking space. Tears leak onto the dark rims under his eyes. "Whatever is the matter?"

Josh's lower lip trembles as I park the Beetle next to Sam's sleek BMW.

"You're not being bullied, are you?"

He shakes his head as the tears fall down his cheeks. Yes, there's definitely a woman in his life. The boy is love-struck! I'll work some of my magic over the holidays and find out who it is.

"Josh, sometimes these things happen. You're an attractive guy. There are plenty of other fish in the sea," I say, taking the carnations off his lap. "Look, why don't you come with me and lay the flowers by the wreath?"

Josh shakes his head. "I can't. I just can't. I have to go."

With that, he bolts out of the car, dashes across the playground and disappears into the great glittering glass tower of the Gilda Ball Academy. It's rather sad but I feel a real sense of relief when he's gone. Taking my briefcase, I walk with the bouquet to the playground and lay it down on the exact spot where Jack died.

I'm heartened to see that the wreath, which I re-hung a couple of days ago, is still there. You see, the kids here do have respect. They really do. It's just a question of believing in them.

8.03am

After that miserable conservation with Ma, I need to change out of these fucking idiot clothes asap.

I transform myself in the nearest Starbucks' toilets. I don my best blue shirt, my green drainpipe trousers and my leather jacket. Check myself in the mirror. I look pretty damn slick: kind of like a mixture of a French philosopher and Simon Cowell.

Although I should go straight to the post office – the queues there can be very bad – I realise that if I'm quick I could squeeze in meeting Josh. I text him and say that I'll be at the school soon.

I get a bus back to Whitechapel and then the train to Hoxton, heading back to the area I know the best. Once outside the station, I buy a banana from a Caribbean grocer, and tootle along the street enjoying the fresh fruit in my mouth. Then I break into a run and make for the Gilda Ball Academy – or the Ballz-up as we term it.

I turn the corner and find Jakaria. He's sitting in his tight-fitting school uniform on top of a litter bin outside the school sucking on a lollipop.

I push him quite hard. A lighter person would have gone flying off the litter bin, but he stays put.

"Ain't you supposed to be in school?" I say.

He faces me and grins.

"What's it to you, Pongy?"

I prod his fat tummy with my finger.

"Have you told the GMF that you're the Countess Feckula?" I say.

"No," Jakaria says.

Just then, at the far end of the street, I see the GreenMuthaFuckas stalking towards the school. I freeze.

Top 3 scariest sights in the world

1. Mercy wearing her trendy glitzy jacket – which she is today. She's the biggest fuck-off sixteen-year-old girl you've seen in your life, with a gold medallion often nestling in between the ballistic missiles of her breasts. She's a bit of a complex case because before she was booted out of the Ballz-up she was on course for top GCSE grades. She's the cleverest girl I've ever met – and the nastiest. She only wears her glitter jacket when she's selling drugs. This also means she's tooled up and ready to shank anyone who annoys her. For some reason, she finds me pretty annoying.

2. The Bentley twins. These two are real psychotics, who will give you a good slap for no reason whatso- ever, other than it makes them chuckle. Like Mercy, they're dressed up in their drug-dealing gear: base- ball caps, sleeveless bullet-proof vests, and low- slung trackie bottoms, the cracks at the top of their arses glistening in the sun.

3. The three of them coming together to form what is known as the GMF, or the GreenMuthaFuckas. This

is the scariest sight of all! If you want some drugs or a good kicking, you go to them.

I seriously think about legging it for my puny life. But I hover for a second and see that they're all distracted, watching Hicky park his LoveBug in his customary school spot. Jakaria turns away from me, and watches his English teacher park the car.

"You're frightened that they'll kick your head in?" I ask Jakaria.

"Who?" he asks in a too-calm voice.

"The GMF."

"No."

"Why not?"

"Because I ain't the paedo what posted porny pics of you knobbing Mercy on the internet."

"You did," I say, stabbing my finger in his direction.

"You think I'm Feckula?" Jakaria asks, pointing an innocent finger at his own chest. "You must have shit for brains."

"Bullshit. You told me you was Feckula on Facebook, innit," I say.

"I didn't."

"You did."

"No, I said I wasn't afraid to be her, coz I aint afraid of nothing. There's a difference. I can't say I'm Feckula or whatever her name is – coz I ain't."

We're silent for a moment as we watch Hicky lumber out of the LoveBug – followed by his son. He tries to say something to him, but old Joshy boy has legged it before he can get the words out. He's carrying a big bunch of red flowers.

With Josh out of the picture now, our eyes follow Hicky across the playground and focus on him as he puts the flowers on the floor.

It's a sad moment for me; I think about poor old Mr Humphreys. The others shift around uneasily in their trainers – and then look in my direction. Mercy sees me. Her great rack perks up.

"So look who it ain't! It's the Countless Feckula herself! Hello, Countless, how are we today, you sick fuck?"

I realise that it's too late to leg it. But I reckon this is as good a time as any to talk to them: they wouldn't pull any serious stuff in front of the school in broad daylight. Perhaps it's a chance to sort out some kind of peace treaty. *Pax nobiscum* as my great-uncle would say. Not that any of the fuckers here would understand Latin. Well, Mercy probably would.

"I'm not the Countess. He is!" I say, pointing at Jakaria, still proudly perched on the bin.

He shrugs. He's far too relaxed.

"Why don't you come over here and tell us why?"

I approach the gang gingerly, trying my best not to stare at the medallion between Mercy's big tits, which are bulging over the top of her green T-shirt. If truth be told, her whole outfit does highlight them extremely well. The tops of them gleam in the sunlight. I have often fantasised about what it must be like to lift that pendant out of the way and touch them.

She catches me looking.

"You are such a dirty fucker. You just can't help it, can you? You is obsessed by my tits, inn-tit?" she says, laughing at her own play on the words. This makes the twins laugh too, not because they understand her verbal game but because they always laugh when she laughs.

"I… I…"

Aware that the worst thing for me to do at the moment is to carry on staring, I carry on staring. I can't help it. It's like my eyes are hypnotised by her breasts.

"God, it's just like when we was doing that play, and instead of you doing your lines and stuff, you just kept staring at my tits. You is an embarrassment, Pongy."

"You were a good Lady Macbeth," I say, feeling that the only way out of my present predicament is compliments.

"Well, you were a shit Macbeth," she says, and then she does this impression of me speaking some of my lines in a camp manner. "Tomorrow, and tomorrow, and tomorrows creeps in a gay pace from day to day and is very gay!"

"Gay!" says Bentley twin number one.

"Gay!" says Bentley twin number two.

"Shit-poker!" says number one.

"Shit-eater!" says number two.

"Him and his bum-chum, Josh!"

"They chomp each other's knobs!"

Then a whole stream of abuse fires out of their mouths: bum-bandit, shirt-lifter, cock-sucker and so on. I'm not too happy about them saying me and Josh are gay, but I know there ain't nothing I can do about it. I just have to take it – like I've done for years. Eventually, even Mercy has to put up her hand and get the twins to stop.

"So, Countess, tell us why you posted that photo of me and you on the internet?" she asks, quite calmly.

"I promise you, it's not me. I know nothing about no Countess. It's Jakaria," I say, pointing to the tub of lard on the litter bin.

Unfortunately, Mercy doesn't seem remotely interested in the thought of Jakaria being the chief suspect.

"Them photos you posted on Twitter is disgusting, you should be locked up. Bluds, I should shank you," she says, pointing her very long black and silver fingernails in my direction.

Like the obedient bodyguards they are, the Bentley twins grab me by both arms and push me towards her. She smiles at me, and then checking no one can see, she pulls out a big kitchen knife from the inside of her Top Shop jacket. The kind of knife that's supposed to cut up cubes of meat, not cubes of Béla.

Its steel blade shines before her big breasts.

Oh shit, why did I even think for a second that she might be feeling well disposed towards me? Why o why?

"I could cut off that tiny dick of yours right now, d'ya know that?"

The Bentley twins push me closer to her. I can smell marijuana and perfume and sweat emanating from her huge body.

"But Mercy, let me explain, I'm not the Countess. Jakaria set me up. I promise I didn't do those photos."

"I known you long enough to recognise your handiwork, Pongy."

The Bentley twins nod stupidly. Mercy licks her lips.

"I might have done the photos, but that doesn't mean I posted them online," I gabble. As soon as I confess to this, I am aware of just how bad it sounds.

"And part of me thinks it's quite 'cute' that you did that."

The word "cute" sounds very strange on Mercy's lips. And for a moment she seems almost affectionate, but she's quickly back to normal. She indicates that the Bentley twins should bring me closer. Suddenly her big hand grabs hold of my balls and squeezes. I yell out but find a smelly, rough palm covering my mouth. I don't know whose coz with them all being so close I can't work out who is doing what. There are hands feeling my bum, chests pressing against my feeble frame, kneecaps and feet jabbing the various sections of my legs. More than anything, there's the overpowering stench of being trapped.

With them all jammed so close, Mercy presses the knife just above my crotch and inserts it in the parting of my blue shirt, running it up through the first two buttons. They ping off without the slightest resistance. Without moving my head, I glance down and see there is a thin line of blood forming across the part of the stomach where she's trailed the knife.

"So tell me, Countess Feckula, why did you bring the GreenMuthaFuckas here? What's the plan, Macbeth, what's the plan?" she whispers. Her breath is warm.

Shivering with fear, I beg for my life: "Please, please, Mercy, I'm not the Countess. I'm not."

"Maybe I should just shank you right here and now?"

Her face is pressed right up to mine, close enough for her to kiss me on the lips. The knife hovers by my ribcage for a few seconds. Then Mercy nods at the twins and they let me go. The smile returns to her face. I want to crumple into the cracks in the pavement, but I manage to keep standing.

"Now," Mercy snarls, "before we clean up, perhaps you could tell me exactly why Feckula wants us here right now?"

Improvising on my wobbly feet, I say: "I want to help you get your revenge on Hicky. After all, he was the one that got us all kicked out of school, and he deserves to pay, don't he?"

Mercy reaches into the top pocket of her jacket, produces an antiseptic wipe and cleans the tip of her knife.

"But what's the plan?"

8.15am

"Have you seen who's hanging around the school this morning?" Julia Webb asks me in the staffroom as I'm pouring some boiling water into my coffee mug. It's rather chipped these days, but I'm still very attached to it: the phrase "I love Scotland" is still visible, if a little faded. It was an anniversary present from Jack.

"Yes, all my old students."

"All your old enemies more like," she says acidly.

"That's all ancient history, you know that," I reply, refusing to be goaded into an emotional state about things. "I'm sure they've come back to ask if they'll be taken back for the Sixth Form. You've got to remember that Mercy was one of my best pupils. She's a pain, but she ain't half clever. Apart from Béla, she's the only student in the year group who should have got an A* in English."

Julia laughs sourly. "It sounds like you're trying to persuade yourself that we should take her back."

I stir my coffee. "I'm just keeping an open mind, that's all."

I add some more sugar to my coffee. Then, when Julia's back is turned, I pop a few chocolates into my mouth from the opened box of Milk Tray that Sam has put on the counter to celebrate the last day of term.

I can't pretend I'm not dubious about Mercy. After all the effort I put in with her over the years, her behaviour a few months ago in May, on Year 11's last day, was a real shock, a real betrayal – and devastating for Jack. I heap more sugar into my cup.

Keen to move away from Julia Webb, I sit down on the sofa near the window overlooking the street and playground, my mouth still full of chocolate. The sofa is right by a framed photograph of Jack: he is smiling broadly, surrounded by happy pupils. He doesn't look that important, with his neat beard and moustache and silvery hair, but he was. Sipping my coffee, I focus upon the portrait of my late friend. He looks so committed in his tweed suit. *You were different from people like Julia. You always thought positively.*

When I first met Jack, over twenty years ago, the school was a comprehensive and the buildings were going to rack and ruin. But it didn't matter because he made the place seem magical. He was Head of English, and he'd been there since his early twenties. He really valued the students and took their education seriously. But he cared about the other members of staff, too. At the end of my first week, he inducted me into the staff sports' club; we would play basketball or tennis every Friday, and then go for a drink at the Birdcage, where Jack would be surrounded by men and women he had taught at the same school ten, fifteen years ago. It was the beginning of a routine that lasted for two decades. It was sacrosanct.

After a couple of years, Jack and his wife became a big fixture in my early married life with Helen; Jack's wife, Glenda, was a social worker and more bullish than Jack – but interesting. We frequently threw joint dinner parties, where the two of us would hold court. I was always more outspoken than Jack, but he was the accepted voice of wisdom. We talked passionately about society; criticising John Major's hapless government, enthusing about Blair's New Labour in the early days. We chewed over everything that happened at school, Helen's hospital and Glenda's department, we discussed the films we'd gone and seen together, we enthused about the holidays we took together, we made the world a better place and then laughed at our naïvety. It was a great, great time. The best, really.

After Josh was born, those evenings more or less stopped. But my friendship with Jack became stronger as I talked to him about my problems with Helen – which started around that time. He was my confidant. He was the one that guided me.

By then Jack was Deputy Head and interviewed Sam for his first job; he didn't want to give it to him, but relented when I persuaded him to give the man a chance. "He's slippery, Mart, not honest," he said. I told him he'd got Sam all wrong. Sam had been in a very bad way, having failed a law course and been unemployed for a year, and was grateful that I had managed to wangle a teaching job for him. He was meek and mild then. Jack watched Sam's ascendancy during the years of the New Labour government with increasing suspicion. "He's going to send this school to the dogs. His airy-fairy, touchy-feely nonsense will lead to the place getting completely out of control. These kids need a firm hand, not constant counselling and mentoring," Jack told me. God, how right he was! And how tragically ironic that he should be the victim of Sam's educational approach.

Bundles of flowers, now yellowing and dying, are placed on the chair underneath his commemorative poster. Around the main photo are lots of other snapshots of Jack in action: dressed up as the pantomime dame on that Charity Day, as the pantomime horse with me on another Charity Day, leading a field studies course in Walton-on-the-Naze, trekking with the kids in Africa, presenting prizes at Prize-giving and, in his most familiar guise, patrolling the school in his smart tweed suit – the one I couldn't fit into.

The rest of the staffroom is typically end-of-termish. Dotted here and there are opened boxes and tins of chocolates with sweet wrappers scattered around their edges. I get up from the window and, seeing that no one is looking now, I chuck a selection of chocolates into my mouth, convincing myself that they won't make me fat because they're not my chocolates. It's a bit like when I smoke now: I believe irrationally that smoking other people's cigarettes won't have the harmful effects of smoking my own. Jack used to joke that I had a miraculous faith in the brand of "OP" – Other People's. Remembering this makes me catch my breath and chew the caramel chocolate in my mouth more slowly.

The staffroom door opens and the blond, shapely form of Miss Kylie Rouse enters. After fetching a coffee, she joins me, looking very pretty and young in a white and red polka-dot dress. I swallow my last chocolate quickly. It is my last chocolate of the day. Definitely. Forever. Well, at least for the holidays. No more chocolate. Only fruit.

"You're very summery today, Miss Rouse!" I say with a wide smile. I straighten my Gucci tie and feel my belly underneath it. I find reminding myself of its largeness quite comforting: having a big belly endows one with gravitas in school.

Kylie blushes. We give each other a meaningful look.

"I've got my playground duty in a sec," I say, lost in her doe eyes.

She leans close, whispering so that Julia won't hear. "Martin, is that wise?"

"What do you mean?"

"It's not right somehow, having that lot hanging around outside. Are you sure they haven't got weapons? I wouldn't put it past them to do something bad."

I glug my coffee and pat Kylie on the wrist. "Oh, I'll be fine. You mustn't overreact."

Down on the street it looks like Mercy, the Bentley twins and Béla are all having a group hug.

"They seem very OK to me," I comment.

Kylie wrinkles her nose. "Just be careful, won't you?"

I get up and head towards my duty, thinking that the trouble with most teachers is that they operate on a "deficit model"; they only see the negatives in children – even great teachers like Kylie. I look up again at the photo of Jack and think: *you weren't like that, were you?*

After wending my way down the spiral staircase and out of the building, I go back to the carnations, which are still sitting nicely on the tarmac.

I wave at my old students standing across the street, watching me doing my last duty of the year. It's right that I don't think badly of them.

Despite the fact that I ensured all of them were permanently excluded, they are smiling at me. Kids are like that: they don't hold grudges in the way adults do. Mercy has her arm around Béla, and the Bentley twins are patting him on the back. He smiles at me. I leave my station next to the carnations and approach the high fence.

"So how is my Lady Macbeth today, and for that matter, my Macbeth and his murderers?"

I'm pleased with my own joke, and it makes me remember just how great they were when they performed the Scottish Play to the school. Béla and Mercy put such a lot of effort into it. The whole class loved updating Shakespeare's play to a "gangsta" setting, but even so, they all tried hard to speak the original language. Mercy was amazing as Lady Macbeth, while Béla made a rather sinister, creepy Macbeth. His delivery of the "Tomorrow, and tomorrow, and tomorrow" speech was chilling in the way he brought out the nihilistic disgust that Macbeth has for life.

"Oh, we're just murdering Béla here," Mercy jokes, putting her arm around Béla. I've always thought she had a big soft spot for the Hungarian boy.

"I hope not! It looks like you guys are friends again to me!" I say.

"Of course we are!" Mercy says. "Innit, Béla?"

"Yes, yes, we are, the best of friends," Béla adds, overwhelmed in her all-encompassing embrace.

Just then I spy Jakaria further along the street. I call out to him but he waltzes towards the main entrance of the school, apparently not hearing my call. "I'll catch up with that boy later on," I say to them. "But I'm glad to see you've made up and you're in a good mood. And I'm glad that there are no hard feelings."

"If you let me back, I'll make sure everyone is good," Mercy says while tousling Béla's hair. He smiles at her sheepishly. They really do look quite good friends. God, maybe they're an item! Who'd have thought it?

"Well, I'm sure the school would consider you returning with the right kind of assurances. But some of my colleagues have the ridiculous thought that you're here for trouble."

Mercy looks surprised. Offended, even. "Us, sir? You've got to be having a laugh."

"So what have you come back for?"

"Pongy will tell you."

Mercy pushes Béla playfully. He stutters forward. To be honest, he looks a bit of mess. I wonder if the GMF are bullying him, or whether it's just horsing around. It's always hard to tell with the GMF and Béla.

"You were right, sir, they were just seeing if you'd let us all come back for the Sixth Form," he jabbers.

"I'm generally right about things," I say.

The grin on Mercy's face sags a little bit. I clap my hands together. "Well, I will certainly investigate the matter with Mr Ndlova. Of course, you realise that you did something very wrong and that may mean it's quite difficult for you to find a place here," I say, adding: "Mercy, you are a very clever girl who should be going to a top university, and you boys are excellent sportsmen. I'm sure, with a revised attitude, Mr Ndlova would consider a place for you here."

I leave them, feeling pleased: there is such a thing as forgiveness and redemption. There is.

8.35am

So I'm standing on my head, my face immersed in rotting bits of food, crushed against old chip wrappers and chicken bones.

The GMF grab my legs and yank me up and down, making my bones rattle, my pockets jangle and my head thud against the slimy bottom of the metal rubbish bin.

My mouth is full of blood from when I got punched by Mercy after the twins caught up with me at the end of the street. It was then that they dragged me kicking and screaming into an alcove on the estate opposite the Ballz-up where all the rubbish bins are and tipped me right into the biggest, dirtiest, smelliest one.

"You gay fuck, where's your mummy now, heh?" I hear one of the twins say.

I yell out that they must stop – the pain is agonising – but my words are swallowed up by the garbage. The GMF shake me again and my phone falls out of my pocket, resting in a mouldy banana skin.

Suddenly, the torture stops. Mercy's phone has gone off – I recognise its hip-hop ringtone – and she seems to be interested in attending to something else. This gives me a chance to edge closer to my phone by hopping on my head. I'm close enough to touch my speed dial. Luckily, Josh picks up right away; his voice is a little distant but I can hear it.

"Hey, where the fuck are you? You were supposed to meet outside school."

"Josh, you gotta help me. I'm fucked, man," I say. "I'm in a rubbish bin. The GMF got me."

"What? Where?"

"Right next to the school. You know, in that estate opposite. You gotta come quick, they're gonna kill me. They're saying I'm Countess Feckula and I posted all those pics on Twitter. Mercy's shanked me, man. I think I might die."

8.35am

The staffroom has filled up when I return from my duty. I notice that behind the throng of coffee and tea drinkers, Julia is standing by Jack's portrait. She hastens towards me.

"Martin, are you OK?" she asks.

"What do you mean?"

"Did the GMF abuse you?"

"Of course not; we just had a chat, that's all!"

Julia looks at me as though I've actually done something wrong; her hands are on her hips, her lips are pursed and her dull grey eyes are contemptuous.

"I was just reminiscing, that's all. That lot don't

frighten me," I say, retrieving the Pot Noodle from the microwave and tucking in with a fork.

"Martin, they're responsible for Jack's death. I just can't believe that you can be as flippant as that. You're not going to write an incident report?"

"I had a talk with them, that's all. And as to Jack's death, yes, their behaviour had quite terrible consequences. But you know very well that none of them intended that a man should die. Ultimately, they're just children. They're babies really – they just think they're tough."

Julia's contempt hurts me because once we were good friends, but Jack's death changed that. She says: "You should write an incident report. They're hanging around outside school. If it turns out there's another riot like last time, questions will be asked."

Looking at her wrinkled cheeks, I think: *oh you sad, embittered old woman, is that all you've got to do in the fag end of your career – insist upon creating more pointless bureaucracy?*

"I dealt with the matter. I don't see that I need to write anything. It's over. Problem sorted."

I flash a smile at her but she doesn't return one. She turns and walks away.

"You're not going to wish me good luck, or anything like that, are you?" I shout out after her. She spins round.

"What for?"

"My interview today."

"Oh that. Well, Sadie is going for the job too, so I'm not sure it's appropriate to wish anyone luck at this juncture."

She turns away and leaves the room. I look through the window at the street below and then again at Jack. *Life was so much easier when you were here, Jack. I never dreamt about getting a promotion of this sort then because life was so stable; you were the true boss.*

Fortunately, Jeff Burlington bundles into the staffroom before I can get too depressed. He greets me with a hearty slap on the back.

"Well, doesn't Martin Hick look all freshly primped and pampered today?"

"Got to look my best for my interview!"

"Interview, my arse, it's a bloody inauguration. You're the only candidate, mate!"

"Haven't you heard? I just learnt Sadie's going for it."

"Oh..." Burlington says. I can tell from his tone of voice that he's revising my prospects now. Sadie is a serious character: a good teacher, a supportive colleague, very well organised and the founder of the Lesbian, Gay, Bi-sexual and Trans-sexual (LGBT) group in school.

"I better gird my loins then!" I say.

"Yes, cover those loins up! No puppetry with the penis now!"

I do my best to laugh, but I find it difficult. The pips go for registration and the two of us walk towards our tutor groups, up the spiral staircase. Kids

are pushing past us but I don't think they're particularly listening, so I say: "It was difficult with Helen
last night."

"You'll be able to work things out in the holidays."

"Yes. But she doesn't want me to go for this job."

"She doesn't?"

"No. She thinks I should go part-time. Spend more
time with Josh and Martha."

We're right outside our classrooms now. Both are
sounding a bit rowdy.

"Look, hang in there, mate. Let's talk later," Jeff
says, squeezing my arm.

I enter my classroom, take the register and ask the
class what they are doing in the holidays. A few of
them are going away, but the vast majority are staying at home. It makes me think about how lucky I am
that I can afford to go away. Except, weirdly enough,
I almost wish I didn't have the money to go on holiday. I'd probably have a much better time at home.
After telling the class to make sure that they get to the
end-of-term assembly on time, I dismiss them a little
early – something I don't normally do, but I'm feeling a bit discombobulated by the news Sadie is going
for the job.

I sneak down to the English resources room for a
few minutes to myself before the first lesson starts.
Sitting at my crowded desk, I think I really need to
tidy up all the mess. I am, it has to be said, pathologic-
ally incapable of throwing anything away.

My stomach feels horribly full from the Pot Noodle

and all those chocolates. I still feel a bit sick. Maybe I should go and throw up?

No. No. It's not that drastic. I know what I need. A little medicine. I unlock my bottom draw – the only one I've got locked – and retrieve my bottle of "orange squash". I take a good long swig and wait for the squash to kick in the back of my throat and line my stomach. Ah, yes, that does the trick! Never fails. Much better. I put it back and lock the draw.

Now I remember I really should file a report on the GMF hanging around outside school. But the prospect doesn't enthuse me. I hate writing reports.

Shutting my eyes, I snatch some random documents and chuck them into the bin. It's fatal to stare. They're like the Gorgon; once you look them straight in the face, you turn to stone! It's generally best to shut your eyes, gather up a great wodge in your arms and chuck them in the bin without once peeking.

"Tidying up, heh?"

I open my eyes. Jeff is standing in the doorway, holding his green mark book like a shield in front of his chest.

"Yeah. Time for a clear-out, I think," I say.

"Look, I was thinking maybe we could go for a drink tonight, away from the hoi polloi?"

"Shall I call you later? I'm not sure what I'm doing."

"OK."

Jeff turns to go. There are still mounds of paperwork before me. I say: "Do you know Helen used to help me clean out my old office, you remember the one in the old building?"

"She did?"

"Yes – nearly every holiday. We had some good times here actually…"

I chuck the papers into the bin with abandon.

"Too much information, my dear Hick!"

"Josh was conceived in that office!"

"Definitely too much information! Look, call me later, heh?"

The moment he's left I regret saying that. What if it gets back to the kids? Then Josh's life will be even harder here. Oh dear. Why am I such idiot? But think positive: think positive. Jeff's a good bloke. I can trust him.

I lean back in my chair, rubbing my eyes, my stressed mind trying to tidy up the confusion of memories: making love to Helen in the creaky old office, the early days of Josh's life, Helen's fierce words last night. I bash my fist against the desk in frustration at the mess.

8.39am

"Whoah, it's Béla's bum-chum!" Mercy shouts out gleefully.

"The one who sucked his dick at the back of his dad's class!"

"And then had their knobs sucked off by his paedo dad!"

"Paedo bum-chum dick-sucking fudge-packing gay day shit-sticker!"

I'm still headfirst in the rubbish so I can't see what's going on but I can hear pretty well. My first thought is: thank fuck! Then, I think: God, what's Josh going to do? He's an even bigger wimp than I am.

"Just let him go, Mercy! He hasn't done anything," Josh says.

There's a round of laughter and then I hear Mercy explain that I've dissed her in the worst possible way by making out that she's fucked a gay fuck like me.

This seems to really irritate Josh. He shouts, "How many fucking times do I have to tell you he's not fucking gay!"

There's a bit of scuffling and the sound of some stuff clattering about in the distance. I hear quite a bit of cussing and Mercy shouting: "Oh you fucking gay cunt, what have you done?"

Suddenly I find the bin tipping over. I wriggle out of it as quickly as I can. Josh helps me a little, too, by pulling at my legs. Eventually, I emerge with the banana skin draped over my face. "We gotta get the fuck out of here!" I say.

I look around and can't see the GMF anywhere. I don't feel it's appropriate at this juncture to ask where they are. Instead, me and Josh run for our lives out of the estate. Once we're safe and standing outside the school, we look at each other, panting.

"What the fuck did you do?" I ask Josh, with my hands on my knees.

"I just grabbed the bag Mercy was holding and flung it

as far as I could. They ran after it. There was loads of crap in it they wanted, I think," Josh says, pushing his long fringe out of his eyes.

I look into his black eyes and think about thanking him for saving my life, but decide against it. It would be a bit too corny.

"Anyway, who do you think Feckula is? I'm beginning to think I better find out before I die!" I say.

Josh shrugs. "I reckon it might be Jakaria. I'll check it out; he's in my class next."

There isn't much more time to have a chat because the GMF suddenly appear at the end of the street. They are running towards us at top speed. Josh and I look at each other and then, without saying any more, we scram in separate directions: he dives back into the Ballz-up, and I run towards home. Just before we go our separate ways, Josh chucks a small rectangular object at me. I catch it without realising what it is, but as I'm running along the street it dawns on me that I'm holding Mercy's mobile phone.

"Hey, you gay fuck, if you don't give me my phone back, I'll kill you!" Mercy yells at Josh as he vanishes into the precincts of the Ballz-up.

8.40am

I find myself doing a rare thing in school: nothing. Just sitting at a desk, staring at the piles of paper I've just chucked in the bin.

My head still hurts a bit. The skin feels taut

underneath my eyes. There's a familiar lingering sadness in my fingers. My chest is constricted. I'm not in
great shape. During the holidays I'll take up jogging,
swimming and cycling again. Maybe go out with
Josh. Down the canal towpath. We could cycle along
the Grand Union Canal, around Vicky Park, down to
Docklands. Yes, I will make things right with Josh.

And Helen can come too. She likes cycling. She
used to be really serious about it.

I notice a DVD poking out of the mass of papers
that are spilling out of the bin. I pick it up and examine it. My heart thuds when I see it. It's labelled
"Jack Humphreys' Teaching Tips".

God, it's the film Jack and I made five years ago for
new teachers. I've been hunting for this for quite a
while. Ever since he died, in fact. I thought I'd lost it.
But no, it's here in the bin.

I stick the DVD into the disk drive and watch the
swirling screen as Windows Media Player boots up.

Then suddenly – although the quality of the film
is rather shoddy and my camera work far too jerky
for someone feeling as queasy as I am – I'm back at
the school five years ago. Jack is standing in the corridor ushering children into lessons, and who should
run by but Josh and Béla! They look so innocent, so
different, so much smaller and happier. They must
have been eleven or so. They make a show of misbe-
having – pulling faces at each other and waving at the
camera. Jack puts his hands on their shoulders and
guides them to the classroom, joking with them, mak-

ing them laugh. He comes up to the camera, about to deliver his first Teaching Tip – the one about keeping control, about the need to distract badly behaved children with good-natured humour, but it's too much. I stop the DVD before he speaks. There's a lump in my throat. Jack is both there – and not there. It's almost like he's alive again.

"Oh Jack, what if I can't distract them anymore?" I whisper.

"What's this you're saying?" a voice says behind me.

I close down the DVD quickly and see that Sadie has entered the office. Her demure skirt suit, her black-stockinged legs, her neatly cut bobbed hair make her look so efficient these days. When she first arrived, years ago, she had spiky bright orange hair and wore a Che Guevara T-shirt. Her desk was littered with copies of *Spare Rib* and feminist books of literary criticism. Now it's all policy documents and training manuals.

"Was that Jack?" she asks tentatively.

"No. No. It was nothing," I say abruptly.

Sadie folds her arms. "I think many of the staff have issues about what happened on the day Jack…"

I look through my messy drawers, refusing to meet her gaze.

"Died?" I volunteer.

Sadie hangs her head down and says: "Yes."

The pips go before we can say anymore. In true Pavlovian fashion, both of us stand to attention and notice that we've both had the same automatic reaction. I fix Sadie with a gimlet grin. She winces. I don't care that she's uneasy. She's a rat trying to rob me of my job. All's fair in love and war. We move on to the first lesson of the last day of term.

9.05am

It's so lovely staying this long in the bath. My wounds feel like they have healed now. I feel comfortable and pensive, so I reflect upon the:

Top 5 mysteries of life

1. Fear. Why does it make you feel so alive?
2. Mr Hick's marriage. Does he know his missus is playing away with old Loverman? Should I talk to Josh about it?
3. What would Mercy's tits be like to feel?
4. If Dad was alive, would I be happier, more successful, loved by everyone?
5. The dead. Is it possible for them to come back?

Thinking of the dead always depresses me because it makes me think of Dad. How he is just gone. And yet he isn't. He is in my head still: *you can be who you want to be, Béla, you can be anyone.*

I get out of the bath, dry myself and go to my drawer of disguises. This always makes me feel better.

Since no one is around to laugh at me, I have a bit of fun trying them on in front of the mirror and taking some pics of myself. I never know when they might come in handy. First, I put on my doctor's outfit which I pinched from the Royal London Hospital; it's so easy to nick stuff there. Mind you, sometimes it does feel like grave robbing.

I look really good in the white coat, with the stethoscope around my neck and pocket microscope in my hand. I take a photo.

Then, I try on the barrister's jacket and wig I got second hand in Chancery Lane a few months back. That looks a bit funny. Snap that.

After that, I put on my city-worker's outfit. I don't have the money to buy a really snazzy suit, but still it looks OK. Snap that. I decide to stay in my suit because I reckon if I get my hair cut, I might be able to avoid long-range detection from the GMF in it when I'm out on the streets again.

Then I spend a bit of time looking at Mercy's phone.

There's not much on it really. No passwords or any of that really useful stuff, but I do find some quite interesting stuff on her texts: she's had a lot of appointments at the doctor's, and at the Ballz-up. They have texted her to come to her exclusion panel meeting; they never did that for me. I don't know why but I get the impression that Mercy really does want to go back to the Sixth Form. As I'm looking through it, the hip-hop tune starts up. Fuck, my own phone is calling Mercy's!

I pick up.

"Josh, you fuck-up, you gotta give me my phone back," Mercy says.

I don't say anything. The last thing I want is Mercy to

know I've got her phone. Thinking this makes me feel guilty though, because it means that Josh is in the firing line. Then an idea comes to me. A really good idea.

"I'm giving it to Ndlova. Collect it from him this afternoon."

I hang up and text Josh from Mercy's phone. I know his number off by heart.

Me: Hey, Josh its Bela on Mercys fone. weve gotta give this fone to Loverman this pm
Josh: Wot the fuck?
Me: Yeah, worked it out. Maybe u cld cum over here at lunch and get it?
Josh: Fuck off. The GMF wll b waiting 4 me
Me: OK
Josh: Aint u gonna thank me?
Me: Fanks. U r a pal
Josh: A pal? I fucking saved your life m8

For some reason I don't want to talk about it. I don't like the idea of owing Josh anything. I'm the one who's normally helping him out.

Me: What lesson r u in?
Josh: English
Me: What is yr Dad teaching u?
Josh: Wot u wanna no 4?
Me: OK to txt?
Josh: Im txting u aint I?
Me: BTW I fink I no who C Feck is

Josh: Who?
Me: It's definitely Jakaria
Josh: U told me that before
Me: And now I'm certain
Josh: It ain't
Me: It is. He confessed to me on Facebook
Josh: He wld say anything to sound hard
Me: U may be rite. I got some investig8ing to do

I switch off Mercy's phone and stare at my computer screen.

I've been looking at Countess Feckula's Twitter page again. There's another tweet:

This is the day Hicky goes down

The Countess is clearly someone in or near school. The most obvious explanation is that it has to be Mercy but I can see from the phone that it isn't her. There's absolutely no evidence of anything like that.

It feels frustrating being stuck at home when all the action seems to be in school. It's safe here, but boring.

I decide to make myself some Hungarian pancakes and some coffee.

9.15am

I'm waiting by the photocopier when Jakaria strolls past seemingly oblivious to the fact that he's in an area forbidden to pupils. To make matters worse, he is sucking a lollipop. This is the sort of indiscipline Sam's reign has brought to this place.

"Now, Jakaria, I hear that you've been saying nasty things about me on the internet?"

"What?" he says with the lollipop still in his mouth. In one deft move, I snatch it from his hand and point the offending sticky sweet at him as I repeat my charge.

"What?"

"Look, Jakaria, I know it was you, so you need to stop it and perhaps apologise to me!"

This evinces a more verbal response: "But sir, it weren't me. I ain't done nuffink. I ain't. It ain't me. I reckon it was Pongy. Pongy and Mercy. Them two are bum-chums and I reckon she put him up to it in return for favours. I mean, you did get them excluded, didn't you, sir? They got a good reason to want you dead, innit."

"Don't lie to me, Jakaria. Just don't lie. I know Béla well enough to know he would never say something like that about me. And Mercy too. She was a very good student."

"You dunna know Pongrácz, sir. He did it. He's Countess Feckula, believe me."

The photocopier has jammed. The screen is flashing red in all sorts of places. As I bend down to fix it, pulling out the relevant paper trays, Jakaria escapes. I shout after him, but he's well away. Still, I'll catch up with him next lesson.

Although most teachers are showing DVDs or

playing trivial games on this last day of term, I am determined to carry on teaching *Death of a Salesman*, which I've been reading with my Year 10 GCSE English class.

Unfortunately, there's something wrong with my interactive whiteboard, which won't let me log on and, when it finally does, only produces a blank screen. As I'm trying to figure it out, the class timidly ask me whether we can play a game or watch a DVD. I'm pissed off that the whiteboard isn't working because I've got this PowerPoint which has a load of quiz questions about the play: we were going to play 'Deal or No Deal' with Arthur Miller, and look at a series of stills from stage productions of the play to match with certain lines. Then I was going to finish it off by showing them clips, taken from YouTube, of various endings to the play, and they were going to judge which were the best. It was going to be a good lesson and I can't bloody well do it because the bloody technology has fucking broken. I know there's no point in calling a technician because they're all on holiday right now.

I have to think on my feet. I put this learning objective on the board: To learn about the issues surrounding suicide.

Then I write the debate question underneath it:

Did Willy Loman do the right thing by committing suicide?

The whole class groan. Jakaria says: "Oh sir, I thought you said we was gonna have a fun lesson!"

"This is a fun lesson! It's fun to think about suicide!" I quip. No one laughs. "Now get out your books and write down the learning objective and the question. I want you to think of three reasons why Willy was right to commit suicide and three reasons why he was wrong. You can do a little chart. A suicide chart."

"But sir, I don't wanna to think about suicide," Jakaria says. "It's against the Koran."

"Put that down as a reason!" I retort.

Jakaria dutifully buys this; I watch him as he laboriously writes down "Willy shouldn't have done himself in coz it's against the Koran."

I walk around the class seeing that no one has much enthusiasm for the suicide chart, with only the swotty girls writing much. Oh God, how I wish the fucking interactive whiteboard was working!

Josh doesn't seem too keen. Despite what everyone says, I really feel it's worked teaching him at the school. I know there have been problems with him being bullied, but they are more or less solved now that the GMF have been excluded.

Our relationship in school is quite unlike the one we have at home; it's much more talkative here. We're constantly sparring with each other; it gives Josh "school cred" because he can be quite cutting. But I'm man enough to take that. The most important thing is that our verbal jousting sparks off all kinds of talk from the other pupils. Although I could have time-tabled Josh with another English teacher, I jumped at the chance to have him because, if I'm honest, I felt it would be an opportunity for him to see me at my best.

But today I can tell he's fiddling around on his mobile phone. The debate is not catching on, and Jakaria doesn't help by saying: "I reckon Béla Pongrácz needs to top himself before everyone finds out he's Countess Feckula."

There are a lot of sniggers around the classroom, which I quell by shouting at Jakaria: "How dare you speak like that in my lesson!"

"He's Countess Feckula, innit!" Jakaria persists.

The sniggers continue. "Jakaria, please, can you let me get on with the lesson?" I say.

The matter is dropped. After a few drab remarks, I pick on Josh.

"Come on, Josh, what do you think?"

Josh hastily shoves his phone in his pocket and looks at me. "What did you say?"

The other children laugh.

"Do you think it might ever be right to commit suicide?"

"Yes."

"Well, when?"

"When you've had all of your dreams and illusions shattered. When you realise how meaningless everything is. When you've betrayed someone you love."

"Like Willy Loman in the play?"

"Yes."

It's just the kind of comment that I needed because it does foster discussion with the pupils, with a lot of them protesting that Willy's ultimate betrayal was to kill himself.

And the lesson becomes a triumphant success. Towards the end, I play Arthur Miller "Word Tennis" with the class; this is where the class are divided into two teams and have to come up with a word connected with the great playwright which is then "hit" over to the other team who have to respond with another "Arthur Miller" word which begins with the last letter of the previous word. So the game begins like this:

"Faith," Josh shouts out, being the leader of team one.

"Hurt," a girl from the other side.

"The stockings," Josh retorts back immediately, a hint of aggression in his voice. As he says it, he looks me right in the eye – something he never usually does at school.

"You can't count 'the', Josh. A point to the other side," I interpose with an uneasy smile: for some reason, Josh bringing up the stockings that Willy Loman buys for his mistress makes me uncomfortable.

The pips go. As the class are making their way to the next lesson, I ask my son to have a word with me.

"You're not mad at me, are you?" I whisper by the interactive whiteboard. The last child has left the classroom and we have the room to ourselves.

Josh runs his hands through his hair in a way that I find quite irritating at home but for some reason don't in school.

"No, not at all," he says, acting far too surprised for my liking.

"It's just that the Word Tennis felt a little… angry."

"It did?"

Seeing his obvious incomprehension, I relax a little.

"It's all right. It doesn't matter."

Then he pauses. "You know, Dad. I reckon Jakaria's right, though. I reckon Béla is the Countess Feckula." His expression is solemn, grim.

"I find that difficult to believe. Isn't he your best friend? Haven't I gone out of my way to help him?"

"Dad, you got him kicked out of the school."

"He's still angry about it?"

"Wouldn't you be? You ruined his life, Dad. He hasn't got a chance."

"Josh, how many times have we been through this? He threw that bloody firework…"

Josh looks angry. "I wish you'd stop saying that, Dad, you don't know that!"

"I saw it with my own eyes, Josh."

"Why are you getting so worked up about it if you're so sure?"

"Just go to your next lesson," I snap. I can't help feeling melancholic about the lugubrious way he walks away.

My Year 8s are starting to dribble in, when the Principal's face pops up outside my room. Kylie tags behind him. Assuming that it's nothing to do with me and that they're simply passing by, I dish out my starter activity, a spelling competition, when Sam enters the room.

"Mr Hick, could I have a word?"

"I'm just about to teach!" I say in my cheeriest voice. "I think my Year 8s would be very disappointed if I didn't!"

Sam isn't to be put off, though.

"Miss Rouse is all set to cover the lesson, don't worry!"

I can see Kylie is carrying a dreaded DVD of *The Karate Kid* behind her back.

"I have an important lesson to teach, Mr Ndlova, can't this wait?"

"It really is a matter of urgency that I speak to you now."

Realising I have no choice but to leave the class, I look at Kylie and say to her, "Instead of showing them that wretched DVD, could you teach them a lesson?"

Kylie gives me a hurt look. I never normally speak to her like this. I pat her gently on the back and apologise. She nods.

"I'll teach them, Martin, I promise."

9.30am

Béla Pongrácz, man of mystery, master of disguises, intrepid detective. The Sherlock Holmes of Bethnal Green. Once again I'm doing the unmentionable because I'm fearless.

After having my pancakes, I sneak into Ma's room carrying a cup of coffee, boot up her computer and try a few new passwords. After all, I managed to get into Loverman's account, so why can't I get into hers?

No good. Still. I've been trying to hack into her account for over a year now.

I try lots of combinations just to make sure – CountessFeckula, FeckulaCountess – adding her date of birth, our postcode and so on. None of them work.

She's probably not Feckula but this messing around has made me think even harder about who she is.

There's a mystery at the heart of Ma. I shut down the laptop and have a go at opening her cupboard, which is always locked. I try to pick the lock, but it's no good.

So I push the cupboard off the wall a little and see if I can pull open the hardboard covering at the back. After fetching a long screwdriver from the tool-box underneath my bed, I manage to loosen a number of screws and get a glimpse. I can't get the whole back panel off so I content myself with peering through a bunch of clothes.

The inside of the cupboard doesn't reassure me. In the murky gloom, I can see what looks like a leather whip with a tasselled head, a big bucket and some kind of uniform.

Do you need this kind of stuff to work in human resources?

Just as I am screwing the back on the cupboard, I hear a key in the lock.

I leave Ma's bedroom quickly. The Count enters the flat. I'm not quite sure whether he's seen me leaving her room.

"Oh my goodness, we do look smart, don't we, Béla?" he says, admiring my suit.

"Well, I thought that maybe I would smarten up after being so scruffy this morning," I say.

The Count tells me that I need to help fetch Ma from downstairs. I ask him how it all went and he tells me, with a superior expression, that it all ran smoothly. I'm turning to get Ma, when he says: "You know, my poor Béla, it is very unwise indeed to enter Bluebeard's castle. Very unwise."

"Bluebeard's castle?"

"Yes. The realm of the forbidden."

It's a strange moment of intimacy between us. He's both patronising me and indicating that he knows some important stuff. Maybe he wants to talk to me?

"But Your Excellency, I can't help being curious… What *does* Ma do during the day?" I ask.

The Count looks at me in alarm.

"It is most unbecoming to ask what a countess does. Aristocratic women have to retain their dignity, especially fallen aristocratic women."

"But Ma certainly isn't one any more."

"One can never deny one's lineage, Béla; you will find this out yourself. Even though you may feel no more than a common street urchin here, one day you will come to realise that your true nature is that of a count."

"I will?"

"Yes, you will. Because blood is thicker than water. Especially blue Hungarian blood... Now your mother is most desirous that you fetch her from downstairs. I had a devil of a job getting her back."

"You won't tell her about...?"

The Count doesn't deign to reply. But I realise that this is not because he intends to dob me in it, but because it's beneath him to answer such a base question. I rush out of the flat and down the piss-streaked stairs to find Ma manoeuvring her wheelchair angrily around the pavement in the morning sunlight.

"Béla, why did you take so long?" she asks.

"I'm sorry, Ma."

"And why are you wearing that suit? Are you planning to get a job in the stock exchange?"

I think about cracking a joke about how that might spare us defrauding insurance companies, but I resist. I value my life.

"I just wanted to look smart, Ma."

"Mmmnnn," she says. She's quite suspicious of my motives. I can tell she thinks I'm up to something.

I think for a moment about saying that there is no need now to pretend that she's disabled but I can see that she's in no mood to be contradicted. I open the broken front door to the block and push her into the stinky entrance hall. The lift is, of course, still broken, so Ma says that I should carry the wheelchair up to the flat and then come back for her. I lift her onto a step and lug the wheelchair back to the flat. Then I drape Ma around my shoulders and carry her up the stairs.

When we are safely in the flat, and she's lit herself a fag, Ma says to me: "Everything went very well at the health centre. The man said no doubt I deserved the disability benefit."

I brush some fluff off my lapel. I feel good in this suit.

"Béla, haven't you forgotten something?"

"No, Ma, I think I've covered everything."

A frown sours her forehead.

"Béla, did you get my cigarettes?"

Shit, shit, shit.

10.10am

By the time I reach the Principal's office, I'm smiling broadly because I'm certain Sam is in some kind of trouble and needs me to come to the rescue. A familiar scenario. Except now there's only me – and no Jack.

"So what hole do you need me to get you out of now?" I ask Sam, as he shuts the door behind me.

But to my astonishment, he faces me with his hands planted on his hips and says: "Look, Martin, it upsets me to have to do this, but there is a problem…"

I blink.

"I feel I have no choice but to suspend you."

Narrow my eyes.

And then I burst out laughing. "I've never chalked you up as a practical joker, Sam, but this is a good one. A very good one. It's the kind of thing Burlington would pull on me, but not you."

Sam looks down at some papers on his desk as he says: "It's no joke, Martin."

I continue laughing. "You're good, do you know that? You're very good!"

"I'm not acting, Martin. This is real."

I hear the word "real", I see Sam's obviously distressed features, and I don't understand. This is the day of my interview, my big day, the day when things go right. The curl of my big, broad smile falls into the yellow sear.

"Why don't you sit down for a second?" Sam says.

I plonk myself in one of the new leather pod-like chairs I helped him pick from IKEA and put my hands over my belly. Sam stands like a centurion in front of his desk.

"What do you mean, suspend me? What's going on?"

Incipient traces of grey are sneaking up the side of Sam Ndlova's finely boned head. Sweat trickles down his temple. I press my point: "I've got an interview.

You can't suspend me today. It's utterly absurd."

Feeling at a disadvantage sitting down, looking up at him, I get up out of the pod chair and move towards Sam's desk. The bulk of my frame stands very close to his much thinner, taller body. Sam does not move.

"Some serious allegations have been made against you. I'm going to have to ask you to leave the premises until this matter has been investigated fully."

"What? What are you talking about?" I ask. The fine spray of my spit dapples Sam's cheek but he doesn't wipe it off.

"I am not at liberty to divulge the identity of the victim. Suffice to say that his allegations are very serious."

At this point, I feel that some consolidated action is required. I dodge past my old friend and hasten behind his desk – the expansive teak bureau I helped him buy when he was appointed to his top position; the position which I helped secure for him.

My eyes scramble over the word-processed document. I recognise the "Memo Style" immediately, the Assistant Vice Principal logo at the top, the Microsoft Word template that she always uses, the complex sentences, the spattering of jargon and the signature at the bottom.

ASSISTANT
VICE PRINCIPAL

MEMO

To: the Principal (the Child Protection Officer)
From: the Assistant Vice Principal
Date: July 20th
Re: Allegations against the Director of English

Highly confidential

Dear Sam,

It's with a very heavy heart that I have to report some serious allegations to you. A pupil has claimed that a teacher has exposed himself to him and has attempted a form of sexual assault. It is with very great shock and sadness that I have to report this teacher as being Martin Hick, who, as you know, is one of my best friends on the staff.

I can scarcely believe these allegations myself, but the note I was sent reads thus:

Dear Mrs Webb,

I am not supposed to say anything but I have to. I was having extra lessons with Mr Hick for my GCSE English after school and I was alone with him. We were talking about the Fall of the Berlin Wall, and he started remembering how he was there just a few days after the Wall came down. He said that there were some very wild theatre groups, doing some very strange things in Berlin at that time, including

puppetry with their penises. I laughed. Then he got it out
and made me touch it. He made me do other stuff that I
can't talk about here.

I don't know what to do. I am not at the school anymore,
and didn't say anything at first because I was ashamed. But
now I realise that this should be dealt with. I like Mr Hick but
what he did was wrong. I can't tell anyone except you. You
must promise not to tell anyone.

Yours the Countess Feckula

(Transcribed by myself this morning after the hand-
written note was put under my door: I will show you
the note today)

I think you must agree that this note has to be taken
seriously – even though it is anonymous. I believe it
is fairly obvious who this pupil is by its content. I will
certainly tell you my hypothesis in person if you want
me to. If these claims are true, we must make sure that
Mr Hick is withdrawn from teaching immediately.
Personally, I think his mental state could have been
affected by the death of Mr Humphreys. He behaved
heroically on that day, but I know his wife well and
have heard he has been behaving strangely. I know
other things about him which I won't say here, but
I will tell you in person. We need to have an urgent
meeting about this.

Julia Webb

I sit down on the swivel chair behind the desk and
try to absorb the full import of the note. With my lips
trembling, I say: "This is outrageous. Nothing like
that took place. It's nonsense. Does Webb have any
proof? Who is this Countess Feckula? Did she actually meet him – or her?"

Sam shakes his head. "I don't think so, but the law
states that an allegation of this sort, even if uncor-
roborated, is enough to warrant immediate suspen-
sion. The precautionary principle applies. And I'm
a bit concerned that these appalling allegations may
be on the internet already. I have to be seen to take
action, Martin, before this gets out of hand."

Sam won't look me in the eye. My heart bludgeons
against my ribs. This is a fucking nightmare. I can't
really think straight. I can see my whole career – and
life – disappearing down the toilet of these lies.

"It's on the internet?" I muster, wiping the sweat
away from my face with the back of my hand. Sam
nods.

"Do you know who this Countess Feckula is?" I
ask, starting to shiver.

"I don't know who Feckula is, but I am going to
investigate it properly. This is a heavy-duty allegation, Martin."

"You've already told me that," I say.

I put my head between my hands and press hard.
I need to think. I need to work out who might have
done this. The Berlin Wall, puppetry with the penis.
Well, yes, I did have a jokey lesson a few months ago

with my GCSE class where these subjects were mentioned; we were doing a comprehension about the collapse of the Soviet Union. A revision lesson after school. So there's a ring of truth about this. But…

"I was never alone with a pupil during that revision class!" I blurt out. "I have registers, Sam. I can get them. I can prove to you that I was never alone. And as for the stuff about the Berlin Wall and the puppetry, it was all banter. It was banter that one child got excited about too…" I say as a dawning realisation comes upon me. "Yes, one child in particular. A Hungarian child – whom I happened to get permanently excluded for chucking a firework at Jack."

I emblazon Sam with my eyes, almost wanting to smile with my dawning revelation.

Sam now meets my gaze – and understands. "And you think it's Béla ?"

"Yes."

Sam harrumphs. "Well, I suppose that might make sense."

I turn around in the swivel chair, trying to reach up for his arm – but in a neat manoeuvre, he turns away from me, seemingly to retrieve pen and paper from his desk. Once he has the pad in his hands, he starts scribbling.

"You've got to give me a chance to speak to him!" I protest.

"Martin, you're not to speak to anyone. It'll just inflame the situation. I'll speak to Béla," he says, still writing.

I get up out of his chair but remain in close proximity.

"But what about my interview?" I ask.

"That's not going to happen today," he says.

"This is ridiculous, Sam. You're making a serious mistake giving any credence to anything Béla Pongrácz says. We all know it's him. And he's got every reason to hate me. After all, it was me who got him permanently excluded; it was me who saw him throw the firework at Jack. The boy is very bad news, Sam, you know that. Nothing he does can be trusted. And you're trusting his word against mine?"

Sam touches my shoulder, indicating that I should stop standing behind his desk. "Martin, I have to ask you to leave the school now. I will contact you as soon as I know any more. In the meantime, I would advise you to get legal representation and try your best to relax. I am sure we will resolve this in due course, but we have to follow the proper procedures."

I move back to the centre of the room.

"Bollocks, Sam. You need to give me a proper chance. You need to assume I'm innocent until proven guilty."

Sam's nostrils flare at my defiance. "Martin, I must ask you to go. I have a great deal to do."

Sam sits down before his computer again, his hands hovering over the keyboard, his eyes darting at what's on the screen – and then he looks at me. I tighten my hands into fists and bury them in my pockets: his lack of sympathy infuriates me but I know I must try my best to keep calm.

"Look, Sam, you've got to give me some time to clear my name. You've got to. We're friends, Sam – or at least we used to be. You were my best man. We were in a band at university. You've got to give me this chance."

Sam nods. Pauses. Then nods again. He looks like he's weighing up a lot of things in his mind.

He stands up and says: "OK, Martin. Theoretically, I suppose, it is possible that I might not have opened this memo until after six this evening... I will try and avoid Julia Webb until then. I don't have any scheduled appointments with her."

Spontaneously, I lunge at my old friend, giving him one of my best bear hugs: my suit crinkling against his Armani one, fabric against fabric. I hug him tightly, smelling that sharp, slightly acrid tang that Sam's body emits under duress, scenting his aftershave as well. Sam's arms linger around my shoulders, and then he pats me on the back.

"Thanks, Sam, thanks," I say as I pull away from him. "Thanks."

"But remember, Martin, don't speak to Béla – that will just inflame the situation. I will deal with him."

I look at my friend and nod gravely. Then I leave his office.

10.20am

Ma digs around in the washing machine and holds up my wet, blue shirt. The blood stains don't seem to have come out.

"Béla! What is this! This shirt was clean this morning. Now it seems ruined."

"Nothing. I just fell over, that's all."

"Your nice new shirt! It was expensive. Have those thugs been after you again?"

"Look, I'll go and get your fags, and then I'll explain everything."

"No, you're not leaving this house today, Béla. You can stay with His Excellency, and I'll get the fags."

"But Ma!"

"I'm not letting you out. And you're going to take that shirt and scrub the stains out of it in the sink."

I pick up the shirt and have a go at scratching the blood out with my fingernails. Ma looks at me with something approaching pity.

"Now, Béla, I'm a good woman, and I see you do need to have fresh air, so I'll rethink my plans for you. You must take the Count to the South Bank. There's a free concert in the place this afternoon. Schubert. The Count will love it. It will be culture for you too. You need cultural things, Béla, otherwise you will become a yob like every other youth in this area."

"What are they playing?" the Count asks.

"Oh something or other," she says, blowing smoke in

our direction. If anyone else was this vague, the Count would complain. But he is silent.

I start coughing from the smoke.

"I'm not sure I want to," I say. "I've got things to do here."

Ma snarls at me: "What? Play on that computer of yours?"

"No. There's other stuff. I could look at other benefits we could claim."

"Béla, shut up! Shut up! You are going to the South Bank and that's it. That is it!" Ma says. "Besides, you stay here, those thugs might come around. I think it's a good idea to get out of the area. And you are dressed for it. You might be able to charm some rich young ladies there. I think a nice rich girlfriend will do you a world of good, instead of that Josh boy!"

She makes for her bedroom. I follow her.

"Ma, I've been wanting to talk to you… You know that job of yours in human resources – what exactly does it involve?"

She flinches. "What do you mean, what does it involve?"

"Well, do you have to tell people off? Do you have to punish them?"

By now, she's reached her bedroom. She opens the door and lets herself in. Then, wedged between the door and the frame, she says: "Why are you asking me stupid questions like this? Now, go and get the Count ready for his trip out."

I slump on the sofa, switch on the box and my laptop.

On TV, there's an inane chat-show about parents who care more about their pets than their children. The Count sits at the piano, tinkering on the keys and writing notes on the staves. He is composing a sonata.

On Facebook and Twitter there's a whole load of stuff from the Countess Feckula. With a gasp, I see it's far worse than the stuff before.

Hick dicks his pupils with his prick!

This time there's a link to a picture of Hicky which has been photoshopped so that it looks like he's got his cock out of his trousers. Fuck me, this is bad, very bad.

Hicky makes his pupils give him blowjobs.

There's the same link to the "penis" picture.

On another new Twitter site, Lady Feckbeth, there is another comment:

Hicky is a bum-bandit, a shit-sticker, a paedo, a gimp.

This time there's a link to another photo of Hicky looking like he's bumming Jakaria. Fucking hell! Lady Feckbeth must be Mercy. It must be; it's exactly the kind of language she uses about me!

The links and updates have covered all of Year 11's Facebook and Twitter pages. It's everywhere! God, this could be national news before the day is out.

Ma emerges from the bedroom with a large rucksack

on her back. It's the gear she always goes to work with. Do you need a large rucksack for human resources?

"You're looking very disabled, Ma," I joke.

"Béla, shut up and help your uncle get ready to go out again."

"He doesn't want to go out," I say, pointing at the Count.

"He does," she says in a softened voice. It's a voice that actually tells me that she knows I'm not going to go to the South Bank and that's OK as long as I don't argue with her anymore.

With that she leaves. Simple as that. No more arguments. She's just gone.

I take a puff on my inhaler and think hard about my options. Do I really want to stay here or do I want to find out what Ma is up to?

So I decide to bribe the Count, saying that I'll get him a big bottle of *palinka* if he says I took him out to the South Bank.

"I suppose my impromptus could do with some work," he says.

Then I go back into my bedroom and change out of my city suit. She'll spot me too easily if I'm in that, but she won't see me if I wear the new disguise I bought for a few quid in Brick Lane Market the other day: my Geek Squad disguise: black plastic-rimmed glasses, checked shirt, black trousers. Then I put my old school uniform in my backpack – I have the strange feeling that I'm going to have to do some hard detective work in school later today if I really want to get to the bottom of all the Countess Feckula stuff.

I dodge out of the flat before the Count can see me. Once I'm out on the street, I feel like I am back in the game again. The real game of life.

10.55am

Jeff rubs his beard. He and I are huddled together in a toilet cubicle. It's the only private space we can find.

"Mart, mate, look, as your union rep, I reckon you should take my advice and go home and watch some TV. Don't approach anyone, take the last day off, put your feet up, have a beer and forget about it."

"But I really think I need to speak to Béla. If I can get him to admit that he's this bloody Countess Feckula and that he's made all this stuff up, I reckon I'm in the clear."

Jeff shakes his head.

"I wouldn't recommend talking to the boy. He's trouble – and his mother is even worse."

"It's definitely him. Definitely him, all that stuff about the Berlin Wall and puppetry with the penis. I remember him laughing about it at the time. He got a real kick out of it, you know?"

"Mart, mate, you can't speak to him. He'll just say you're trying to bully him. It'll make things worse for you. You won't change his mind and you'll get angry and it'll make things far worse."

"But it's so unfair, Jeff!" I say with clenched fists. "Just when I'm about to sort everything out, now this comes along!"

I look at Jeff's thinning, grey hair and remember a time – not so long ago – when his tonsure was bright and brown.

"It'll come to nowt. Sam will investigate it, find that Béla was making it all up and it'll be forgotten next term. It's far better that he does that than you."

"But Jeff, I just don't think I could bear to have this whole thing hanging over me during the holidays. Things haven't been so good between Helen and me. And I just know that getting this job will make all the difference. We'll have some extra cash, for one thing. Cash I can spend on her. I need to take her away for a romantic holiday, get away from all of this and the kids, and just be with her. I want to romance her, to show her I really care, but I can't at the moment."

"You don't have to take her on an expensive holiday to do that."

"It's more than that. I'm not sure she really respects me. Although she says she wants me to be on hand for the kids, I think actually that's the last thing I should do. I think if I had this job I'd gain status in her eyes; I'd show her I'm going somewhere. I feel she just thinks of me as a has-been. She's done so well and I've just stagnated. This promotion would change that."

I can see that Jeff thinks about squeezing my arm,

but doesn't. "No-one thinks of you as a has-been, Martin," he says.

I swallow down my emotion. "Oh Jeff, how I wish Jack was here. It's made everything so much harder to bear here. I felt as if I could manage things when he was around... It was his idea that I should take Helen on a holiday. He was even going to give me some money to help pay for it."

And then, before I can prevent myself, I find I am on the verge of crying. I let out a strange, barking sob, and my eyes prickle with tears. God, this is embarrassing. I look up to Jeff, trying to reassure him that I am back under control. But he looks distinctly uneasy. He turns away and unlatches the door to the cubicle.

"Jack was right, you need a break, Mart. You really do. You don't look well."

"He was right about a lot of things. He warned me about Sam, he warned me years ago. He warned me. And I didn't listen!"

"Jack was bitter about Sam, there's no two ways about it."

I follow Jeff out of the cubicle to the sink. I look at him again, catching him off-guard. In that split second I see repulsion ripple through his features. The bluff, jovial mask that he wears for most of the time in school, and in his life generally, disappears and I see what's really there: rank suspicion. Why?

I feel quite nauseous, but bite back the bile.

"I'll go home," I say, walking away from the sink while he is washing his hands.

Although I know I shouldn't, I return to the staff-room. It's the end of break. Most of the teachers have abandoned their cups of tea and coffee and are draining away towards their classrooms. Some nod and say hello like it's a perfectly normal day, one or two even ask me what I'm doing for the holidays. I mutter some small talk and move on.

I catch sight of Sadie and follow her up the stairs. Just outside her classroom, I ask for a quick word.

My big body feels awkward and lumpy next to her small, compact frame, her neat skirt suit, her crisp, perfectly bobbed hair. Pupils are chattering to themselves, earphones and mobiles dangling around their necks and ears. They pass by, oblivious to our conversation.

"Look, Sadie, I know this is really a bit out of the blue and completely uncalled for, but I was wondering if you could sort of say you're sick today and not go for the interview?"

Sadie looks at me quizzically. "Why?"

"I can't really explain."

As soon as I've made the request, I realise how stupid it sounds.

Sadie looks down at me. I tuck my shirt into my trousers, waiting for a response.

"What's going on, Martin?"

I shift around on my feet.

"It's just that I'm not going to be interviewed today, and I thought maybe you could wait till next term as well. After all, it really is asinine having an important interview like this on the last day of term."

"But if Sam didn't interview anyone now, there'd be no one in place for September."

"Yes, I suppose that's right," I concede.

Fake concern spreads over Sadie's face as I linger in the hi-tech, carpeted corridor. God, I hate this architecture, with its sci-fi walls, its chrome banisters, its flat-screen noticeboards, its grinning furniture. Jack and I much preferred the run-down, tatty Sixties pokiness of the old comprehensive. We felt at home there: it was a wild, energising place full of freedom. I remember that Sadie liked it too: she could wear her Che Guevara T-shirts there and say "All men are pigs", and people would laugh. Now everyone's so corporate – it is all very uninspiring.

"Are you all right, Martin?" Sadie asks. "You seem... distracted..."

I edge away from her, gulping a little.

"Good luck with the interview, Sadie. Forget that I ever said anything," I reply.

As I walk downstairs, I realise that I don't really know what I'm going to do. Should I leave the school as ordered or should I stay? I hum The Clash tune to myself, "Should I Stay or Should I Go?", finding in the punky melody a dry crumb of comfort. Really, at a time like this I should be phoning Helen.

I visit my own class. I see the blond, polka-dot form of Kylie moving in and out of the desks of my Year 8s. She's been a good girl and has opted to teach the lesson plan on my desk, instead of showing *The Karate Kid*. I look jealously at her, safely sealed with those children, safely ensconced in her job, facing no ridiculous allegations, free to teach.

I tap on the window. She approaches, eyeing my pupils cautiously as she does so. Shutting the class-room door behind her, she looks up at me with her blue eyes.

"Hi, Kylie," I say with false jocularity. "I just thought I'd said goodbye."

"Goodbye? What's going on?"

"I'm leaving school early. There's a problem. I have to go home. That's why you had to cover my last period."

"But why?"

"It doesn't matter. It's not anything serious," I say, trying my best to look very nonchalant. "Tell me, are you going away this holiday?"

Kylie runs her hands through her hair. "Ibiza. I'm going with some college friends."

"It'll be very hot in Ibiza, I expect."

Kylie touches my arm, asking me if I'm OK.

Can I trust her? If I tell her and she blabs, the allegations will be all round the staff by the end of the day. Her sympathetic cornflower eyes make me want to confide in her.

I clear my throat and take the plunge: "The Principal, in his wisdom, has decreed that I have to go home. Béla Pongrácz has been making up false allegations against me."

Kylie puts her hand over her mouth. "Oh God, Béla."

I nod grimly. "Exactly. Oh God, Béla. That boy, when I think about it, has done his best to ruin my life. I don't know why I've been so bloody nice to him. But I have. How many times have I let him come to my house? How many times have I made supper for him? How many times have I listened to him and Josh playing their music? How many times have I really tried to do my best for him? I really tried not to get him excluded, Kylie, but what he did was so wrong, I couldn't just do nothing."

This confession makes the air sizzle. Kylie and I stare at each other. She takes my hand. Her skin is a little cold, but it feels nice. She looks up at me with wide eyes as she says: "Martin, you did the right thing. That boy should be shot for what he is doing to you. You were amazing. The only one right from the start of all this who tried to take control. There they were, all those mentors, the Principal, all these teachers, and they couldn't do anything, just blustered around, but when you started speaking, the kids listened. It was like you were the one they respected. And then the way you tried to save Jack's life."

"But I didn't," I say, swallowing hard and withdrawing my hand from hers.

"You mustn't blame yourself," she says. Her sweet breath is close. Her face is smooth with make-up. In the sunlit corridor, her polka-dots shimmer.

"But I do, Kylie, I should have got to him quicker.

If I had been thinking of him first and not of playing the hero, trying to stop the riot, he might be alive now."

"Martin, I saw what was going on, and you did what was right. You had to stop them setting off all those fireworks. You had to. I was terrified. We all were. You *were* a hero. Only the people who were there know, and I was there."

We are silent. We can both hear that the class is getting restless; there are lots of scuffles and noisy shouts. I wish she didn't have to go.

She hesitates for a moment, thinking of what to say, then, taking my hand again, she goes on: "Look, why don't you call me if there's anything I can do to help? I know you're the good guy, Martin."

I tighten my grip on her hand. If I wasn't so sweaty, I'd kiss her. I feel her physical proximity: I can't ignore the fact of her body – pert, fresh, enticing.

"Yes. I'll do that, Kylie. I'll call you. Thanks."

We nod goodbye like sad lovers. I have a lump in my throat. Why can't Helen be as understanding as her? I bet she'll think I'm to blame somehow for this mess.

I push these thoughts to the back of my mind as I track down Josh. The least I can do is keep him informed; otherwise he'll get all the news second- or third-hand.

Annoyingly, I find he's in the treacherous Julia Webb's French class. She gives me a really poisonous glance as I put my head around the door and ask for my son. He leaves the class quickly.

"Josh, I'm going to have to go home," I say.

"Why? What's happened?" he asks, looking down at the carpeted floor.

"That bloody friend of yours wrote a note saying… Well, I don't like to say. Basically enough to put me in jail and get the sack and just about any other humiliation you can imagine!"

"You mean Béla?"

Josh fiddles with his fingers. He's surprised, but he isn't shocked. He knows what that Hungarian weirdo is like, I suppose.

"Yes! Who else? You practically told me yourself he is the Countess Feckula. So did Jakaria. And everything else points to him."

Josh nods lugubriously.

"Look, Josh, perhaps you could talk to him and get him to tell Sam that it's all made up. If I lose this job and get jailed for being a paedophile…"

"Oh come on, Dad, you're overreacting. They'll find out it's lies sooner or later – with or without Béla's help."

"But not before they've given the job to fucking Sadie Renton!"

Josh peers down at his black school shoes. They are scuffed and the laces are undone. The kind of thing that would normally really aggravate me. Not right now.

"What are you going to do, Dad?"

"Josh, can't you talk to Béla, please?"

Josh puts his hands up. "OK, OK, I'll do it. But it

won't make any difference. You know what he's like. Once he's made his mind up about something, that's it. I have no influence over him."

"Didn't he tell you he was going to do this? You're his best friend, Josh. Didn't he give you a clue?"

"Of course he didn't. All I know is that he's really angry with you. He says you screwed up his life."

"And now he's screwing up mine! God, Josh, you have to speak to him."

"OK, OK!"

"And you can give me his number as well," I add, holding up my index finger.

"I'll text it to you," Josh says, putting his hands in his pockets.

"No, you can give me it right now!" My voice is boiling with impatience.

"He's lost his phone."

"That's very convenient!" I say, shaking my head.

"Really, he has."

"I'm going to have to visit him then!" I stamp my foot down on the ground.

Josh takes his hands out of his pockets and faces me with a nervous grimace contorting his lips. "Dad, don't do that. Just leave it; it'll make things worse."

"Whose side are you on, Josh? Do you really want me to get the sack?"

"Dad, I never said that. But I can tell you one thing: there are better jobs than this one."

"Don't talk like that, Josh!"

"Dad, I've had nothing but aggro here. It's shit being the teacher's son."

"The GMF are out, Josh. Out. They won't be back. Finito. Caput. What they did in May was unconscionable. They can never be forgiven. Nor can Béla," I snarl.

"Béla wasn't really part of it. He was bullied by them into throwing that firework."

"So this is what it's about, is it? If I get Béla's place at the school back, he'll get me my job back?"

"No, Dad, I don't know what it's about. I don't know! I don't know!" Josh shouts at me.

He runs away before saying anymore. I think for a foolish moment about chasing him, grabbing him and shaking the truth out of him, but I know this won't work. I sag against the wall. I'm sweating. It's a hot day. The new school building traps the heat in a way that the old building never did.

I wipe my brow and trudge wearily down the stairs.

11.05am

It's quite difficult keeping a tail on Ma without her seeing me, but I manage it, hunkering down low behind cars and then dashing commando-style to the nearest darkened doorway.

I follow her bobbling, rucksacked back to Shoreditch High Street overground station, and then hang back at the bottom of the platform, with my hood up. When she boards, I get on at the end of the compartment. I sneak a peek of her reading the *Metro* paper and thrumming her fingers. She wants a fag!

She changes at Shadwell, where she puts the rucksack at her feet and then lights up. When she boards the DLR at Canary Wharf she crushes the fag on the platform. This is a particularly tricky point. It involves lots of dodging in between pillars. It's much easier in the Canary Wharf shopping centre because there are quite a few people around. Ma doesn't seem to suspect anything. I am a master at blending in if I want to.

At the end of the shopping centre, she leaves the mall, and enters a large residential tower block. Unfortunately, I don't get what floor she gets off at because there's security on the door and I can't go in.

I think: God, can a human resources department be in a building like this?

Not knowing quite what to do now, I hang back, watching the building.

Mercy's mobile vibrates in my pocket: Josh is calling.

I pick up.

"Béla, my dad just got suspended!"

"He did? Why?" I ask.

"Yeah. He was fucking hysterical, Béla. I don't know what to do."

"What?"

"The really scary thing is, he's blaming you."

I stop looking at Ma's building and concentrate on the call.

"Me? What the fuck?"

"He's got it into his head that you're the Countess

Feckula. It's what all the kids are saying. Apparently, the Countess wrote this note saying he abused you or something."

"I promise, Josh, I'm not the Countess. Someone's out to frame me, I swear."

"But look, if you get called in by the head or anything, I'd be careful if I were you."

"What do you mean?"

"Just think carefully about what you say."

"Josh, you don't think I'm the Countess, do you?"

"All I'm saying is that I wouldn't be mad at you if you were. I could kind of understand why you might have done it. After all, my dad did completely fuck you over."

Josh hangs up before I can reply. Just then, my heart leaps for a second because a woman in a smart suit, looking like Ma, leaves the building. But then I see it isn't her.

Much as I am burning to know what Ma is up to, I realise that it's more important to discover the identity of the Countess. Otherwise, I'm in some very smelly doo-doo.

Most of all, I need to interview Jakaria. The most obvious explanation is that the GMF set him up to be the Countess; he's probably too stupid to do it by himself, but I can easily see how he might have been "persuaded" by Mercy into becoming her.

I feel like I'm a proper detective again.

I decide to take the bold step of calling Jakaria on Mercy's phone.

"Hello," a nervous voice says.

"You're Countess Feckula, ain't you?"

"Pongy? Is that you? How come you got Mercy's phone?"

"Yeah, it's me and don't worry about the phone. I just need some answers. Look, if you tell me who the Countess is, I'll promise to do all your coursework for you. Completely promise. I know how to get an A* and everything. You've got shit for brains."

"You will?"

"I promise, man. But I need to know."

"It ain't me, Pongy, I promise. I reckon it's Mercy."

"You reckon?"

"I know it. I heard her talking to the twins about it this morning. When I was sitting on the bin."

"And you weren't bullied into being the Countess by the GMF?"

"Course not, I'm not a weakling like you. The GMF don't boss me around."

He's bullshitting. He's trying to blame Mercy because he knows I'll never dare challenge her.

"I think I'm going to come into school to talk to you about this. I'll see you soon," I say, striding boldly towards the DLR.

"But Pongy, you're not allowed in school!"

"I'm a master of disguises, Jakaria. Believe me, I'll get in... I'll find you today..."

"OK, Pongy, whatever you say," he says. "It hasn't been nearly so good without you in school... Will you really do my coursework for me?"

"If you help me find the Countess, I will."

11.17am

I'm just about to get into the VW when I find Sadie rushing up to me, flustered.

"Martin, Martin! Wait," Her smart jacket is slightly askew and her hair is ruffled. "I just wanted to say that I'm not going to do it. I've cancelled the interview. It's just not right. It's just not."

I don't know what to say.

"You shouldn't on my account…" I try.

"I should! It's what Jack would have wanted. He always saw you as his successor. I can't go against his wishes."

I nod. I would like to disagree with her, but I can't.

"So you feel him too?"

Sadie shivers. "I do, Martin, I really do."

She turns away from me as I start up the car, and when I look up again, she's gone.

I pull out of the school and turn onto the Kingsland Road at the traffic lights by the mosque.

And suddenly, miraculously, it's as if I've got Jack sitting right beside me, giving me advice, thinking things through. *Call Helen, Martin old chap, call Helen. Talk it through with her. She's good in crises like this. You know that. Go on, just swallow your pride a little and call her. Apart from me, she's the one you trust the most.*

I turn down a sideroad and drive into a quiet residential area full of old Victorian houses and a pretty, gated square. Once I've parked, I press the label WIFE on my mobile and walk into the square, enjoying the fresh smell of the roses and the summer air.

After what seems like a century, Helen picks up. "Martin, are you OK?"

I rarely call her during school hours unless there's something up.

I explain the situation. There is a pause.

"Martin, please be absolutely honest with me. Is there any truth to these allegations at all?"

"What? No, Helen! Of course not! None at all. I mean, I suppose I *did* bring up that stupid puppetry stuff in front of the kids, but it was a harmless joke!"

"Oh, Martin, that was very foolish in the current climate."

"Look, Helen, I have never, ever abused any child. I wasn't even alone with the Hungarian – and I haven't been at home either. That's the point."

"Well, Sam will find that out."

"He might, but somehow I don't trust him. He looks at me in a very odd way these days. It's like I'm on the wrong side somehow, as if I am the sort of person who might have done it. I think he might believe Béla!"

"Don't be ridiculous. You're getting paranoid."

"He's got it in for me! Do you remember when we used to be such great mates, and used to talk about everything? Since all the trouble, he's barely spoken a word to me. In fact, today is the first time I've actually had a conversation with him since then."

"He's been busy, Martin. Look, I'm going to have to go…"

"This is a set-up, Helen. I can feel it in my bones. The pupils who were responsible for Jack's death were standing around the school gates this morning, looking like they knew something was going to happen. Béla was with them. He was actually hugging Mercy. I think he told her about the note he sent, that's what I think. Or they were in it together," I say, piecing things together in my mind as I speak. I continue: "All the pupils I got booted out from the school are getting their revenge. That's what's going on."

"The ones in *Macbeth*?"

"Yes. The ones in the Scottish Play. I put so much work into them… God, this is a nightmare."

"I haven't heard you talk like this before. Are you OK?"

I'm thinking things through now. "They killed Jack, Helen. I've been so bloody naïve!"

"This is your panic speaking, Martin," Helen says in the slow voice she reserves for difficult patients. "What you're saying isn't rational. Now I need you to stop right now and take a deep breath. Just shut your eyes and slowly draw in the breath right into your stomach and hold it there for a minute and then release it…"

"I'm not doing your bloody breathing exercises, Helen. I need some support, not fucking yoga lessons."

Helen waits for me to calm down, and then says: "You need to go home and rest. Those pupils didn't kill Jack – as you yourself pointed out at the time. They contributed, yes. But he wasn't well, Martin. And you're not in great nick either. I can't pretend I'm not concerned. Please could you just go home? I'll see you as soon as I can but I'm a bit tied up here. I'm getting ready to put a guy under who's about to have a liver transplant."

"An alcoholic?"

"Sadly, he is."

Suddenly, I hear Jack's voice in my head again. Since I said his name out loud I can feel him much more vividly with me. Not in a nutty, hallucinogenic way, but in a clear-headed logical fashion: his sensible voice and advice. *Get her to call Sam. She can sweet-talk Sam for you.*

"Helen? Just, please, take a sec, to phone Sam. He likes you. Tell him to cut me some slack. Tell him he should interview me for the job as normal. Ask him to give me the holiday at least before he suspends me. Give me some more time to get to the bottom of this." My voice is surprisingly calm.

"If I call him, will you call the doctor and make an appointment?"

"OK."

Pause.

"I'll call Sam if you promise to go home. And not speak to anyone. And definitely not to Béla. That'll just inflame the situation."

This phrase sends a shock through me; it's the exact phrase that Sam used when I left his office.

"Have you talked to Sam already?" I snap.

"No, of course not."

"Because he used exactly the same phrase with me. 'It'll just inflame the situation'."

"For God's sake, Martin, you're crazy!" she says. "It's a common phrase." But there's something in her voice, a sort of defiance. She's lying, I'm certain of it! Fuck, fuck, fuck. What is going on?

I ring off before things get too heated. I know that when I feel like this, it's no good speaking to her; she always runs rings around me when I'm angry.

I drive home. I'm nearly there when I see the GMF mucking around in Ravenscroft playground. Mercy's green T-shirt is bobbing up and down on a swing, a fag in her mouth, as the Bentley twins push her high into the blue sky.

I park the car and get out, approaching the group slowly but confidently. The twins stop pushing and coagulate around Mercy as I draw near, smelling the sweet, sickly scent of marijuana as I do so. The big girl blows smoke in my direction as she whoops: "Hey, muthafuckas, it's Hicky! Hicky, Hicky, come here, let me give you a hug! Mind you, I better not, 'cause you might get your knob out!" She laughs and points her long, painted fingernails at me.

"Mercy, cut it out, will you? I want to ask you something. You got Béla to send that note, didn't you? That's why you came down to the school... You knew he sent it, didn't you?"

Mercy nods knowingly at me. Now I'm sure she's in on it.

"Maybe we did, maybe we didn't! What are you going to do about it?"

"I'm going to tell Mr Ndlova. And then I'm going to call the police and tell them what you did to Mr Humphreys."

More raucous laughter from Mercy.

"Like I'm scared," she says, her fingernails playing with her hair extensions.

"You should have been arrested for what you did to him."

It feels good to express these long-buried thoughts. I realise that Sam did a terrible thing in refusing to call the police over Jack's death. There should have at least been an inquest.

Over the summer I promise I will press for an inquest, Jack.

"Why are you here anyway? What's happened? You get suspended or something?" Mercy says.

I retreat a little.

"I'm going to tell Mr Ndlova about you guys and then I'm going to ask for an inquest. And then you're going to go down. You really are. Because you can't just waltz around thinking that you can do whatever you like."

Mercy stops fiddling with her extensions and shows me the finger. Her bright, long fingernail shines in the summer light.

"Like I'm going to do that, heh? You fucking got us expelled, man. You fucked up my whole education. I couldn't take my GCSEs because of you."

Her anger is rising to match mine. My chest twinges.

"You were lucky not to get a criminal record. Think yourself lucky. I saved you from that."

"You fucked up my life, man. You fucked up the twins' life," she says, spreading her fingernails like a fan before the twins.

"So you set out to get your revenge?"

"What if we did? What's it to you?"

"And you're in cahoots with Béla, I presume... Feckula, or whatever he calls himself?"

"Sure, he's Feckula, everyone knows that."

I turn, and half walk, half run my way back to the car and drive away. I am just outside our house when Helen calls again. Since there's no traffic around, I feel free to stop the car in the middle of the street before I've parked and take the call.

"Did you speak to Sam?"

"No, I didn't but I left a message for him to call me."

"Can you keep trying? I've just learnt some important news: Béla definitely wrote that note. If I can get him to retract his statement, then I think I'll be all right."

"Martin, don't do that. Please, please tell me you won't."

"You don't get it, do you? You don't realise how

much trouble I'm in."

There's a worrying pause.

"Look, is there something you might have forgotten about?"

"What?"

"Martin, this is no joke. You really haven't got a grip, have you?"

"Helen, we've been through this."

"Martin, how could you forget your daughter unless you're really not thinking straight? Do you remember that she breaks up at noon?"

Helen always gets the better of me in the end. A horn blasts behind me. I've been blocking the street for a few minutes. I slap my forehead and start up the car.

12.01pm

Great detectives are always prepared. Sure enough, I do need my school uniform! I change behind the bins outside school and easily get past reception; I just tell the stupid secretary that I've had a doctor's appointment and need to go back into school. She doesn't even ask to see my ID.

12.15pm

I find Martha tucked away in a corner of a corridor, reading *Harry Potter and the Goblet of Fire* beside her mini bassoon and guitar. She acknowledges me with a tip of her eyes. It's a gesture she's picked up from Helen.

Josh was so different! He'd emerge smiling and scruffy in his jeans and T-shirt from his local primary school, and bound up to me, yelling at the top of his voice "Dad! Dad!", pummelling me with his fists, dragooning me into a toy fight. Josh was wild then. Although I found it hard work at the time, I miss that zaniness. Martha is so controlled and measured.

I gather up her instruments and guide her along the corridor. She continues reading as I jostle past the polished mothers who are clearing out their children's lockers, picking out sweet wrappers, dirty socks, dog-eared books. I know I don't have to do the same with Martha's locker, but it's worth checking. I tap her lightly on the shoulder, my finger pressing against the shoulder strap of her pretty gingham uniform.

"You have cleared your locker, haven't you?"

Martha gives me a look of withering contempt. "I did that two days ago, Dad," she replies and then resumes reading her book.

I smile at the only working mothers, Felicity and Sarah-Kate, who have children in Martha's class. I've been intermittently doing the school pick-up for four years now and have got to know the mothers well. Felicity is a partner in a firm of accountants and Sarah-Kate runs her own firm of "head-hunters" in the City. Their children, like Martha, stay on for the daily clubs – dance, art, computer, games and karate – because they can't make the 3.30pm pick-up – the end of "normal" school.

Sarah-Kate sweeps her hair behind her ears, looking stressed as her son, Hector, tussles with all the crap that he's accumulated in his locker over the year.

"At the local primary where my son went, it was simple because there were no lockers!" I offer in sympathy.

Sarah-Kate smiles a weary smile. "Ah yes, the complications of wealth!" she comments.

Martha looks up from her book and asks: "Why is wealth complicated?"

I'm a little taken aback by her peremptory and precocious question, but Sarah-Kate enjoys the challenge. "Well, as your dad said, it was easier at the local primary because there were no lockers which material possessions could be stuffed into. The fact that the school can afford lockers has made your lives more complicated because you've been able to bring more stuff to school."

"But if you were truly wealthy then there'd be less complications because you'd just pay for a nanny to do the clearing-out with Hector and not have to worry about it yourself," Martha retorts.

"Martha! Don't be rude now!" I say.

"She's not being rude!" Sarah-Kate laughs. She now dives down to the locker and starts pulling out the detritus crumpled up in the corner of Hector's locker. The hapless Hector stands back, looking sweaty and lost. "The truth is, Martha, I can afford a nanny, but wealth also creates guilt so I feel obliged to pick up Hector as much as I can."

Hector is a stupid boy who doesn't really understand the conversation, but he believes that somehow he is being mocked. He bursts into tears. Sarah-Kate has to comfort him with her arms full of dog-eared books.

12.18pm

It's strange being back here, sloping around in this old uniform, smelling the schooly smells: the chippy wafts of the dinners, the plastic aroma of the new building, the farty stinks of the pupils. I decide to adapt myself into an altogether new personality, who is a mixture of Jakaria, Josh and myself. Part idiot, part cynic, part foreigner. I decide I will call myself Jack, in honour of Mr Humphreys.

I test out this new character in the toilets, saying hello to myself repeatedly until I get the right effect. A huge part of me changes: my voice, my accent, my whole character. It's like I've stepped into this mashed-up mirror world where bits and pieces of me are really distorted, guarded, always on the look-out for clues.

12.24pm

Once we're back home and I've put all of Martha's school stuff in the cool hallway, I sit down on the bottom step of the stairs and think: *I've lost my fucking job.*

There's a terrible swirling feeling in my stomach. A

sense of utter humiliation. I had been so convinced at the beginning of the day that I would get the promotion, but now I have nothing.

"Can we go to the playground, Daddy?" Martha asks, standing before me with a lock of shiny brown hair dangling before her eyes.

I shake my head. "No, not right now."

"Why not, Daddy?"

I think about trying to invent some excuse, but I decide to tell her the truth. "Things are not very good for me at the moment, Martha," I say.

"Is it you and Mummy?"

This question surprises me. "What do you mean?"

"Are you getting a divorce?"

"Whatever gave you that idea?"

"It's just that you and Mummy are always shouting at each other," she says in such a matter-of-fact tone that it's difficult to take the comment seriously.

I grip her wrists and say: "Mummy and I are not getting a divorce. It's nothing to do with that. It's just that I lost my job today. I got suspended. A pupil made up some stuff about me and got me suspended."

"Is it Béla?"

"Yes, it's Béla. How do you know that?"

"I heard Josh talking about it."

So Josh knew a lot more than he was letting on. That doesn't surprise me.

I get off the bottom stair and wander towards Martha's musical instruments, which are still languishing in the hallway. I need to take them to the living room and put them by the piano. But I don't. Instead, I look down at their cases and think: what is all this for?

"But I don't think it's him. Béla is nice. He likes you, even though you did get him kicked out of school."

"I need to speak to him, that's what I need to do."

"Why can't you?"

"Because I'm not allowed to."

Martha tries to pick up her big bassoon case and lug it into the living room but has difficulty. I relieve her of it and carry it into the room.

"I could speak to Béla," Martha says. "He likes me."

12.25pm

I check the messages on Mercy's phone. I've got it switched off most of the time because I don't particularly want her to call me, but I know Josh has got the number so I figure it will be good to see if he's left any messages. Mercy has left quite a few. After listening to the first one, in which she is threatening to chop off my cock, I delete the others from the same number. However, there is one from a different number. A little girl's voice pipes up: "Béla, this is Martha. Josh texted me this phone number and I decided to phone you but don't tell Daddy. My daddy says you have been saying nasty things about him. He is not allowed to speak to you but I think you can speak to me."

I call the number back straight away.

Hicky picks up. "Yes?"

"It's me, Béla. Are you allowed to speak to me?"

"Béla, can you tell me what you're up to?"

"Mr Hick, is that really you?"

"Of course it's me, and I need you to tell me quickly what you're up to."

"I'm just…" I hesitate. Does he know about me spying in school?

"I know, Béla. I know everything."

His tone is pretty menacing. It feels like he's talking about his wife shagging Loverman. I gulp. "You do?"

"Yes, I'm not too happy with you."

"With me? I only found out."

"What do you mean found out? You are the cause of everything," Hicky says.

"I didn't do anything, sir. I swear."

"I bet you did. In fact, I'm sure you did."

God, has he lost his mind? Is he so mad about his wife shagging someone else that he's gone insane? How could I have anything to do with that??

"How could I? I'm only a kid, they're adults."

"They're not adults, they're morons. Stupid, silly school children who were obviously instructed by someone to ruin my life."

"I don't think they're school children, sir. They're grown-ups!"

"They're not grown-ups, you idiot!"

"I didn't have anything to do with it. I just found out. I promise," I say, feeling panic rising in my limbs. Hicky sounds like he wants to kill me.

"Béla, why did you write that note about me?"

Oh-my-God, he's talking about me writing the note, and not me finding out about the affair! How stupid am I?

"I didn't write anything. I promise."

"Everyone knows you're posing as this ridiculous internet character, Béla. The Countess Feckula, if that's what she's called... You can't lie to me."

I think for a moment about what Josh said: be careful about admitting or denying anything. But that's Josh. He's more devious than me. With me, the truth comes first.

"I'm not her! I'm not, I promise!" I blurt out.

There's an awkward silence.

"Well, I need you to tell Mr Ndlova that! You need to tell him that those allegations are made up."

"I will, if you want me to, sir."

"Good. Where are you at the moment?"

I hesitate to tell him this. "I'm... er..."

"I want you to meet me back at school in ten minutes or so. By the reception. We need to get this sorted out. This is my job that's on the line here. I don't think you realise how serious this situation is."

12.35pm

Think positive: things are going to be all right. I make myself a quick cheese toastie, filling it with my favourite ingredients, lashings of chutney, a bit of tomato and a slice of ham. I give some of it to Martha and chomp into the rest. It's one of my best;

the melted cheese is delicious.

Once I'm stocked up, Martha and I get into the car. As I pull the VW back into the Gilda Ball Academy, after a brief cloudy period, the sun comes out again. I sing "I Got You Babe" for Martha. She giggles.

However, my mood darkens when I get out of the car. Mercy and the Bentley twins are sitting on the wall opposite the high, barricaded fence of the academy, smoking. If they didn't seem quite so menacing, they would be very sad.

Martha stares at the gang with avid attention, asking what they are doing there. I don't answer, but hurry her indoors, shouting behind me: "Haven't you got anything better to do than upset my daughter?"

The GMF hoik themselves off their wall and stalk over to the school fence.

"This is where the action is today," Mercy states, pointing at my chest. "You ain't been on Twitter, have you?"

"I don't bother with that kind of online rubbish."

"You should. There's a lot of Hicky-Dicky tweets on Twitter."

I see my carnations are still lying on the tarmac of the playground quite untouched. I'm not going to let this girl disturb my equanimity.

"I'm coming back to school because I'm going to be made Deputy Head! Maybe you should stick that up your Twitter!" I say, the words coming out like they are my destiny.

Mercy looks unruffled. "I heard that you was

sacked for good."

"You heard wrong," I say with the firmest smile I can hold in the circumstances.

With my head held high, I stride into school, narrowly avoiding being hit by a missile clearly aimed at me. My daughter and I escape into the sanctuary of the building.

"Dad, who are they?" Martha asks.

"Just some very misguided individuals. They thought they could destroy me, but they thought wrong."

To my relief, I find Béla waiting for me in the reception area. For some reason, he's in his school uniform. Martha looks at him darkly, waggling her finger at him. "Béla, why have you been saying nasty things about Daddy?"

"I haven't. I promise I haven't, Mr Hick," Béla says, looking at me with his mysterious Hungarian eyes and comically pointy nose.

His words are painfully comforting to hear. I grab his soiled sleeve.

"You're not going to discuss this with me, you're going to tell Mr Ndlova this! Please follow me."

If Sam is surprised to see me, he's even more alarmed to see Béla. He is just about to leave his office to get lunch, but he agrees to see us nevertheless. Martha is happy to sit outside by the photocopier.

"This is not good, Mr Hick, not good," he says, looking at me, wearing the formal Principal mask he puts on in front of all his pupils. "You were supposed to stay at home. I was going to speak to Béla in my own good time. And Béla, what are you doing here in school uniform? I thought I made it clear that you were permanently excluded."

"I had to come, sir. For justice's sake."

Sam plants his legs firmly on the floor and seems determined not to sit down, or to invite us to either.

"There is no time, Sam, I don't want this hanging over me all summer. I want this sorted out now. I want my name cleared so I can go for the job! Now, Béla, can you explain what's happened here?"

Béla sweeps his head to one side and says with a Hungarian-Cockney lilt in his voice: "Yes, that's true Mr Ndlova, it's all lies. It's the GMF, sir, they're behind it. They hate Mr Hick for getting them excluded."

"They bullied you into writing the note, is that what you're saying?" Sam asks.

Béla frowns at me. Luckily, Sam doesn't see him exchange glances with me because he's peering at some paperwork on his desk. Then he looks up and harrumphs. "Béla, what have you got to gain by telling me all this now?"

"Well, sir, I was hoping that maybe if I told the truth then you'd take me back."

Sam's face darkens.

"Oh, I see, so you're expecting favours in return for first making up a whole load of lies about Mr Hick and then retracting your testimony, is that it?"

Béla shakes his head wildly. "No, sir! I never wrote

the note in the first place!"

Sam's eyes light up. Fuck, Béla shouldn't have said that. That's not good.

"So, if you didn't write the note, who did? The allegations still stand − even if you're not their author."

I interject sharply: "Sam, you can't be serious! The note was clearly written to make it look like it was Béla. If the note isn't written by him, it's a forgery."

But as I am saying this, I feel my whole argument getting tangled up in knots.

Sam makes for the door and has his hand on the doorknob as he says: "Look, this needs to be properly investigated. You may not be this 'Countess Feckula' figure, Béla, and you may not have written that anonymous note, but someone did!"

I hang my head. It's clear that Sam is determined not to give me the benefit of the doubt.

"Sir, er... can I please have a quick word with you alone?" Béla says.

Sam's hand comes off the doorknob.

"What do you mean?" he asks Béla.

"I mean that I've got some information... something else, that I would like to put to you. We could always meet in Daquise, of course − you know, that Polish restaurant by the Albert Hall?"

I'm not quite sure what Béla is going on about − and I'm not sure I want to know − but whatever it is, it's got Sam's attention. He stretches out his fingers as though he's got cramp in his hand, and shoots me a glance.

12.45pm

As soon as Hicky is out of the room and the door is shut, old Loverman snarls: "Béla, you'd better not be mucking me around. Make it quick. What do you want to say?"

I hold my nerve. I sweep my hair to one side and direct my pointy nose straight at Loverman's face.

"You know Daquise then? It's a nice place to meet someone," I say with a sheepish grin.

He slides towards me and leans close as he asks: "What are you on about?"

"I certainly know about meeting doctors there."

This does it. Loverman edges away. He knows I know. I know he knows I know. We're all clear. Irritation and fear flicker through his features. "You've been snooping, haven't you? Have you been following me? Is that it?"

I shrug. "I am a good detective, if that's what you mean. My father was one too. He was a detective in Budapest. One of the best."

"I'm not interested in your father, I'm interested…"

"Who might be reading your emails, sir?"

Loverman interrogates me about hacking into his account, but I deny it. Then he gives up with a weary sigh. "Have you said anything to Mr Hick?"

"No, sir."

"Have you told anyone else?"

"No, sir."

"Why should I believe you?"

"Because I'm trustworthy, sir."

Loverman lets out a little snort. "Are you?"

"What I don't think anyone here realises is that I'm a Hungarian aristocrat. I'm really a count. Hungarians are people of honour."

Loverman squints. "Are you having me on?"

"No, sir. It's true. You can phone my home right now and talk to my great-uncle, the Count Zoltan Pongrácz. He can tell you all about my distinguished lineage."

Loverman sits down beside his computer. I can see that he's logged onto his email account, the one I hacked into earlier in the day. Clocking that I'm looking, he twists the screen away.

"Swear and hope to die, sir," I say.

Loverman types some stuff and then looks up. Fuck, has he changed his password?

"It has to stay that way. Mr Hick must never, ever learn about Daquise or anything else. Do I make myself clear?" he says.

"Yes, sir. He will never learn about the way you treat Mrs Hick. Nothing like that. And no one else will. If I can just get my place at the school back, sir?"

Hope glimmers in Loverman's eyes. He pauses, then says: "There would have to be certain conditions. You'd have to come back on a school contract."

"I'd do that," I say, standing to attention.

Loverman sniffs heavily and then makes for the door. "I want you to leave the school now and not come back until next term. I will send you a letter but you must leave right now. And speak to no one. Understood?"

As he's saying this, he gets a mobile phone out of a drawer. He tosses it from hand to hand as he speaks to me. It's not the one he normally uses in school. It's an older version. A bit of a brick.

"Yes, sir!"

With that, he opens the door and asks Hicky to step back into the office.

12.47pm

Sam stands by the window and looks out at the playground where Jack died as he says: "I thought about things and discussed the evidence again with Béla, and I've decided that you should be reinstated in your position, Martin."

Relief floods through me. I almost want to cry.

"Thanks Sam, thanks, you are making the right decision."

"There is the matter of the interview too. Gilda Ball is arriving shortly for it. I think it's only fair now that we give you a crack at it today. But you have to understand, Martin, if you were to gain the position, we would have to work together. We need to show Gilda that you and I can collaborate. Perhaps we can even be friends again. Since Jack's tragic accident, I feel things haven't been good between us, but perhaps that can change."

"Yes, I think we can be friends again."

12.47pm

As soon as I'm out of the door, I crouch down beside the photocopier and log onto the internet on Mercy's phone, and then try to log onto Loverman's email. But he's fucking well changed the password.

I have no proof of anything now. Like the stupid dickhead I was, I didn't cut and paste the emails into a document.

Béla, don't despair. Don't give up. Firstly, old Loverman doesn't know you have no proof. Secondly, you can get proof if you need it.

"Béla, what are you doing?"

Two big, brown eyes poke around the feeder tray of the photocopier and stare at me in astonishment. I put my finger to my mouth and indicate to Martha that she shouldn't let on to anyone that I'm here. She laughs.

"What's going on, Béla? Is Daddy in really big trouble?"

"No, I got him his job back."

Martha crouches down beside me in this nook and giggles some more. "Did you, Béla?"

"I did."

"You did! Oh Béla, you are my hero!"

"I am?"

Martha squeezes my arm and then rests her brown hair against it. I feel all swelled up inside. This is the first really nice thing someone has said to me in a very long time.

"Béla, why are you hiding here?"

"Sssh! There's one final mission I need to do to make sure your dad is really going to be all right."

"There is? What is it?"

"I can't tell you, it's top secret."

I look straight into her eyes and think: God, what was old Loverman thinking banging her mum? Does he know the harm he's causing?

I can smell my dad as I hide behind the photocopier. I can scent the tobacco on his tweed jacket, I can inhale the scent of cherry *palinka*, I can remember him reading *Emile and the Detectives* to me in Hungarian. I can feel he is back again.

I say to Martha: "Do you know what my dad said to me? Always investigate, Béla, always investigate. Being a detective, Béla, is a duty!"

"Do you think Daddy still needs your help?" Martha asks with her mouth open.

"Yes. And I think he needs your help as well. I need you to be my spy around the school. Do you promise you'll do that? I'll come and get your report at the end of the day, and we can compare notes, heh?"

When I see the door to Loverman's office begin to open, I whisper to Martha that she must say I've left the building. She returns to her chair. Now I hunker down out of view, safely hidden by wrapped blocks of A4 paper and the plastic bulk of the photocopier.

"Where's Béla?" I hear Hicky ask.

"He's gone home," Martha says. Good girl! Good girl!

"I will contact him during the holidays," Loverman says. "But Martin, I think perhaps you should take some time to prepare for your interview. I could take Martha to lunch, if you want."

"I like it when you take me to lunch," Martha says.

Both men laugh. Hicky's laughter is louder than Loverman's, though.

Then the three of them leave, heading towards the staffroom and the canteen.

I see my chance. Bent down low like a commando, I run into the office and start to scout around. I check the place where Loverman last got the phone from his drawers. There's nothing except papers and reports and that kind of crap.

Then I see Mr Loverman's briefcase.

I try to open it but the latch is secure, and there's no way I can prise it open.

Kneeling down on the floor, cussing in whispers, my heart flip-flapping, I feel the strand of a belt dangling on my shoulders. Swivelling around, I realise that it's Ndlova's raincoat. Suddenly this voice that sounds very like my dad says, *Look there, look there…*

I grope around the coat and find nothing in the main pockets, but there is something bulging in a hidden compartment at the bottom of it. I have to unzip a number of pockets and there, finally, is the old mobile phone.

I weigh it in my hands, feeling its chunkiness in my palms. Then I stuff it into the inside pocket of my jacket.

Once I shut the door, I have the office to myself. For a moment, I feel what it must be like to be a headteacher. A lovely, gorgeous, amazing feeling.

With my heart racing, I take a seat in Loverman's swivel

chair and pick up the landline phone. It's fantastic feeling important. Oh the privileges of power!

Suddenly, I'm gripped by another amazing idea. I put my handkerchief over the mouthpiece of the landline, and dial my own number.

Mercy picks up.

"Yes," she says. Her voice is quite different from the one she airs around the street. It's quite posh. She must have seen that it's the school phoning.

"This is Mr Smith, Mr Ndlova's new PA. Are you called Mercy?" I say in my deepest, poshest voice.

"How do you know that?"

"Good. I'm calling because Mr Ndlova wishes to talk to you and your two friends, known as the Bentley twins, about your futures at the academy. He has been reconsidering things after meeting with Béla and wishes to give you places at the Sixth Form Academy on certain conditions he wishes to discuss with you this afternoon. Can you come into the school to talk to him?"

"Is this for real?"

"Of course it is!"

"I mean, you kidding me or anything?"

"Why would I do that? This is deadly serious."

"Is this coz you've sacked Mr Hick?"

"I can't divulge any private information. Suffice it to say, we have been reconsidering things."

"So Mr Hick is definitely getting sacked?"

"I can't possibly comment on that."

"Coz I would never come back if he was there."

"So, you will come back and be interviewed by Mr Ndlova later on this afternoon?"

"Yes."

"There is another matter. I believe this is Béla Pongrácz's phone. Is this correct?"

"He stole my phone. And left his one with me," says Mercy, sounding particularly lame, almost nervous.

"Béla would like his phone back. Perhaps we could arrange a swap?"

"OK."

God, she sounds pleased! This is what she wanted!

"Good. I would like you to present yourself at Mr Ndlova's office at 3pm. You could meet Béla shortly before that in the reception area of the school. That will be all now. Thank you!"

I slam down the phone and clap my hands together. Just as I do, the office door opens and Loverman is staring me whack in the face.

I leap up from his chair, leaving it spinning in my wake.

"Béla! What are you doing?" he shouts as he runs towards me.

"I… just dropped something…" I say.

"It's off! The deal is off! I knew I couldn't trust you. I knew it! Get out of here and never, ever come back," Loverman yells, flinging his arms wildly in the air.

It's actually quite scary because I've never seen him lose his temper like this before.

"But sir…"

"Get out! Get out before I do something I regret!"

Sensing that I may have used up my time in Loverman's

office, and not wanting to hang around in case he discovers what I have in my pocket, I bolt for the door, open it quickly and dive into the scrotum of the Ballz-up.

12.59pm

I love the silence of Hicky's resources room. This is just about the safest, snuggliest place to be right now. I sniff the air, inhaling the dry scent of old books, loving the feeling that I am completely shielded by the shelves. This is the room where the English department keeps all their stock. I know it very well coz over the years I've helped tidy it up.

Six floors below, outside the massive wire mesh fence of the school, I can see Mercy and the Bentley twins hanging around, clearly discussing her conversation with Mr Ndlova's PA. Somewhere in the bowels of the building, old Loverman is fuming about me. I bet he doesn't realise that I'm still here!

I scroll through the messages. Unlike the emails, which were a bit guarded, these messages don't hold back. I read in the inbox:

I don't know how I'm going to get by without you xxxxx.

You are the only reason I want to go on xxx

It's on Wigmore Street, the Ramada. Got a swimming pool! Xxx

Finished with surgery at 9pm. Straight to u after.xxx

I need you to discipline me. Can't stop thinking about your beautiful cock, even during surgery! xxx

There's a noise, a rustling, and a cracked cough. I'm jammed at the end of a row of text books, holding Loverman's mobile phone – and feeling a humungous hard-on coming on.

I see a pair of brogues pacing along the polished floor.

Fuck! It's Hicky.

As he turns towards my row of books, my heart gibbers. I can smell Hicky now. He's put on this cool aftershave, this sophisticated eau de Cologne.

As I sniff, I can also catch that faint trace of body sweat that he gets when he's stressed. I'm just about to jump out and squeeze his hand when a deep-throated voice says behind him: "Martin, it's truly a time to celebrate, mate! You're going to get the job!"

I recognise the speaker now; it's Mr Burlington, a teacher who always spends his time in lessons on the phone to his mate in the National Union of Teachers.

"I think I'm gonna do it!" Hicky says, but not with such a kick as Burlington.

Burlington slaps Hicky on the back and they laugh.

Then Burlington gets out a bottle of vodka from his bag.

"God, I better not! Not before my interview!" Hicky says. "I can't go in pissed!"

Through a crack in the books, I see Mr Burlington with his big bushy beard and belly goading Hicky to have a drink.

"It's vodka, mate! You can't smell it on the breath! Dutch courage and all that?"

"No, no, better not!" Hicky says, but then Burlington pours some into a plastic cup and both of them drink the hooch.

It's weird but I realise Hicky is very like Josh, who does exactly the same thing; he says no to my mum offering him fags, but then he goes and smokes them anyway. Josh will say he's never going to play in a band again but the next thing you know we're practising. He has these great hissy fits but then he's my friend again pretty soon afterwards.

"I think you've got a very good chance of getting the job as long as you don't turn up pissed!" Burlington chortles.

"No, I'm sure Sadie will get it," Hick says, drinking from his plastic cup.

Burlington laughs. "Don't talk rubbish! You're the only person who can keep order here, you're the Terminator, you're the puppet master."

"Careful now!"

Both men start laughing. They walk to the door of the resources room, still laughing, and then Hicky says he really needs to get his head together for the interview. So Burlington says goodbye, wishing Hicky good luck with it all.

"Drink down the boozer later on?" he offers.

Hicky ducks his head. "I think I might have to stay in tonight. But I'll call you."

Burlington lightly taps his friend on the back and disappears.

Feeling nervous now, I crawl along to the end of the bookshelves thinking that, considering everything, it's best that Hicky doesn't find me here.

But then again, I kind of want him to.

In a way, he deserves to know the truth. He needs to know what a bastard old Loverman is. There's a real rhubarb-and-custard chew of feelings inside me.

Suddenly it's all solved when a very strong but soft voice says: "Béla, what are you doing here?"

There's so much I want to say, so much, but it's like I've got this huge gobstopper in my mouth. My lips twist this way and that, and I try to swallow.

"I thought you might like some help with tidying up the stock, you know, ready for next year."

Mr Hick smiles gratefully. I love it when he smiles: his eyes crinkle and suddenly his quiff of thin hair looks "debonair" – a brilliant word he taught me.

"How long have you been here?"

I shake my head, but he knows I'm lying. He's a pretty good mind-reader: I mean, even a great detective like me can't fool him.

"Where's Josh?" he asks, peering around.

"I don't know," I say. "He's got classes in a few minutes."

"And he told you to spy on me, didn't he?"

"No, he didn't, sir. I promise. This is nothing to do with Josh."

Hicky switches on his computer. A big PowerPoint presentation balloons into view, with the front-page slide saying: *"My Vision Of A Deputy Head's Role At The Gilda Ball Academy."*

"I'm only trying to help you, sir. I mean, I think I've helped you a lot."

"Whatever it was you said to Mr Ndlova, it worked. I must admit I was a bit puzzled by it. You completely changed his attitude to everything. How?"

Hicky pats the chair next to him and urges me to sit down.

Suddenly, I see a door in the wall. A door which I kick open when I say in a great rush: "It's something I've found out, sir. I mean, that's what I had this hunch about and then I found the proof. I mean, sir, you can't say I'm not a great detective because I am. I mean, my dad was a detective in Hungary. A great one and I kind of learnt from him to be suspicious, you know, and I just had this feeling about Mr Ndlova and so I went and investigated, you know, and I found this in Mr Ndlova's office."

"You've been snooping in his office?"

"Yes, he wanted to speak to me again, and then left the room and I found this."

"Béla, what have you been doing?"

I hold out the old mobile phone before he can ask any more questions.

Hicky takes the phone from me. I study him closely as he scrolls through. There's something both thrilling and more than a little terrifying as I see his expression change from confusion to comprehension to horror.

1.30pm

It is the end of lunch. The last lunchtime of the year.

My pupils are sauntering up the stairs chanting, pushing each other against the banisters, chewing gum, biting into half-finished sandwiches, wiping fruit juice from their lips with the sleeves of their uniforms. A few of them holler hello to me. I don't really hear them. A few look curiously at me as I stagger to the staffroom, and then they move on.

Jack, where are you? I need to talk to you right now and you're not here.

Yes, more than ever, I need to speak to you, Jack. I need to hear your voice in my ear, feel the gentle touch of your big hand on my back. I know what you'd say, you'd tell me to go for the job – and then talk things through with Helen. I hear the light Yorkshire brogue in your voice as you tell me: "These things happen in marriages, Mart, they do. You just need to keep calm and talk things through. Just do that... Yes, you did it..."

You did it. His last words to me in the playground. *Yes, you did it.*

In the staffroom, Sadie Renton greets me cheerfully. She rubs her hands together.

"So, Mart, I heard that you've sorted everything out. That's great."

I shrug numbly. Her face falls. "Mart, are you OK? You seem a little..."

"I'm OK."

"Is it because I'm going for it as well?"

"You are?"

"Well, yes, I thought since you were back in the running, it would be OK. But if you…" she says, tailing away, making it unclear what she was going to say.

"It's all right. You should go for it. It doesn't matter," I say.

A few minutes ago, I would have been a bit suspicious as to how she came to learn about the interview, and deeply bothered that she's decided to put herself back in the running, but I'm not now. I look at her smart clothes, her short hair and her efficient demeanour and think: *you're a fraud*.

I manage to muster the ghost of a smile, but no more than that. Most of the staff are popping end-of-term chocolates into their mouths and grumbling about having to supervise their tutor groups for half an hour before the end-of-year assembly.

The pips go and the staffroom empties.

I find Martha sitting quietly in the corner of the room reading her Harry Potter book; she hasn't missed me one bit.

But Jack, I don't understand. Helen seems to care about me. She's always worrying about my health, about my workload, sometimes she rubs my back on the sofa – but she's gone and done this.

I just don't understand, Jack.

"*Women are inscrutable,*" *you say.*

But your wife never did this to you.

"*Yes, I was lucky. Very lucky. But we all do things*

THE LAST DAY OF TERM

that are mysterious. Even me, I had to go and look for comfort elsewhere."

What am I going to do, Jack? I used to listen to Helen when she would talk about how I should "work on" paying more attention to my children, about how I should "think about" cooking more for all of them, about how I should "consider" my health, but how can I take anything she says seriously again? Her words seem so hollow now.

The truth is, her words were a disguise for her deception. She was pretending she cared.

I can feel that my old friend is forced to agree with me. He is. He definitely is nodding in agreement from beyond the grave.

"Come on, Martha, we're going," I say gently, trying to hide the upset in my voice.

"But Dad, haven't you got your interview?"

"How do you know about that?"

I sit down beside her, gazing around at the staffroom, which is sapped of teachers. Dirty water down the plughole.

"Duh! I mean, it's all you've been talking about for the last few weeks," she says. I examine her bright eyes and see Helen there. Alert, watchful, intense. The opposite to Josh with his hopeless, dreamy vagueness. Leaning closer to me, she whispers: "Did you really do a puppet with your penis?"

I freeze. My God, has Sam spread the malicious lies all around the staffroom? How low can the man stoop?

161

"No. Where did you hear that?"

"Everyone's talking about it here. They said you made a joke about playing puppets with your penis! And then you got into trouble. It was something like that. I didn't really understand the rest."

I grip Martha's hand tightly and examine her features. Has she been disturbed by what she's heard?

She seems surprisingly cheerful.

"It's all rubbish. Nonsense. I've been cleared of everything. You mustn't believe any of it." Martha wraps her small arms around my considerable girth and presses her head against my stomach. She has too much faith in me. I shake my head again and again. No, it couldn't have been Sam. It must have been Julia. That makes much more sense. It's exactly the kind of thing she'd love spreading around. "You mustn't believe any of it, Martha. It's all lies. There are people here who are out to get me."

"They were all talking about it! It was quite funny. I mean, it is rather funny, isn't it, Daddy?" Martha says in a giggly voice, blithely unaware of the little stress-induced spasms in my face.

"Come on, we're getting out of here," I say, loosening the belt of my trousers.

"But Dad, I'm fine here. You can do your interview and I'll sit here and read. Besides, I can spy some more for you."

"You're beginning to sound like Béla."

"He taught me how to do it. I met him behind the photocopier."

"Behind the photocopier?"

"Yes, he taught me how to become invisible. Putting headphones on and reading a book is a great way of spying. They all think you're not listening. But you are. Did you know his dad was one the greatest detectives who ever lived? Did you know that? How cool is that?"

I'm sweating now. Béla makes me feel very uneasy. Although I'm glad he showed me the texts, I'm concerned that he might tell other people. I definitely don't want anyone else knowing that my wife has done the dirty on me – especially with my boss.

"You'll need to make sure the boy keeps quiet," I hear Jack say.

My chest churns and nausea rises in my stomach.

"Are you all right, Dad?"

I don't speak for a minute as my head pulses. I shut my eyes and lean my head against the wall behind the chair. It feels like the first time I have ever sat down in the whole of my life. I feel the heft of my big bottom in the seat. God, I'm overweight. With my eyes still shut, I pat my daughter's hand and say: "I'm fine. I'm just tired, that's all. So tired… I just need to rest my eyes."

"You're sweating, Dad!"

I open my eyes and look down at my clothes. I've been sweating so badly that the armpits of my jacket are saturated.

"Do you think it will matter?" Martha asks.

"What will matter?"

"Wearing a jacket like that at your interview?"

"I'm not going to do my interview. I'm not going," I say, dabbing my upper lip with a paper hanky I've pulled from my pocket.

But I can hear Jack insisting that I must.

"No ,I can't do it, I can't, Jack, I can't," I say out loud.

"Jack isn't here, Daddy, he isn't," Martha says in a surprisingly calm and piercingly sane voice.

I expect my daughter to ask me why I've said his name, but she doesn't. Instead, she clasps me even more tightly around my stomach, pushing her head against my ribcage.

"I love you, Daddy."

I'm too exhausted to think, but I find my daughter's sudden rush of affection peculiarly moving and restful. I shut my eyes again and find myself thinking about my days at university. That night of the summer solstice. Until now, I'd always considered it to be a perfect night.

It was the summer of 1988, the summer after the terrible hurricane when the trees were still lying rucked and ripped on the ground. Sam and I had written a great set of songs about the hurricane which we performed on the summer solstice in the woods at midnight.

We didn't advertise the event much, but word got round and there was a candle-lit procession from the Sussex campus into the woods. Helen had made these amazing paper lanterns which she hung in the grove where Sam and I performed. I was on guitar and Sam was singing. The pair of us both dressed up as tree spirits and sang about the hurricane. The terrible wind. The idiot wind.

Sam was possessed by the music. I can remember his neck glistening in the lantern-light, his voice soaring into the starlit sky, all the other students listening hushed and reverent. He'd really thought we could make it as a duo then.

But more to the point, just remember Helen! How pliant and lovely and devoted she was! And how great we were as a couple! I was the artist and she was the scientist; I was studying English Literature and she was doing Medicine. A union of opposites, a communion of the objective and subjective, a perfect merger.

Sitting perspiring in the staffroom, my mind fixed on my wife, I think about the very first time I made love to her. I'd never been so in love with someone, before or since.

But was it love? Or was it the intoxication of the moment, of youth, of having no responsibilities?

And Sam. Faithful Sam! Had he been loyal to me then? Or had he been shagging Helen since that time? Had the affair been going on for that long? No, it couldn't have happened then! What would there have been to stop him and Helen running off then and there if they were in love? After all, they had no children, no mortgages, no responsibilities.

I open my eyes and look at my daughter. No, there

was no way it happened then.

"Come on, Martha, it's time to pay your mother a visit, I think!" I say.

"But Dad, I like it here!" Martha protests, tugging on my hand. "Stay here and do your interview and then we'll go and see Mum. When you've got the job!"

1.55pm

I wasn't expecting to feel like this. I guess I secretly thought that when I told Hicky about his wife, he would appreciate my detective skills and thank me. But it's turned out to be a bit like my "last" last day of school, when I got excluded. Back then, I also thought I was doing the "cool" thing, the right thing, but of course I wasn't.

I see Josh emerge from around a corner, follow his form towards the assembly hall and watch his sad, hunched steps. I feel guilty. What if Hicky and his missus get a divorce? Will I be responsible for it?

A lot of the other kids are horsing around but Josh isn't. He's got his earphones on, looking down at the ground. Somehow it makes me feel even guiltier.

I realise it's assembly time. Joggling behind a group of Year 8ers, I enter the gym. My uniform feels sticky and small. It's muggy in the hall. Being in a Year 8 class, I am forced to sit cross-legged at the front, while Josh's class are way at the back.

Nevertheless, I manage to position myself at the edge

and get a pretty good view of him.

To my surprise, I see that Hicky is one of the many staff standing on the fringes. He told me he was leaving the school straight away, but there he is. His arms are crossed and he doesn't look too happy. I think about catching his eye but decide not to. I am invisible at the moment; no-one has noticed me, and I need to let it stay that way.

A few months ago, in May, on Year 11's last day of term, back when we were friends, me and Jakaria snuck into the staffroom one lesson time when I'd calculated that there would be no one around. As per normal, I was right.

I'd just wanted to have a snoop around but Jakaria caused real trouble. He saw that Miss Rouse's workstation was unlocked and decided to Facebook rape her, despite my pleas with him not to. He posted this photo I'd made of Hicky as the Terminator in her photos folder and then wrote as a status update:

I SUCK HICK DICK.

I was just about to delete this stupid obscenity when a teacher came into the staffroom and we had to skedaddle. Jakaria was triumphant and told everyone about his amazing Facebook rape. Everyone reached for their mobiles and saw the update on Rouse's profile. Quite soon after this, Mercy made up this chant, which everyone quickly started singing:

Hickory dickory dock,
Rouse sucked the cock!

The clock struck one,
The cock spunked
On her tongue
Hickory dickory dock,
Rouse sucked the cock!

The contrast between that raucous riot and the quietness of the children in this assembly now is incredible. It all makes me remember how everything got out of control.

At first it was just bits of paper that were chucked around in assembly but things got much worse because the GMF got involved. Soon eggs and flour were being flung around the corridors.

A few kids stripped off and ran naked through the school, bursting into lessons. Some of the girls got down to their bras and flashed their tits at teachers they fancied.

I suppose it was all pretty harmless to begin with, but then it turned nasty when everyone got wind of the chant. It echoed through the school, making the walls shiver:

Hickory dickory dock,
Rouse sucked the cock!
The clock struck one,
The cock spunked
On her tongue
Hickory dickory dock,
Rouse sucked the cock!

And then, once we were out in the playground, after some windows were smashed, things really went mad.

The fireworks started. Mercy and the Bentley twins had brought them along and started firing them off like nobody's business.

With the sky exploding, the GMF pelted the front of the school with stones, shattering the whole of the front entrance. It was like watching a Niagara Falls of glass. I've never seen anything like it!

I was standing watching the cascade with an open mouth when Mercy appeared by my side and shoved a smoking firework into my hand. I could see immediately that she was high: her pupils were dilated and she had this mad expression on her face.

I leapt backwards in fright and flung the firework away. Until then the fireworks had just gone off in the sky, well away from anyone – pupils or teachers – but this one headed into the crowd and straight towards Mr Humphreys, who seemed already to be struggling from the effort of trying to stop the Ballz-up being stoned.

I really don't think the firework hit him. I really don't think it did.

But the truth of that whole riot is so jumbled up in my mind that I can't even be sure if the glass front of the academy smashed first, and then I threw the firework and then Humphreys fell down. Sometimes I have flashbacks of Humphreys falling down before any silly stuff happened in the playground and all the kids flinging the stones because they saw that he'd lost it. Sometimes I see him falling because my firework hit him.

I just can't get it straight in my mind.

Hicky was certain my firework hit Mr Humphreys. And that's why I got permanently excluded. Because there were mitigating circumstances – Ndlova believed me that Mercy shoved the firework into my hand – I was allowed to take my GCSEs, unlike the GMF.

One thing is for sure, if Humphreys hadn't gone and died, I would be OK.

Death is like that. It changes everything. Forever.

Another reason things are dead quiet now, on this last day of term, is because the learning mentors are going around shushing everyone. They're even shushing the staff!

Mr Ndlova walks in and I see Hicky put his hands into his pockets. Total silence. God, how different things are now!

Ndlova takes off his jacket and walks up to the podium and starts talking. And talking. And talking. The trouble is, he's got quite a soft voice and I can't really make out what he's saying. The stuff I do catch is the normal shit: what a great year the school has had; the sporting achievements of some kids; the prizes won by some others; the staff who are leaving; and a special mention for the Deputy Head who died while doing his job. A memorial tree will be planted at the beginning of the next term. There is no talk of the riot.

I glance at Hicky. He still looks sick.

Somehow I feel like I've fucked things up again.

I'm basically a total fuck-up.

Just as I am beginning to feel like I'm better off dead, Mr Ndlova says: "Remember to be nice to your care-givers, and have a great holiday!"

And then I recall a line Hicky taught us from *Macbet*: "screw your courage to the sticking place/and we'll not fail."

Hicky's a good teacher like that. Lines stick in your mind after his lessons. Particularly since I feel this line is very relevant to me: I can't lose my bottle now. I have to believe in myself, believe in my intuitions – because they are the right ones.

Hicky had to know that his wife is playing away. Loverman is a traitor who wanted to get rid of Hicky because he was banging Helen Hick. That's the truth!

And it's also true that I did something very wrong in throwing the firework.

But the past can't be changed.

I mustn't mix everything up. I must see that there's a real value in the truth.

As the assembly draws to a close, my mind moves away from my doubts and on to more relevant questions: will Hicky go for the Deputy Head job now? It's really my only hope of staying on at the school and rescuing my academic career. Saving myself from looking after my great-uncle for the rest of my life.

The thing is that Hicky doesn't look like he's in any shape to do it at all.

Maybe he needs the kind of talk I've just given myself?

I don't think he's got my powers of resilience. My

ability to defeat the bad things in my head.

After we are dismissed to the music of Michael Jackson's *Thriller*, I have a quick word with one of the learning mentors, a big burly bloke in a fluorescent yellow bib – all the learning mentors wear them – and shaven head.

"Hey, mate, I thought I better tell you that the GMF are planning an attack on the school today. At about 3pm."

He looks at me. He doesn't know me – thank God – but he's heard of the GMF, I can see that.

"What, the big girl and the twin body-builders?" he says. "I thought they were kicked out."

"Yeah, they were. But they're planning a revenge attack, what with it being the last day of term and all. It's all over the school. Everyone's talking about it. Three o'clock."

That's enough for him. I see him whispering furiously to the other learning mentors and teachers. Suddenly all the staff are very, very anxious to get every single kid off the premises.

But they haven't reckoned on my powers of invisibility: I follow Hicky into the staff toilets. Luckily, we're alone.

I notice that the staff toilets are a lot less stinky than the boys' toilets.

"Béla, what are you doing here?" Hicky says just as he's about to go into a cubicle.

"I was just coming to wish you luck."

"What for?"

"For your job interview."

"Oh that," he says like he's not interested.

I pounce into action.

"Hey, sir, you've got to go for it. You've got to. I mean, he owes you. He owes you the job now. He owes you."

"You haven't got the phone still, have you, Béla? Could I look at it again?"

I hand it over.

Hicky scrolls through the messages, his face becoming more and more droopy.

"Sir, maybe you should look at it later? I mean, someone might come in..."

"And maybe you should get out of the staff toilets!" he snaps back, putting the phone in his pocket.

He eyes me suspiciously as he asks, "You haven't told anyone else this, have you Béla? You haven't told Josh, have you?"

"I haven't told anyone. And I won't tell Josh. I want to help you get this job. I believe in you, sir. After all, you are the only person who can get me my place at the school back."

"Is that why you're doing this?"

"No! It's not that. I want to help you. I know we had our differences over the Humphreys thing. But you've always been kind to me. And you're my friend's dad. That's why I'm doing it."

My words bring tears to Hicky's eyes. "You know, Béla, I think you're the only person who really cares about me. I really do."

He slumps against the wall and slides down it so that he's sitting right by the rotating hand towel machine.

I stand above him. "I wouldn't say that."

"I've lost everything, Béla. Everything. I just can't see how I can go on teaching here now. This news makes it impossible. Totally impossible. That woman Webb spread all those lies around the staffroom… I wonder if she's in on it as well. I'll probably lose my kids in the divorce settlement. And I bet that Sam will find some way of getting me the sack in the end."

"You need to fight Mr Ndlova. You can't give up now. You need to get up, sir."

I grab at his hand and try to yank him up, but he's quite heavy. So I crouch down, put his arm around my shoulder and pull him up. He smells of sweat and his expensive aftershave.

Slowly, with me groaning underneath him, he gets up.

2.30pm

I hesitate as Gilda Ball, the sponsor of the academy, invites me to sit down. She is a well-put-together woman in her mid-fifties, heavily made up, in a grey skirt suit and shiny red shoes. Her long fingernails are the same cherry red as her shoes.

"Mr Hick, please take a seat. We heard you were sick – but you look in the pink to me!"

The rest of the panel laugh, but I remain impassive. I stare hard at Sam, who shifts uneasily in his chair.

Sam seems so smart, so plausible now. How many people know the truth about him? I think back to the time when Sam came to stay at ours in the mid-1990s.

Things hadn't been going well for him then. He had a pretty serious drug habit, no house, no job and not much of a future: after he'd failed his law degree his family had disowned him. No one would take him in. No one, that is, except his old college friend, Martin Hick. Had the affair started then? Had Helen snuck down in the night and fucked him on the sofa?

"Mr Hick? Are you sure you are OK? Would you like to take a minute?" Gilda Ball has her clipboard ready.

I sit upright. "Yes, yes, fire away."

"So, Mr Hick, what made you want to apply for this job?" Gilda asks, clicking the top of her pen.

"I thought I might sort things out. Totally sort them out, once and for all."

Gilda muses over my mysterious words, but Sam's face freezes. He puts down his pen. He's known me for a very long time. He can tell when something is wrong.

"You're not being very clear, Mr Hick," Gilda retorts, unaware of the glances Sam and I are exchanging.

Suddenly, out of the foggy befuddlement that's afflicted me since lunchtime, I see some clarity. "I would like to explain what's been going on."

"Martin! You have to be careful with your words," Sam says, fiddling with the paperwork in front of him.

I am rarely angry with anyone other than Helen, and, in fact, until this moment, I've never really been angry with Sam. But I feel a new emotion over-whelm me.

Fury.

It has been seething and bubbling in me ever since I heard Sam give credence to the ridiculous lies in Julia Webb's absurd memo. And now, with those texts on the old mobile phone... My fingers itch. If I could legitimately get up and smack him in the mouth, I would.

"You see, Mrs Ball, I think there are some things you should know. Sam is my friend. Was my friend. He's been running this school for a while now. And during that time, he has managed to bring the whole institution to its knees. He has overloaded the teachers with initiative after initiative, bam-boozling them with paperwork and his ridiculous talk about the well-being of the children and meeting their unique needs. But this has just caused chaos. The culmination of this was witnessed in May, a few weeks ago, on the day the Year 11s left school, when Sam's Deputy had a heart attack trying to quell the bad behaviour Sam himself stoked up during assembly."

"This isn't true!" Sam blurts out. "This is a total misrepresentation of the facts. This school's results have improved by 35% since I took over; our value-added is one of the best in the country. The simple fact of the matter is that Jack Humphreys had a heart attack when a firework was thrown at him, completely out of the blue. The inquiry judged the whole thing to be a freak, tragic accident."

Gilda shifts in her chair, looking uncomfortable. For a moment she looks as if she is going to intervene. But then she just settles back, throwing me a questioning look.

I feel permitted to go on. "The improvement in the results, Sam, has been due to the efforts of the teachers here, nothing to do with you. You have done everything in your power to hamper them. More to the point, fireworks wouldn't have been let off if there had been some order in the school. If, for example, there had been more teachers in the playground to confront the ringleaders. As it was, there was only Jack and myself. But no, did you listen? No, you didn't! You have his blood on your hands!"

"That is not what the inquiry judged to be the case. You are becoming highly emotional about this, and I feel it's time you left!" Sam shouts back.

"Mr Ndlova, would you please let Mr Hick finish!" Gilda snaps.

I calm down a little and lean forward. "Sam doesn't have a grip, Mrs Ball. He encourages the children to express themselves and turns a blind eye to their bullying, their spitting, their chewing, their talking in lessons, their rudeness, their violence. In his eyes, everything is the teachers' fault. He's put these learning mentors in place who take the issue of discipline out of the teachers' hands and only deal with the situations they know they can handle. Moreover, they tell the kids that they're not to blame for anything, that they're victims and they need more sympathy, when what they need is a good kick up the backside. Meanwhile, the rest of us are left to pick up the pieces. If I was Deputy, I would make this man do his job properly. I would give power back to the teachers, I would insist upon some decent standards of behaviour in this place! Everything that Sam is doing here is causing mayhem. He can't even organise a decent interview! What's he doing leaving this job interview until the last day of term? And that assembly he just took. What was that? Trotting out the same old clichés about staff who are leaving, saying that they are committed, creative teachers but not remembering a single detail about what they've done at the school. He was just going through the motions. He has no appreciation of how to run the school at all."

I'm yelling now. I'm out of my seat and jabbing my finger at Sam. In stark contrast to the animated indignation of a few moments before, he's rigidly impassive with his eyes averted from me.

"This is nonsense," Sam hisses.

Gilda is still taking notes. "You can sit down now, Mr Hick," she says as she finishes writing.

"I think we can safely consider your interview terminated," my former friend says finally.

2.50pm

I meet Mercy and the Bentley twins in the school reception.

178

They've changed out of their ragamuffin street-fighting gear and are dressed smartly: Mercy in a nice black skirt and white blouse, the twins in two sharp, fake designer suits. They smile gingerly at me.

I'm the boss because they think I'm Loverman's bum-chum. They look surprised I'm in school uniform but don't question me about it: I think they assume I've already got my place back.

Standing tall by the reception desk, I nod to the secretary that Mr Ndlova wants to see these three.

"You'd better sign in!" I say. Dutifully, they troop up to the desk and write their names down. The secretary gives them plastic wallets to put their name tags in.

"Mr Ndlova wants you to wait in the vestibule until he comes to see you," I say with suitable authority.

Mercy and the twins sit down on the school side of the barrier, looking quite pleased and a little bit nervous. For all their bad behaviour and the trouble they got into, they enjoyed school. I can see they've realised that it's a hell of a lot better than hanging around the streets all day smoking dope and getting into trouble.

For a moment, I feel a twinge of guilt because they look so bloody grateful that they've been given another chance.

For all their bad-ass front, they are babies. Big, big babies.

But then I remember the knife Mercy pulled on me this morning and it hardens my resolve.

"Have you got something to say to me?" I ask, looking at them sternly and confidently.

Mercy can't look me in the eye.

"I'm sorry, Béla…"

I wait for a minute for her apology to sink in and then, leaning close to her, I say: "Look, good luck. But I have to warn you, Mr Hick is not very happy about you coming back, so if you see him I would run if I were you! And you'd better give me my phone back."

Mercy and I swap phones. Even though my phone isn't nearly as good as Mercy's, it feels good to have the old fucker back. I can see Mercy feels the same way too.

I step back and say: "Mr Ndlova will come and see you soon," knowing that the interviews are due to finish.

With that, I leave them and return to my hiding place behind the photocopier, outside the Principal's office, and wait for Hicky to emerge.

I check my mobile, feeling the familiar texture of the keypad. I text Josh: "Hey, got my fone back, fink got yr Dads job back! Why don't we have a practice this pm to celebr8?"

Shortly afterwards, I get a text back: "OK. Where r u?"

I give him the info. He says he'll come over and see me when his form tutor has dismissed him.

A little later, the man himself strides out of the office like some gangster who's just left a whole load of dead bodies in the bank and swanned off with the swag. I rush up to Hicky. "Sir, sir, I think the GMF have come back. I think they're going to attack the school, sir! They've got past reception!"

The reaction in Hick is immediate. He tucks his shirt into his trousers and snorts with flaring nostrils. "Show me where they are; I think it's time to sort that lot out once and for all."

I direct him around the corner. The GMF happen to be sitting quite innocently on the soft chairs by the display board which trumpets the achievements of the Ballz-up, but the moment they see Hick, they look frightened.

"I thought it was made clear to you that you were never to come back. Get out of here, the lot of you!" Hick screams at them. "Get out of here and never come back!"

The way he storms over to them makes me feel a bit guilty about engineering this: things seem to be getting out of control.

Mercy stands up, making Hicky think she's looking for a fight. The big man grabs her arm. The Bentley twins rise to the Queen Bee's defence and touch his chest lightly, saying: "Hey, hey, hey!"

Hick lashes out at them, hitting one of them on the face, and then wrestles Mercy to the floor. It's a deft move for such a fat man. He really has got the better of her!

Just at that moment, the reception secretary starts screaming hysterically: "It's happening again!"

Hicky tussles with the GMF until Loverman appears with four learning mentors in their yellow bibs. What they see confirms their worst fears: Hick is being attacked by the GMF. Looking on in astonishment, they observe him struggling as the twins overpower him and push him onto the sofa.

"Get out of here! Get out of here!" Hicky screams.

By now, Mercy has lost it: "You fucking tosser! You fucking tosser! This is the day you go down mate!"

She tries to smack his face but, even though his arms are pinioned by the Bentley twins, he manages to dodge her fist and kick her in the leg. She dances up and down in rage and pain.

She's just about to really hit him when the learning mentors surge onto the twins and pluck them off poor old Hicky.

With a bit of struggling, the learning mentors manage to get the better of the GMF by pushing them towards the exit. Things are made even more awkward because the automatic doors keep opening and shutting on them as they push the writhing gang over the threshold.

But eventually, after lots of noisy swearing, they manage it. Then Loverman shouts at the terrified secretary: "Lock the doors. Lock the doors! Lock the bloody doors!"

I've never heard him swear before, but now seems a good time to do it.

Mercy and the twins bash on the glass doors, shouting and screaming at us. But it's useless because the glass is pretty thick and their cries are muffled.

3.15pm

"Thanks, Béla," I say as the Hungarian helps me towards the medical room. I feel a little woozy and my cheek is bleeding. My friend takes my jacket and helps me lie down.

"Shall I get Martha?" he asks.

"No. I don't think I want Martha to see me like this.

But it would be good if you would look after her."

"I'll look after her," he says, retreating as the door opens and someone else comes in. I look up and see that it's Kylie.

"Martin!"

She hurries over to the bed and leans over me. I lean back and tell her that I'm fine.

"What are you doing?" I ask. Her breasts press against my arm as she examines my cheek.

"I'm a first aider, Martin. Sam sent me."

"He did, did he?"

"Look, I'm going to put some TCP on that cut and then cover it with a plaster. Would that be OK?"

"Yeah, whatever."

I shut my eyes. I feel very, very tired. After all, I scarcely slept last night. I smell the young, fresh odour of Kylie's body mingle with her perfume and feel her dabbing me with antiseptic and think that she doesn't do it like a doctor. Helen is so ruthlessly efficient doing something like this; not tender in the way Kylie is.

"Is that OK?" she asks after a while.

"It's good," I say with my eyes still shut.

"How's your head? I heard they gave you quite a battering."

"It's fine. I'm just a little tired, that's all."

"Perhaps I should call an ambulance? You could have concussion."

"No, no, I'm fine."

"Should I call your wife?"

"No, no. No need for that."

"Do you just want a rest?"

"Yes. Just a little rest."

"I should call your wife."

I turn over. The keys in my trouser pocket crunch against the upper part of my leg. I have my back to Kylie now.

"I don't want you to do that. No. It wouldn't do any good."

"Shall I go?"

"Can you stay with me for a little bit?"

I face her again and find her doe eyes looking at me with real sympathy. Her breasts are heaving underneath her polka-dot dress.

"I'll get you a blanket," she says. She goes over to a shelf and retrieves a blanket, which she then puts over my chest and legs with a kind-heartedness that makes my throat ache.

"This feels like what my mum did when I was little and I was ill."

We smile at each other. I feel like I could fall forever into that smile of hers.

"Where is everyone else?" I ask.

"I think Sam is deciding whether to call the police or not. There's some big meeting in his office about it."

"And Mercy and her dear friends?"

"They've gone. They ran off when the learning mentors went out to talk to them."

"They were here for trouble."

Kylie comes up close to the bed and feels my fore-head. She has magenta fingernails.

"I told you to look after yourself, Martin. I told you."

"No one tells me that."

"And you didn't listen!"

"I never listen!"

We both laugh gently. The flirtation makes my wooziness disappear. I take Kylie's hand in mine.

"Have you ever been to Scotland?" I ask her.

"No!" she says, surprised.

"I think you'd like it there. The Outer Hebrides. Uist. You can go swimming there and there's absolutely no one around."

I'm about to tell her about the seal when I notice Béla standing by the door. Has he been there all this time? Kylie lets out a little yelp.

"Béla, what are you doing here?"

"Oh sir, I'm sorry. It's Josh. He told me to come and get you. He's upstairs. He's with Martha. He says he needs to see you."

I sit up. "Oh God, Martha... And I'm supposed to be at the staff leaving do."

I swing myself off the bed. Kylie tries to stop me, while still staring at Béla in a horrified fashion.

"You need to rest. You stay here and I'll go and see them."

Béla leaves. "Martin, what was he doing here? Hasn't he left the school? He looks so weird in that school uniform!"

"Oh, it's all right. He's looking after Martha. I'd better go and see how she is," I say, moving towards the door. Kylie follows me as I climb slowly up the spiral staircase.

"Is that wise, Martin? Hasn't that boy got some kind of vendetta against you?" she asks, concern suffusing her gorgeous features. I tell her not to worry about it.

I find Josh and Béla hovering before the staffroom door.

"Dad, are you all right?" Josh asks.

I pat him on the hand. "I'm fine. Totally fine. In fact," I say, glancing at Kylie, "I never felt better."

And it's true. The dizziness has completely gone and I have that satisfied feeling you get when you know you've done the right thing. I say: "Look, why don't you two go on home and I'll come and join you a little later. I'll bring back Martha."

"Is it all right if Béla comes back with me? We're going to practise," Josh asks.

"OK." With that, they scamper off to God knows where.

As soon as I enter the staffroom, I find the staff clustering around me. They listen aghast to my tale. They want to hear both bits: my interview and my fight.

I say: "I just gave it to all of them."

A huge cheer rises spontaneously from the staff. It makes me realise just how despised Sam and those yobs are. I feel reluctant to talk much about my ruck with Mercy and the twins, but simply say: "As soon as I went out to reception, they flew at me. I had to defend myself. It was pure self-defence."

Then I put up my hands. "Hey, look, I don't want to talk anymore because I might get reported for keeping good order."

There are a few knowing chuckles from Burlington and our mates. I give Julia Webb a pointed look. She is hovering on the outer edge of the melee. She averts her eyes.

"But I will tell you about my interview." And off I go...

There are a lot of nodding heads.

"Do you think he will give you the job?" Kylie asks, handing me a glass of summer punch.

"I'm afraid I haven't been offered it, and never will be," I confess. "But I've never had such a therapeutic interview in my life!"

Even though the staff look a little crestfallen, the compliments fall thick and fast. God, to think this lot were gossiping about my "penis puppetry" an hour ago.

Burlington says: "We never thought you'd do it, considering Sam is, or should I say was, your best friend!"

The only people who don't offer their congratulations are Sadie Renton and Julia Webb, who continue to linger on the periphery. Yes, they were definitely the ones who told the staff about the contents of Countess Feckula's note. I can see the guilt and anger in their eyes.

"But come on, Martin, even if you think you haven't got a chance, they've got to see sense, haven't they?" Burlington says, after the gasps have died down.

I laugh. "Me? Get the job? After that interview? I'll get the sack, more like!"

I feel temporarily intoxicated by my outburst – but I am dimly aware that there will be a very big come-down soon.

"Ndlova can't do that! You've just spoken your mind, that's all! And those kids had it coming. After what they did to Jack. It was shocking they didn't get arrested."

"Oh, you don't know him. I've known him for nearly thirty years now, and I've come to realise a few things about him."

"But Dad, you and Sam are friends," Martha says, peering up from her book. Heads swing in her direction, surprised to find her there. Then they chortle kindly at a child making such a pertinent point.

"I am still friends with him!" I say, opening my arms to the group. "I just think he's an incompetent idiot, that's all."

More laughter.

Then the staff break away from me, leaving me with my daughter. Only Kylie remains close, watching me with a tender smile – which flickers a little when Sam enters the room.

Although the staff try to pretend they haven't noticed his arrival, they can't help but lower their voices. I swallow a mouthful of summer punch. It's very fruity and it's quite difficult to gauge just how alcoholic it is.

Grimacing, Sam says in the jolliest voice he can muster: "I apologise for my lateness! I promise to be with you in a few minutes for the leavers' speeches but currently I just need to sort a few things out."

Then he adds as a whispered aside, which everyone hears: "Mr Hick, if you would be so kind, could you come with me?"

I follow him out of the staffroom, where I find Josh and Béla still hanging around. "You boys need to go home," I say. They traipse behind me and wait outside Sam's office while I go in.

Sam shuts the door. Gilda Ball and her lackey have disappeared.

"Where's Gilda?" I ask.

"Martin, may I ask what is going on?" Sam spits out, ignoring my question. But I am not going to be intimidated. I stand tall, pushing my big belly proudly in his direction.

"You should know, Sam. You should know."

"I think you must have taken leave of your senses! I can't believe what I just witnessed. That interview was a total car-crash."

Sam stalks around the room, weaving angrily in and out of his pod-like chairs.

"I take it I haven't got the job."

"Of course you haven't. The only question that remains is whether you resign now, or later."

"I'll resign now if that's what you want."

I look straight into his hard, brown eyes. Funny how he and Helen have the same colour eyes. From the way he's peering at me, I can see that he's still not sure whether I know or not. He sits down and rubs his greying temples. I remain standing.

"I think we should wait a little. Give you time to find another job," he says, looking down at some papers on his coffee table. "In the meantime, I'd like to know what you've got against me."

"You had me suspended, Sam, on a completely false charge."

"That's been dropped now."

"You seemed to take those ridiculous allegations very seriously."

"I had to. That's my job. It's the precautionary principle, Martin. I had to."

He really is too pathetic for his own weasel words.

"Look, I'm going home now to think things through. When I have, I'll call you," I say, reaching into my pocket and feeling his phone still safe and sound.

4.00pm

Me and Josh are hiding in the PE stock cupboard, surrounded by lots of hockey sticks, footballs and goalposts. It smells of old socks. Josh flings open the window and pulls out his gear, skinning up on a cricket bat.

"Do you think that's a good idea? I mean, what if a teacher finds us?" I ask him tentatively, because he seems in a really bad mood.

"I'd be pleased if they kicked me out of here."

I'm not so sure about that. Having got my place back and then got kicked out again all in the space of a couple of hours, I can certainly say being excluded is not a great feeling. I'd still give anything to be in Josh's position.

"The GMF are not coming back so things are better for you, innit?"

"Yeah, but my dad's probably still going to be teaching here."

"I don't get why you're so down on him teaching here."

"Can't you see the way everyone picks on me having a teacher for a dad? It automatically makes me gay," Josh says, holding the spliff to his lips and getting out his lighter.

"That was the GMF and they've gone."

"But everyone else as well. My dad is such a mong. Every mongy thing he does reflects badly on me. Every time he loses his temper, every time he puts someone in detention, every time he fails some kid… It's a fucking mess, man! I'm automatically the gayest kid in the school coz I've got him for a dad."

He lights his spliff and puffs some greenish smoke out of the window.

I was going to tell Josh about how I'd saved his dad, but I don't now. In fact, his attitude annoys me. Josh simply doesn't realise how lucky he is.

"Look, mate, the GMF have gone. Your dad hasn't been sacked. He might even become the Deputy Head. You've gotta look on the positive side."

"My life is crap."

"Is that coz you don't like your mum either?"

"What's my mum got to do with it?" Josh says, turning to face me. The blue light at the window shines behind his hair, illuminating his face. He has soft features: a soft, round nose – not all pointy like mine – and big, red lips. He actually looks quite like his mum.

"I don't know. I was trying to figure out why you're so depressed, that's why. It just don't make sense to me. It's like you've got a pretty nice Dad, who gets you whatever you want, and your mum's really clever, a doctor and all, and you live in a big house with your own big room, and you've got an iPod, and an iPhone, and an Apple Mac, and all the instruments you want, and you're doing really well at school. And look at me – I've no school to go to, I've got this cheap old laptop, a crappy mobile phone, no dad, a mum who's like a commandant in a concentration camp, and I share my room with a horrible old uncle. But I'm happier than you!"

Josh responds immediately. "Oh boo-hoo! Let's all cry for poor little Béla!"

"You're spoilt, Josh! That's what you are!"

"Why don't you fuck off and leave me alone!" he says, putting out the spliff with the tips of his fingers and heading out of the door.

I have forgotten that he's got a master key from his dad until I hear him lock the door behind him, leaving me a prisoner in the smelly PE cupboard.

4.20pm

I spend a fruitless few minutes trying to look for Josh around the school, but he's nowhere to be found. Martha tags along but obviously isn't much help.

"Could he have gone home?" Martha suggests.

We wander into the gym and hear a loud knocking coming from the cupboard where the kit is kept. I unlock it and Béla emerges, stinking of marijuana.

"Béla! What's going on?"

The Hungarian looks at me in alarm. "I don't know."

Martha giggles. "You're really stinky!"

"Have you been smoking dope?" I ask.

"No, sir, I got locked in there, that's all."

"Who locked you in?"

"Somebody, sir."

"But who?"

"I don't know. I was just in there and I got locked in."

The truth is that I feel quite sorry for Béla. He's always been bullied in some way or other.

"Look, why don't you come back with us and you can practise with Josh. I think he's gone home," I suggest.

"I'm not sure, I think my mum wants me home," Béla says.

"Oh come on, Béla, Josh will like it; he's been wanting to practise with you for ages. This morning he even suggested to me that I took you both to the Cardiff Harp Symposium."

"If it's OK with you, can I go home and change, then come around?"

"I tell you what," I say, feeling quite expansive with all the relief now. "I'll drive you!"

4.38pm

It's lucky that Ma isn't home when Hicky drops me off. The Count is still playing the piano. I run to my room, strip off my uniform, root around my disguises drawer and change into my trendy gear: my skinny jeans, my white shirt and my leather jacket.

The Count stops playing the piano when he sees I'm leaving so soon. He wants me to stay in the prison of the flat. But today I've escaped. I'm free!

I jump back into Hicky's VW and off I go.

If it wasn't for the fact that Josh is being so horrible to me and I didn't get my place back at the school, this would be the best day of my life!

4.45pm

My phone rings as I'm opening the door to our home. Pushing open the door with one hand and holding the phone to my ear with the other, I listen to my wife.

"Martin, what's happened?"

Béla and Martha follow me into the cool hallway. The haunting chords of Josh's harp ripple through the house. It's a relief to know that he's home.

For the first time in a very long time, I actually

feel positive about the instrument. Josh is a good player. As if she is chasing the elusive notes through the house, Martha dashes upstairs. Béla seems much more reluctant; he looks around at the furnishings in the house with a wistful look. I shoo him upstairs as I answer Helen: "Perhaps I should ask you the same question."

"I've heard all about your antics at the interview, Martin."

"Oh, did you indeed?"

"What do you mean by that?"

Just then I hear some shouting from upstairs. Josh is swearing at the top of his voice: "Fuck off, fuck off out of here!"

"I'll call you back in a sec. There's something I need to sort out!"

"What?"

"I'll tell you in a minute."

I put the phone in my pocket and shout out Josh's name as I go up the stairs. I had thought it was Josh yelling at Martha, but as I draw close I realise that he was cussing Béla. The poor boy is hovering nervously just outside Josh's room, fiddling with his fingers.

"Hey, Josh, what's up?" I say in my jolliest voice as I peer around the door. Martha stares at Josh in astonishment. My son has picked up a ruler and is waving it around with scant regard for anyone's safety. I surmise the boys have fallen out. I'm good at dealing with situations like this.

"Martha, maybe you could get Béla to show you

some stuff on the computer downstairs while I have a chat with Josh?"

"Cool," Martha says.

Béla agrees somewhat lugubriously and leads Martha downstairs. In a sweet gesture of trust, she takes him by the hand.

Josh puts down the ruler and looks at me.

"What's going on, Josh? I thought Béla was your friend."

"Well, he's not, he's a cunt."

"Don't use that language, please! What on earth has got into you?"

"It doesn't matter."

Josh takes hold of his harp and, leaning his cheek against its frame, plays it softly.

"Are you feeling very bad about things, Josh? Is that what's going on?"

Josh stops plucking and looks at me.

"Did you get the job, Dad?"

"That's not what I'm talking about."

"But I'm asking you a question. You answer my questions, I answer yours."

"No, of course I didn't."

Josh looks at me with intense, hard eyes.

"Dad, why did you run off last night?"

"I've answered a question. Now, you answer mine. Why have you and Béla fallen out?"

"He was bullying me."

"I can't believe that, somehow. Béla isn't the bullying type."

"What? This is the boy you had excluded from school, remember? I can't see why you're suddenly his biggest defender," Josh says in an exaggeratedly aggrieved tone.

"Well, yes, but that was something else. I'm trying to help here, Josh. Béla is your best friend. I don't want you two to fall out. I mean, Béla didn't tell you anything that annoyed you, did he?"

"What do you mean?"

"He didn't say anything…"

"Maybe he did."

"What did he say?" I ask a little too anxiously.

Has Béla told Josh about his mother's infidelity? Is that what's happened?

"Why did you run off last night, Dad?"

"That's not what I'm talking about. I'm asking you about what Béla said to you."

"Why did you run off?" he persists.

"Josh, you know that Mum and I are going to sort everything out, don't you? You know you don't have to worry, don't you?"

"Why did you go off last night, Dad?"

"Your mother and I had a row."

This feels like very dangerous territory. What the fuck does he know?

"I know," Josh says.

"If you know, why are you asking me about it then? Did you hear it?" I ask.

To be honest, I am not sure what exactly we're talking about. It's one of those weird conversations where there's one secret too many.

"I hate it when you shout at each other," Josh says.

I breathe in deeply. This feels safer territory. I say: "But the whole thing is academic because I didn't get the job and I think I'm going to be around a lot at home next year. I'll probably be unemployed."

"Have you told Mum that?"

I get up off the bed and walk to his window. There are loads of roach ends on the windowsill – Josh doesn't even try and clear them away now. It'll probably be my job soon to be cleaning up all this muck.

"No. I haven't."

"Can you phone her and tell her?"

Josh's fingers jitter on the harp strings. I sit back down on the bed. I'm pretty sure that he doesn't know about Helen's betrayal.

"OK, OK, I'll phone her and tell her."

"Now, please," he says, leaning his harp on the wall. He is keenly attentive.

"What? In front of you?"

"Yes, Dad. And I don't want you shouting at her, or saying anything. I just want you to admit that she was right."

I pull my phone out of my pocket and toss it from hand to hand.

"I'll phone her and do as you say. But she wasn't right, you know. Things would have been far better off if I had got the job."

"Dad, you're hardly ever around as it is. If you

were Deputy Head we wouldn't see you till Christmas. You might as well put your bed in the school."

God, he's even using Helen's phrases.

"I have a wider duty, Josh. I know I can do great things at that school, but in order to do them I have to have a position of power. Just being a head of department isn't enough to make real changes. Besides, I owe it to Jack."

"Jack died because of the job, and you might too, Dad, if you're not careful."

"Josh, I'm a lot tougher than Jack. I'm not going to die."

"Mum says that your health isn't good, Dad. She's really worried about you."

"Mum has her other reasons for saying that."

"She's a doctor, Dad!"

"She has her reasons."

For a crazy moment, I think about telling him everything. Then he would see who was truly the good person in this situation. Helen has really brainwashed him into thinking that she is the one in the right.

"What is all this about me having to be at home?" I dig my hands into my pockets. "You and Martha are fine! You're both doing really well, except for the odd bit of histrionics, which is perfectly normal."

"How do you know that? Do you actually know what really goes on here? Do you actually know how I feel about anything?"

"Of course I do. I know you've got your music,

you've got your friends, you've got your computer."

I run out of things to say.

"Dad, I've spent the last few years being called gay all the time because you teach at that school. It's been non-stop. It's completely fucked me up," he says, lowering his voice to a shamed whisper.

His words pierce me. But then I remind myself that he's the kind of kid who would have got bullied wherever he went. He's got an awkward manner. A nasty way of irritating people. And besides, I have eradicated the source of the bullying. No. I must not feel guilty.

"But Josh, the GMF have been booted out. That's going to stop."

Josh sighs. "I never go out. I just stay in my room playing my music and doing Facebook and Twitter shit pretending that I have loads of friends, but I don't. A lot of the time, I'm just baby-minding Martha."

"Oh Joshy, don't be so negative. Think positive! It's great that you've got Martha."

"Is it? She irritates the hell out of me sometimes. Let's face it, she's a bit of a stuck-up, prissy little bitch."

"She's your little sister, Josh, you shouldn't speak like that about her. Come on, Josh! Lighten up!"

"I might feel more positive if you started acting like you're part of the family."

I shake my head wearily. We are truly going round in circles.

"I am part of this family, Josh. It's tough because Mum is out a lot of the time. I think we should seriously think about putting some pressure on her to cut down her work hours instead of picking on me all the time."

"Don't drag Mum into it like that. She's not to blame for this. She's got an important job."

"And I haven't?"

"You're a two-bit teacher, Dad. She's a consultant in one of the biggest hospitals in the world. There's no comparison. You have to accept that she's the big cheese around here."

I twist my fingers into fists. "I'm not going to be insulted, Josh."

I hasten to the threshold of the room and I'm just about to leave when Josh says darkly: "Dad, I know what you get up to."

I wrinkle my forehead, peering back into the room.

"What do you mean?"

"I know, Dad. I saw you once."

My heart is beating quite a bit faster now.

"I saw you, Dad. I saw you going into one of those places."

"What are you talking about? Josh, I'm going," I say, not rising to the bait.

Suddenly, he jumps up on the bed and bounds towards me, bouncing on the springs of the mattress. His face looks demonic as he punches his fist in my direction: "You're going to call Mum and tell her that you're going to spend much more time at home and take your responsibilities seriously. That's what you're going to do!"

"You could use some of your own words sometimes, you know, instead of quoting your mother all the time!"

"You're going to do that!"

I avert my eyes as I say: "Yes, yes, keep your hair on, I will. I'll do it now. But I would appreciate the chance to do that alone."

I go into our bedroom and shut the door. Staring at the marital bed, I touch WIFE and listen to the phone ring. With any luck, she'll be in surgery and I'll be spared this conversation until the evening, when I'll be insulated by a few beers.

She picks up.

"Helen? Are you able to talk? Josh is fine. I was just calling you to say that."

"What's happened?" Her voice is urgent. I can tell without asking that she's not got much time.

"Oh, he was worried about some things, but we've straightened them out now," I say in a soothing voice.

"What's been going on, Martin? I got a call from Sam earlier on. He said you were behaving like a total lunatic."

"What did he say?"

I straighten the duvet on our bed and sit down, hesitating. Should I tell her I know?

"Did you get the job, Martin?"

"I'll probably be a house-husband next term. I think Sam will definitely sack me – if he can. He tried earlier in the day; that failed, but I'm pretty sure he's going to try again."

"That wasn't what I heard. He told me that Gilda loved you, particularly after you put on a James Bond show of beating up the local yobs. Sam was saying that you'll probably be running the school with him next term. He was sounding quite disconsolate."

I don't know what to say. If that's true, then maybe things will be OK...

"Look," she sounds kinder now, a trace of the old nice Helen seeping into her words, "I'm very busy today, but tomorrow can we talk calmly about things? Will you promise not to drink too much tonight so that I can have a conversation with you in the morning? I'm not on call, and it's going to be much better to talk to you then."

After the call, I make my way to the kitchen, feeling like I deserve a beer. I see, with a twinge of irritation, that Béla has decided to help Martha on my school laptop. I consider telling him off for not asking my permission first, but then, feeling generous, I change my mind. I grab a cold can of beer from the fridge and, gesticulating with it in their direction, I say: "Tally ho! The term's over! Long live the holidays!"

With that, I head into the living room, kick off my shoes, shrug off my jacket and switch on the cricket. I lean back and sip the beer. Despite all my efforts not to think about it, I can't stop dwelling upon those texts. I get Sam's phone out and examine the messages again. This time I look at the messages he's sent her.

> Helen, I love you, you know that, don't you? I have spoken to M but he won't listen to reason. Sx.

> You know, more than anything, it's talking to you that counts. I feel like we are kindred minds. Sxxxx

Her ones are less effusive but more to the point:

> I want you inside me, you know I do. I always have.

It's a weirdly sado-masochistic exercise: each word simultaneously stabs and heals me. But then I put my thinking cap on. Taking a somewhat dispassionate view, I consider their texts to be rather weirdly formal and yet romantic. Sam seems keen to say Helen's name again and again. The word "Helen" is clearly a totem for him in the same way it was for me at the beginning of our relationship. Sam and I, for all our differences, are quite similar. Romantics at heart. In love with the same woman.

I feel dizzy as I recast my memories in the light of the affair. Sam's friendliness with Helen at university, the holidays that we have shared with Sam's family, the dinners, the parties, the barbecues, the coffees and the glasses of wine, the football games and the hours spent jamming on their guitars, the chats, the revelations. Memories bounce and twist and spin around in my mind.

Sam used to be my best friend!

It is only now that I remember that Helen is going away on conference next week, giving a talk on the trials of her new anaesthetic techniques, which include showing DVDs to patients while they are having surgery.

Isn't Sam going away on a conference too? God, why haven't I seen all of this before?

Should I call her again and just tell her I know?

No. I'm not going to have a phone-row with Helen. I am above that particular indignity.

Instead, I'm going to have some peace watching the cricket.

The thing is, I just can't begin to think of what to say to Helen. I could call her a whore, but my mind balks at this. She's not a whore at all; I can see that from the texts. She loves Sam. But does that mean she doesn't love me?

Thinking these half-charitable thoughts, I feel quite Zen about my wife's infidelity and Sam's treachery. In a way, it's a relief to know that there's a proper reason for Helen's coldness towards me recently. It's a relief to know that it isn't me. It isn't my mind, body or being that she hates; it's just that Sam has seduced her.

Yes, when I think about it, I am well and truly off the hook; in fact, as far as I can judge, the bloody hook has been wrenched off the wall. I can't be apportioned any blame. Sam is the scapegoat now. Helen can't hold me responsible for the breakdown of the marriage.

My phone rings again. I see it's the school calling. Do I really want to speak to Sam at this juncture? Mind you, it might be Gilda herself.

And it is.

"Mr Hick, I'd like to ask you formally if you would accept the post of Deputy Head. Initially, we had decided to make the post temporary, but I've decided that I want you permanently in post."

I'm so shocked to hear this that the phone nearly falls out of my hands. I tighten my grip around it.

"Is this some kind of joke?" I ask

"No, I can assure you it's no joke."

My mind tries to compute all the implications of accepting the job: my new status in the eyes of Helen, the extra money, the power to change for the better at the school.

"Well, I'd be delighted to accept. Yes, I'll take it," I say. "I accept!"

"I am so glad. I was very impressed with your performance today. You were courageous in many ways. You have my full backing. I am aware that there are certain differences of opinion between you and the Principal. I have decided to put you in charge of discipline in the school."

"That's fantastic news."

"We can't have a tragedy like the one that afflicted Mr Humphreys again. As an academy, we're under extra pressure to get results quickly. I feel confident that with you at the helm we will stamp out the appalling behaviour we've been seeing in the school recently."

"Yes, that is certainly true. But what about Sam? How does he feel about things?"

"Mr Ndlova will have to accept the decision of the sponsors of the academy – namely me! This isn't a local authority school where the governing body decides things. My word is law around here. It's as simple as that. If Mr Ndlova decides to leave the school as a result of my decision, I feel confident that you could take the reins until the formal process of appointing a new principal has been gone through."

"He used to be my friend, you know."

"And mine. Unfortunately, Mr Ndlova seems to have become distracted recently. But let's discuss this next week. I think you deserve to raise a glass to your success with your family. I'll call you next week. Well done, Mr Hick!"

After I finish the call, I know the first thing I should do is call Helen, but I decide not to.

Instead, I look at the empty air before me and see it fill up with the image of Jack.

"I did it," I say. "I did it, Jack. I am going to be you!"

I take a big slug of beer and the image flickers and fades. There's a lurking sadness that I don't want to think about, so I switch off my phone and bound into the kitchen, where Martha and Béla are sitting, crouched in concentration over her mathematical equations. They're the people I most want to share this news with.

4.47pm

It's one of the best feelings ever because what does Hicky do the moment that he learns he's got the job? Does he rush up to see his son sulking up in his bedroom? Or does he come and see yours truly?

Yes, he rushes up to me first! Me, Béla Pongrácz, the immortal secret detective who's helped him out so much! He shakes my hand first and says with tears in his eyes: "I did it! I got the job!"

I kind of know this already because in between helping Martha and having a surreptitious nose around Hicky's school computer – it's only full of boring lesson plans as far as I can see – I've been listening in to his conversation with Gilda Ball. That's the kind of detective I am. Martha don't suspect a thing. She thinks I've got a bladder problem because I keep going to the toilet. "Oh Béla, you don't have to go again, do you!"

Still, I do a great job at being amazed because the truth is: I am amazed. Amazed that Hicky should be telling me first. And amazed that I'm going to be back at the Gilda Ball Academy next term. There's no way that Hicky will keep me out after I've helped him so much.

I watch him with watery eyes and think: fucking hell, old Béla had to put in some work to get Hicky that job.

I am, at bottom, a total and utter genius.

As I watch Martha shrieking with delight, I muse to

myself whether it's time that Hicky learnt just how hard I did work today.

"I got the job, Martha! I showed everyone. I showed everyone," Hicky says.

"Well done, sir! We did it!"

"Daddy! You did it!"

Hicky takes Martha by the hand and dances around the room with her. Martha reaches out for me too and soon I'm dancing around with them as well.

Hicky gets out of breath quite quickly and stops. It's quite interesting that he doesn't tell Josh his good news. Or that Josh hasn't come down to find out what all the fuss is about.

Hicky heads back to the front room. I follow him. Just before he's about to go back to the cricket, I say: "So, sir, do you think you might, well, you know, find a way to get me a place back at the school, next term?"

Hicky doesn't hesitate. He slaps me on the back. "Of course, of course!"

Now there's real gratitude in my eyes. "Thanks, sir, you don't know how much it's going to mean to me."

"Béla, remember though, there are certain things…"

He doesn't have to say anymore because I know exactly what he's thinking.

"I will never, ever say anything! I promise!" I say.

"Good, now I'm going to watch the cricket and put my feet up! It's been quite a day!"

Once Hicky has sealed himself off in the front room, I return to Martha in the kitchen. My hands tremble with the enormity of the thought of going back to school. I never, ever thought I would be so thankful to return to school!

"I'm a bit hungry," Martha says, giggling a little. "I haven't had anything to eat all afternoon. You won't tell Mum that, will you? I mean, if Mum found out, she'd yell at Dad. He's supposed to feed me, but sometimes he forgets. Then I eat crisps. Which make you obese."

"You're not fat at all," I say.

"But Daddy is!"

"Why don't we go and tell Josh the good news, and then I'll get you something to eat. I'm a good cook," I say, puffed up with Pongrácz pride.

"Do we have to? He won't be pleased."

"Why not?"

"He hates Daddy. He thinks Daddy is a bad man."

"He does?"

"Yes. He and Mummy think Daddy is a very bad man. But that's just stupid. I know that Daddy is really like Dumbledore. A very, very good teacher who has a hard job."

"I still think we should tell Josh, just to see what he says."

I smile at Martha. She smiles back. We mount the stairs and hover for a brief moment outside Josh's bedroom, listening to him playing the harp and singing. He's very good.

"Sail away, sail away from the bloody day," he's singing.

I wait for him to finish, then I rush into the room and say: "Josh, your dad got the job! He's going to be the Deputy Head."

But the thing is, as Martha predicted, Josh doesn't seem pleased at all. He stops playing his harp and gets up, approaching me and Martha jaggedly, like a snake that's been trodden on.

"Are you saying my dad actually got the job?" he says, plucking at his temples with the tips of his fingers.

Martha chuckles.

"Yes, Daddy did it! Even though Mum said he wouldn't! Daddy did it! I reckon Daddy's a lot cleverer than Mum thinks he is! I used to think he was a bit like Professor Snape, but now I think he might be Dumbledore!"

It's funny but I can see that part of Martha is super-clever, and that part of her is far older and wiser than me, but there's also this tiny, tiny girl aspect to her, particularly when she talks about Hicky.

"Dumbledore! You don't know what you're talking about!" Josh snaps.

"But Josh, why aren't you pleased? I mean, you're the son of the king of the school," I say, feeling myself getting more impassioned the more I think about it. "I mean, your dad whopped the GMF today and got the job. I don't get it!"

Josh wrinkles his nose at me like I've farted. I think it's probably a good idea that I don't tell him that I'm returning to the school either. "God, you hero-worship my dad, don't you? How sad is that?" he asks.

"He's a good bloke."

"He's not a good bloke, you Hungarian fuck-wit. He's not, so why don't you fuck off? Who said you could stay in my house, anyway?"

5.00pm

Martha puts her chin on her hands as she watches me from the kitchen table.

"Why are you Josh's friend?"

"We're in a band," I say, as I peel her carrots and chop them up into thin slivers.

"Yes, but Joshy is horrible to you. He said you were a Hungarian fuck-wit. I mean, if you think about it, that isn't a very nice thing to say to a friend, is it?"

I make a face and then laugh. "I remember the first time I ever, ever met him…"

"In the whole of the universe?"

"Yes," I say, smiling at Martha. Somehow, I feel she's got my way of thinking, even more than Josh. "It was when I was eleven and I was put into Year 8 even though I should have been in Year 7 so I got stuck with this bunch of psychos in my year, Mercy and the Bentley twins, and they were chasing me all around school, beating me up, and I didn't understand nothing then, coz I'd just come from Hungary, where nothing really like that happens, not that bad, there aren't the kind of kids you get here, and I was shitting myself when this face pops out of a hole in the wall, with long hair over his eyes, and he says here, come in here, you can be in my band. And it was Josh. And he was hiding in the music block, which is all protected from the kids coz it's full of equipment, and so that's when it began, every break time I'd play in the practice room with Joshy boy."

"So Josh saved you from the GMF?"

"You know about the GMF?"

"I know everything. I know all about how babies are made, which is yuck. I know all about the Tudors, the Reformation, and how solids turn into liquids."

"I know about those things as well."

"You know how to cook. That's more than my dad does. My mum is always going on at him about that. When she's not here, he just makes us pizza or spaghetti hoops."

"I like spaghetti hoops."

"Me too."

"I like pizza too but I like Hungarian food the best."

"Who taught you how to cook?"

"My ma. I have to cook every night for her and my great-uncle. Except this night, of course, because I am here!" I say very cheerfully.

"Josh doesn't know how to cook."

I ask her why her mum thought her dad wouldn't get the job.

"Mum and Dad had a big row last night, and the night before that, and the night before that, and then the day before that, because it was the weekend. Dad gets annoyed and shouts but Mum never shouts. She gets disappointed," she says with wide eyes like it wasn't really a problem at all, but this huge game. "Mum said that Dad would never get the job. That he wasn't good enough. Daddy didn't even sleep in their bed. I did!"

Although the fish fingers aren't ready yet, I put the vegetables before her and she munches them merrily. Her forehead furrows.

"But seriously, I still don't get why you are Josh's friend."

"I already told you."

"But just playing music with someone doesn't make you their friend."

"It made John Lennon friends with Paul McCartney."

"Who are they?"

"They formed The Beatles. John Lennon fought against capitalism. He wrote songs attacking our corrupt society. Josh is a musician. He's like Beethoven. Temperamental. He lives for his music. Besides, like my mum says, being nice is overrated. Being nice is about subscribing to the values of our capitalist society."

"I don't know what you're talking about," Martha says.

I puff out my chest. I do know more than Martha! This gives me an excuse to give her a lecture about capitalism: how it seduces you, how it exploits the workers, how it's doomed to fail. And how it will all end soon.

"As Ma says, the revolution will come. This recession, all these wars, all this global warming means that everything is collapsing," I say.

"Does your mum know everything?" Martha asks.

I think about this for a moment – and hesitate.

"She doesn't know about healthy living," I say, adding with a little constriction of my airways: "She smokes too much."

"Josh smokes too. Dad and Mum are always going on at him about it – how it's really unhealthy and everything. He wants to die young he says. I hope he does too.

I look at her earnest face and can't help smiling. It's like she knows absolutely everything – but somehow knows nothing.

"I think it's more serious with my ma. I think I have asthma and get coughs really easily coz of her."

"That's bad," Martha muses. "Does she know how bad it makes you?"

No one has asked me this question before.

"I don't know," I croak.

"If she loves you properly then she wouldn't do it around you, that's what I reckon," Martha says decisively.

"But she does know about a lot of other stuff," I say. As these words are coming out, I'm thinking, does Ma really know about much?

"Then she's like my mum too. My mum knows everything. Except that my dad might know more."

We're silent as I put the fish fingers onto two plates. I'm pretty hungry too. The last thing I had was some Hungarian pancakes and a banana in the morning. God, that seems like years ago. Martha and I tuck in.

"This is delicious!" Martha says. "You're a great cook, do you know that? Like Jamie Oliver!"

I am smiling with real pride when Martha adds without any sense that she's doing me down: "Except Jamie Oliver wouldn't cook fish fingers."

I go back upstairs a little reluctantly; I'm not looking forward to facing Josh again. He's still pretty mad at me. But I know also that speaking to him is my duty. It's like my duty too when Ma has a go at me. I am one of those people who have to face people's anger all the time – even when I don't deserve it.

Luckily, Josh is still plucking at his harp and doesn't seem to notice me at all. I pick up his acoustic guitar and strum along as best I can, making up the words as I go along.

"July day, sail away..."

As I am strumming, I think: yes, this is the reason why I like Josh. I like the way I am just free with him to sing or strum whatever I like. Somehow even though he's a really critical person, he never criticises my singing or strumming. Instead, after I've been singing for a while, he'll join in. Only today he breaks off pretty quickly, and rolls a spliff. And today, all of a sudden, I don't like the idea of breathing in all that smoke.

"I don't think you should do that," I say. "It isn't good for you."

Josh sneers at me. "What the fuck's the matter with you? Course it ain't good for you. But it's good to die young," he says.

But somehow this joke ain't funny anymore. "Your life is good, Josh, you shouldn't want to die young."

"Oh fuck off! You don't know fuck all about my life, you cunt," he says, lighting up the spliff. Today, he doesn't even bother with puffing the scented smoke out of the window. "Besides, you never complain when your mum smokes. What's the matter with you?"

"How do you know I don't complain?" I say.

"Course you don't, you fish-faced cunt!" he laughs. "You're the biggest mummy's boy I've met in my life."

"I'm not," I say firmly. I know Josh pretty well and I know that he's still mad at me for saying he was spoilt earlier. But now, when I think about it, I think that perhaps I was wrong. I've seen a bit more closely today what Hicky is like with him, and there's something very wrong between them. "I'm sorry I said you was spoilt, Josh. I don't think you are really. I was just joking."

"Don't give me this bullshit, Béla. Of course, I'm fucking spoilt. You ain't got nothing compared with me but somehow you're happier. I don't know quite how it happened coz your mum is a fucking nightmare, and my mum is OK, but it did. It just did."

I should be insulted to hear him speak about Ma like that but her rejection of me outside the health clinic still stings. Josh is right: she is a nightmare.

"What makes your mum OK?" I ask.

As he speaks, his voice changes from Cockney to being quite posh. He drops his "innits" and "ain'ts" as he says: "She knows everything about everything. She's the kind of person if you were dying, you'd want her doing the surgery. And when I'm on holiday, she takes me for long walks by the seaside and shows me the seashells and the cliffs and the sea and explains how it was all formed and we look at the sun and she tells me how we're this small blue planet, so delicate, so small, and how we have to protect it."

"That sounds nice." And very removed from anything my mum would do. The only walks I do with her nowadays are pushing her wheelchair down to places like the health centre. "I remember how my Dad was a bit like that when he took me down to the Danube in Budapest."

I trail away. I don't want to speak any more. It's too

upsetting. There's silence as Josh smokes his spliff. He tries to hand me some but I shake my head.

"I can't believe my Dad got that fucking job," Josh says at last.

"But Josh, I just don't get why you're so against him."

Josh starts playing his harp quietly again.

"Béla, you don't know what my Dad is like. You don't have to live with him," he says, resting his head against the frame of the harp.

Suddenly, a mega-Béla brainwave comes upon me. I lean forward, narrow my eyes at him and whisper: "You're the Countess Feckula, ain't you?"

5.15pm

My wife stands before me. I pause the cricket. Her mouth is pursed and her chest is pushed out, her cleavage highlighted underneath her blouse. The sun has returned and now streams through the front bay windows of the house, gilding the marble mantelpiece that we paid so much money to renovate.

"Aren't you supposed to be in surgery?" I say, jolting forwards on the sofa. This is the first time Helen has ever come home on a "surgery" day. Clearly something is wrong.

Her tongue flicks over her lips as she says: "Was there any reason why you switched off your phone?"

"I'm sorry, I've been busy. But what are you doing home? This is insane. You're due in surgery, aren't you? You'll be getting sacked next!"

Helen ignores my disingenuous concern and steams ahead with what's troubling her: "But Martin, you didn't tell me you've been promoted, did you?"

I pat the empty cushion next to me on the sofa. "I was just about to tell you!"

Helen hesitates.

"It was quite embarrassing, to tell you the truth, Martin, having Sam phone and tell me something I should have heard from you. He said you learnt about it a while ago."

"It wasn't that long ago."

"Well, an hour or so ago."

"That's not that long ago."

She looks at me – and then sighs. She looms over me as she concedes: "I'm not surprised, actually. After all, I haven't been exactly positive about you getting the job."

"No, you haven't."

She sits down beside me, smelling of antiseptic. It's not an appealing perfume.

"And I'm still not that keen. It's going to be very difficult. You two are at loggerheads over a lot of things."

"Is that what Sam said?"

I shake my beer can. It's empty and I don't feel tipsy at all. I definitely need another.

"Sam can't work out why you're so mad at him."

"He can't?"

I get up, leave the room and move briskly into the kitchen. Helen follows me. We find Martha there with her Harry Potter book resting on a plate of half-eaten fish fingers and beans.

"Oh Martin…" Helen sighs, picking up the plate the book was resting on. I can see there's a line of tomato ketchup running along the bottom edge of the book. Helen has spotted this too.

I shrug. This seems a trivial worry, considering everything else. I hand Helen a sponge to clean the book with. As she scrubs away, Martha says: "Daddy got his promotion, Mum! I think he's very clever, because you said he wouldn't, but he did! Don't you think Daddy is clever?"

It's ironic that although I hardly make an effort with Martha, she seems to adore me.

"We're all very pleased for him," Helen says flatly.

"Martha is, at least," I say, opening a fresh can of Stella.

Helen hisses that she needs to talk to me alone. I head back into the front room, and she follows. I feel exhausted suddenly at the thought of another marital "chat". I've had my day of triumph, of sweet revenge. I feel at peace with the living – and the dead. I'd rather leave it at that. But Helen won't drop it. She informs me that she's got a couple of hours before she has to return to the hospital to catch up with some paperwork.

"So what happened to your patient? Did the transplant go OK?" I ask.

Helen exhales loudly. "We decided not to go ahead with it."

"Why?"

"It's not a perfect match. It wasn't worth the risk. We spent the afternoon weighing everything up and decided against it."

I pat my stomach, thinking about my own liver. I take another swig of my Stella.

"What did he do?" I ask.

"What do you mean?"

"What was his job?"

"He was a manager."

"Where?"

"At Homebase."

I give a hollow laugh.

"What section?"

Helen thrums her fingers impatiently but answers nevertheless, telling me that he was in his early fifties and supervised the garden furniture departments at a number of Homebases. He drank heavily at work.

"What did he drink?"

"Vodka, I think," she says.

"Anything else?"

"I'm not sure. Vodka can destroy your liver pretty fast."

I know my questions simultaneously irritate and engage her. It's the one thing she prides herself on: she gets to know the human side of things – unlike most of her colleagues. In the early days of our relationship, I used to talk to her endlessly about her professional life: her patients, the doctors, the other surgeons, the consultants, the managers, the nurses, even the orderlies. Helen made it her business to know about all of them.

"Do you think he'll live?"

"Depends on whether we can find a better liver for him. He's doing fine at the moment. He could live for a while with his current liver, but he's going to need a new one soon."

"And you haven't got another one knocking about?"

Helen sighs. "No. Like I said, not at the moment."

There's a pause in the conversation.

"So it's perfectly fine for you to come home and talk to me? You're not endangering anyone's life by speaking to your mug of a husband?" I ask with a wry smile.

"Yes. It's perfectly OK to talk."

"OK, Helen, what do you want to talk about?" I ask, watching a ball getting knocked for four across the grass.

Helen spreads her hands across her smart skirt.

"I just don't know if we can carry on like this," she says.

This makes me sit up. "What's that supposed to mean?"

Helen looks down at her clipped, clean, unvarnished fingernails – what a contrast to Mercy's – and then looks at me. "It means that I just don't know if we can carry on with these sorts of disagreements. This isn't what marriage is about. Or life, for that matter. It's not fair on us, or our children. Martin, you don't listen to anything I say. It's just not working. And I'm beginning to think that it's best if I just let go; just stop feeling so responsible for you."

"Stop deciding for me," I say.

"Yes, if you want to put it that way. It's not good for me, or for our relationship. Ultimately, you can do what you want. I can't force you to behave in any particular way."

I shut my eyes and try to get some clarity in my tipsy brain. I open them again. "So, what you're saying is... if I don't give up the Deputy Head job, you'll divorce me. That's the choice you're giving me, isn't it?"

I switch off the TV with the remote and stare at her.

Helen presses her two hands together and then points them at my face. "Look, I'm putting this to you because I'm so worried about you, Martin. You can take this job, but you won't survive it. Or at least the marriage won't... If the threat of divorce is the only thing that will stop you getting it then so be it."

"So you want to divorce me for my own good?"

"Now you're trying to make me sound stupid. Obviously, it's more than that. It's about me too. It's about what I want."

"What do you want?"

Helen puts her hands through her hair and then paces down towards the window.

"I just want a chance to start again, Martin. That's

what I want. And I think that's best for you, best for me, best for our kids."

As if to emphasise this, she touches the window pane, her hands imprinting on the glass. Outside, the summery evening insinuates itself into the street.

"Are you really serious? I can't believe you're talking like this," I say, shaking my head and walking over to her. She flinches as I approach.

I'm close enough now to catch a tiny scent of perfume.

"You haven't even let me have a go at the job yet. You haven't even given me a chance."

Helen considers edging away from me, but she decides not to. She wants to show me that she's not frightened of me. She should be because my fingers are itching. I feel like I could hit her at any moment. I really could.

"What you need is to take things easy and stop getting so stressed. And what this family needs is someone at home, to help Josh and Martha. As we both know, it makes far more sense if you do that. Come on, Martin, you know what Jack's life was like. He came home at midnight. He was forever trying to sort out everything. And you're a lot like Jack – only more disorganised."

"Thanks for the vote of confidence. That's the thing, Helen: you've never believed in me," I say, examining my palm.

"I've always believed in you – as a father. And what I'm saying is a big vote of confidence in you in that regard. Josh and Martha really need you."

I fetch my beer from the coffee table by the sofa, finish it and then crumple the empty can in my hand.

"You know, it's always puzzled me why you're so against me doing well in my career. It always has. Until today."

"What do you mean?"

Under Helen's withering gaze, the crumpled can suddenly looks like a metaphor for my soul.

"Well, it's always nagged at me because it's never really made sense, but today I found out the reason why. It's not only you that doesn't want me doing the job. It's Sam. You *and* Sam..."

It's out! His name is in the ether! Flung like a stone at a window. I watch her face feel the impact of his name and try and withstand the blow. But she can't. No matter how she tries, her eyes, her cheeks, her mouth register the shock. Like glass gradually cracking.

"I'm sure that's right. I'm sure Sam thinks that he could work better with someone else," she says, weakly. But it's pointless pretending.

"He told you that, did he?" I ask, picking over the shards of her respectability.

"Yes, he did but..." Helen mumbles vaguely, turning her face away from me and colouring. She looks out onto the street. The rich evening sunlight is gilding my VW Beetle and the other cars in the street. There is a real beauty in the light, but a sadness too. It is orangey, tinged with the evening, and a feeling that things are moving on.

I have to defy the melancholy. I have to be triumphant. I stand beside her as the sunlight floods against her middle-aged skin, exposing its flaws. My belly touches her back. She moves away.

"And when was that? In a hotel room? In his office? On a business trip you took together?" I say breathily.

Her moment of shock has passed. Instead, my questions seem to provoke a mournful curiosity in her.

"How did you find out?" Helen asks.

"Maybe Sam told me."

Helen relinquishes her melancholic pose and folds her arms. She is rearming herself. I had surprised her with my knowledge, ambushed her even, but now she's adapted and is redeploying her forces.

She tuts. "Don't play games with me, Martin."

She sits down on the chair beside the window. I grab a chair by the bookcase and pull it up next to her. This surprises her. I think she's expecting me to be more aggressive.

"How did you find out?" she asks again, contorting her lips in a way that might suggest that she's either being self-righteous, or just curious.

"It was Béla," I say, patting her reassuringly on the back. She doesn't flinch this time at my touch. Now this is out in the open she seems less afraid of me. "He found Sam's phone."

Helen takes a moment to compute the implications

of this. She looks briefly into my eyes and seems almost apologetic, then she turns her head away from me but remains on her chair.

"He stole it from Sam?" she asks.

"I don't know," I say a little uneasily.

"Well, it doesn't take a rocket scientist to work out that either Sam must have given it to him – or he stole it."

"No, I don't think so. He just found it."

Helen leans forward slightly. I can smell the operating theatre on her.

"Don't be like this, Martin," she pleads with me, touching me with an infuriating lack of commitment on my forearm. I pull away from her.

"I think I'm being pretty reasonable considering you've been having an affair with my best friend," I spit out. Finally, my words have caught up with my feelings. There's real disgust in them.

Helen gets up from the chair and she makes her way towards the door. "I've been meaning to tell you for a while," she says.

It's as if she can't see me, as if I don't exist... For a moment, I want to scream, shout at her, try and get her to show some remorse.

I get up off the chair and put my hand on the door so that she can't escape. She is trapped by my big right arm, pressed against the door. I lean close as I say: "Bollocks! You weren't ever going to tell me, were you? You were planning to divorce me without me having the slightest clue about what was going on.

I think you were going to cite my unreasonable behaviour. That's what I think."

She's frightened now. Genuinely scared that I might be violent.

"That's your paranoia speaking, Martin. I hadn't even thought about divorcing you until today," she says.

My hand remains planted on the door. "I don't believe you," I say.

Very gently, in an almost tender gesture, she puts her hand on my chest and guides me away from the door. It isn't an aggressive move but it is an assertive one. I pull back. I don't want to hurt her. I just want her back, that's all.

She follows me as I retreat back into the room. This feels like a positive move.

"The truth is, Martin, I've been trying to pretend that things are OK. I'm beginning to think now that the affair was my way of saving the marriage. As long as I was so busy at work and swept off my feet by Sam, things felt OK. Felt manageable," she says.

I laugh hollowly. "I like that. Of all the excuses for having an affair that's the most lame. Trying to save the marriage! Do you have any idea what a betrayal this is? Do you have any idea? When did it start, Helen? Was it years ago?"

We're standing facing each other now. "Of course it wasn't. It's only happened in the last few months."

"In the last few months?"

"It was Jack's death, Martin, that made Sam really

think about his own life. The day after he died, he came to me, he said he had to say what he'd always felt before he died. He came to the hospital."

"I don't want to hear the sordid details," I say, sweeping my hand before her. "The main thing is that he must have been carrying a very long-burning torch for you."

"Perhaps he was."

"And perhaps you were for him."

"Perhaps I was."

"So why didn't you choose him all those years ago?"

"You were the confident, pushy one, weren't you? Sam was always so much quieter, so much less confident."

"And then I helped him get into teaching and he changed into a person who's confident enough to fuck my wife."

"I'm sure none of this would have happened if Jack hadn't died. I'm sure of it," Helen says emphatically. "But it's like the pillar that held up the building has gone, Martin."

"I don't believe it. Sam never cared that much about Jack."

"You've got Sam very wrong, Martin."

Helen falls silent. Then she turns to face me again. "It's over, Martin. Let's stop pretending. You've got your promotion. Let's just try and be civil. We've got the kids to think about."

There had been a moment when we were really

talking. Properly in the zone. Properly communicating. But it's gone now. Finito.

"Helen, we were talking just then. We were actually saying stuff to each other that we haven't said in years. I think we can work this stuff out. I really do. You can't just chuck it all away, without trying."

I can see that these words make an impact by the moistness in her eyes. She is that young girl I fell in love with again. She really is. Vulnerable. Thoughtful. Sensitive. Considerate. Appreciative of me.

Then the moment is gone. A siren whirrs in the distance. The noises of London intrude in the room. Everything's fucked.

My wife's gone. She left ages ago. Just one more weary adulterer.

Later, I hear speedy footsteps stomping down the stairs, the door slamming and then see the vanishing figures of Josh and Béla running past the window.

I go out to look for them, but they seem to have disappeared. Instead, I go to the local offie and stock up on more beer, Pringles and Nachos. It's going to be a long night. I need sustenance.

6pm

I'm running fast again but this time I'm the hunter, not the hunted. I've got to move quick coz Josh is running like a fuckwit with a firework up his arse. Even though there is no oxygen in my lungs and I feel like I'm drowning, I am keeping up.

Running. Running. Running.

Running past the neat houses on Quilter Street, past the picnicking families on Jesus Green, round the corner, past the chemist's, past the green-boarded newsagent's, past the Birdcage pub. A couple of drunks stagger back as they emerge from the betting shop and I fly past, pursuing Josh.

It's a weird day. A moment ago there was strong sunlight, but now there are dark clouds overhead and it's beginning to spit rain. I stop for a moment, gasp for air, then suck on my inhaler.

"Josh!" I shout. "What's the matter with you?"

"Get away from me!"

We've reached the playground. Josh climbs to the top of the climbing frame. I try to follow him but he kicks me away with the soles of his shoes.

"I said, fuck off! Didn't you hear me?"

His words wither in the empty playground. All the little children have gone home.

"Josh, are you Countess Feckula?"

Although he hasn't admitted it, DCI Béla Pongrácz can definitely detect that his behaviour is that of a guilty man. Joshua Hick is now my prime suspect.

"Fuck off."

I mount the frame, but don't climb to the top in case he kicks me in the head. I'm good like that; I avoid unnecessary physical abuse.

"Look, mate, I'm not trying to fuck you over. I'm just trying to find out what the fuck is going on."

"Fuck off."

"Please, Josh, I'm your mate. I ain't gonna say nothing to anyone else. You can trust me. It's me. It's Béla. I'm not going to tell anyone. I just want to work out what's going on."

"Fuck off."

My gaze is fortified by a sudden shaft of sunlight emerging from the dark clouds. I look up at the sky. The rain clouds are heading for the City. The change in the weather signals a change in Josh's mood: he makes room for me on the climbing frame.

"You won't tell anyone, will you?" he says, his eyes flickering this way and that.

I pull my most solemn face. "You can trust me, mate. I reckon you probably need to get all this stuff off your tits."

Josh's mood lightens: he laughs. "Chest! Off your chest! You're obsessed with tits."

"That's coz I ain't gay!"

I reach out and squeeze Josh's hand. He doesn't recoil. We look around. The Birdcage pub is just up the road and there are loads of doors and windows in the tower blocks, flats and houses that surround us.

I let go of his hand. "Let's go down there."

Josh agrees and we leave the playground and find a secluded spot underneath some grotty flats, by some rubbish bins. It smells quite a bit but no one can hear us here.

"So you posed as Countess Feckula?" I ask, digging my hands deep into the pockets of my leather jacket.

"Yes," he says, his face now hidden by shadow.

I have to take another puff on my inhaler just to steady my nerves. But the steroids make me more jittery.

"But that means you must have framed me!" I say, feeling the full force of this revelation enter my bloodstream. Thinking aloud, I say: "You made me look like I was the Countess Feckula by posting the photos on the memory stick. It wasn't Mercy at all, but you! Why didn't I think of that? You had that memory stick!"

Josh kicks the rubbish bin with his trainers, not looking at me. "I thought you would be pleased! My dad got you permanently excluded, man! He chucked you out! I was doing you a favour."

I feel a shiver swoop through my spine. "Oh my God, you thought I would say the allegations were true!"

"It would have been no skin off your nose!"

"But why didn't you let me in on it then?"

Josh sighs. "I didn't know I could trust you. And I was proved right. You fucking well backed up my dad, you cunt!"

I walk to the edge of the underpass and look up at Sivill House, the grim walkways, the miserable balconies, and the deep blue air beyond.

"Josh, you're really fucked up, man. Really fucked. I would never have done that to your dad – or you!"

I'm going mad on the inhaler now. It's the only comfort I've got. Josh turns away from me, looking up at the summer sky as he says: "Look, I know you may not like it but my dad has to stop teaching at that fucking school. It's destroying everything."

I direct my gaze now at the road that curls around the tatty shops. In the distance, we can see some riders on motorcycles approaching. I put away my inhaler and grit my teeth.

This situation is fucked. My best friend betrayed his dad and me. Nothing is as it seems.

6.30pm

There's a diminutive knock on the living-room door. I recognise it immediately as Martha's. I put down my beer on the coffee table, get up from the couch and open the door.

"Come in, Your Royal Highness! Would you like some Pringles?" I ask, tipping the opened cardboard tube towards her. She takes a few, I grab even more, and we stare at each other for a moment, munching merrily. Once she's finished, I look at Martha's smile shimmering in the shadows. She starts walking around the room.

"Where's Mum?"

"She's had to go back to work."

Martha surveys the space before her, as if looking for traces of her mother. She's trying her best to be cheerful. She asks for some Nachos and I oblige. I eat some too.

"Why don't you come and sit down on the sofa with me?" I say, after swallowing my Nachos.

My lips feel all powdery and crispy. And my mouth is rather dry. I sip some more beer.

"Why did she go back to work?"

"She's got some paperwork to finish off."

Martha nuzzles into me as I lean back on the sofa and sip at my beer.

"Did she go out because she wants to divorce you?"

Now she's sitting beside me, the glowing images of the television are flickering over her face. Her eyes look watery.

"Mum is not going to divorce me. It's not going to happen. We just had a bit of row, that's all."

"Is it because Béla found a phone?"

"Martha, have you been listening in on other people's conversations?"

Martha ducks her head down. "Only a little."

"Look, I'm sorry, Martha. Things are difficult but we're going to sort them out. In a minute Josh will come back and he'll look after you, and I'm going to go and sort this out."

"Are you going to see Mum and say sorry?"

"Sorry for what?"

"For being cross with her."

"It's not quite as simple as that."

Just then, there's a knock on the front door. I glance through the window and I'm shocked to see Sam, hovering anxiously on the doorstep. He is dressed in jeans and a golfing shirt; he looks more like Tiger Woods than a headteacher.

I jump up, leave the front room and open the front door swiftly.

"Yes," I say stiffly. "What do you want?"

He returns my stony stare with one of his own.

"Is Béla here?"

"No, he isn't."

"He stole my phone. I need it back urgently. Do you know where he is?"

I shrug my shoulders, trying to look as nonchalant as possible: I realise that Helen hasn't yet told him that I now know. This makes me feel weirdly powerful. But just then, Martha pokes her head around my hips and pipes up: "Oh hello, Sam! Have you come to see Mummy?"

Sam tries his best not to seem embarrassed as he retreats down the steps. "No. It's something else."

"That's good, because she's not here! She's got some paperwork to do."

"I was looking for Béla, actually. You don't know where he is, do you?"

"He ran out with Josh a bit ago. They nearly always go to the playground or the farm."

"Thanks, Martha," Sam says, stepping away from the house and hastening down the street before I can get another word in. I shut the front door and walk back with Martha into the kitchen. I ask her whether Sam has come round to the house much.

"Once or twice, he comes to see Mummy. They always talk about their work together. Then I go to bed."

"Is Josh here in the house?"

"No. He's usually out with Béla somewhere."

I call Josh on his mobile.

"Where are you?" I ask.

"I'm just out with Béla."

"Well, just a word of warning: you might see Ndlova while you're out."

"Mr Ndlova?" Josh sounds startled.

"Yes. Look, if you see him you should both run away. Don't talk to him. In fact, I'd quite like it if you both came back here. There's some stuff I need to discuss with you."

6.40pm

I'm coming out of Haggerston Park, feeling like splitting totally from Josh, who is trailing behind me, when this bloke in a Mercedes starts honking at us. At first, I think it's some nutter because the beeping has this crazy rhythmic insistence, but then I see it's old Loverman.

When he sees me he screeches the car to a halt and dives out, shouting: "Béla, give me my phone now!"

Without thinking, I bolt. Josh shouts after me and then follows. Together we run into Hackney City Farm with Loverman in hot pursuit.

We run past the café, past the open-air washbasins, jump over the wooden fence and dive into the piggery. Realising that Loverman will see us if we don't jump into the pen, I climb over and duck down with Bella the gigantic ginger pig. Josh copies me.

With Bella's great wet snout nuzzling next to us, sniffling and snuffling, Josh looks at me in confusion. I put my finger to my mouth to shut him up.

We wait there, smelling the dungy smell of the pig pen with Bella nosing around us. I catch a glimpse of Loverman poking his head around the door and then disappearing.

After a few minutes, feeling that the coast is clear, I climb out of the pig pen.

"Béla, why was he asking for his phone?" Josh asks, vaulting the wall.

I say sullenly: "It was nothing. I think the GMF stole it and he wants to blame it on me."

"The GMF? They stole Loverman's phone?"

"It doesn't matter," I say. "The main thing is to get away from him, like your dad said."

"But why do you need to get away if you didn't do anything?" Josh asks, frowning.

I don't answer. We cross Hackney Road in silence and creep down the top of Columbia Road where the cobblestones are. We're safe from Loverman now because cars can't come up here. We pass by Stingray, the pizza pub, and look enviously at all the students drinking lager and eating their pizzas. They look like they're having fun.

The fucker tried to frame me!

I think I should probably go home but there's a big problem: I'm covered in pig crap. Ma would kill me if I came home in a state like this.

6.50pm

When I hear the boys' voices coming up the street, I get up off the sofa and open the front door, ready for them. They look up at me – both cartoonishly unkempt and rough, with bits of straw sticking out of their long hair. Although they have quite different features – Béla has a pointy face and Josh's is round – the similar hairstyles, their leather jackets, their jeans and shirts make them look like brothers of a sort.

I wave my hand in front of my face. "God, you guys really smell bad. Where have you been?"

Josh points at Béla, who looks down at the pavement moodily. "We had an encounter with Bella the pig," he says.

They step into the hallway. I make them take off their shoes and jackets, and then suggest that they get cleaned up. Both of them seem a little unsure about this, but when Martha surfaces in the hall and says "Poo!", they both agree to have a shower.

"Are you sure that would be all right?" Béla asks.

"Of course, and maybe Josh could give you some clean clothes to wear until you get home. You seem to have got dung all over your trousers. Martha, why don't you show Béla the way to the bathroom and get him a towel?"

Josh eyes me suspiciously. He knows I am up to something, but he can't work out what. When Béla has disappeared upstairs with Martha, Josh turns to me. "What I don't get is why you wanted me and Béla to stay away from Ndlova. I mean, I just don't understand why he was asking for his phone from Béla. Did Béla steal it or something? What's going on?"

"Get cleaned up and I'll tell you. I can't tell you right now."

"Dad, just tell me now!" Josh says.

"It's difficult with Béla here. I need to have a proper talk with you about things. But I need to calm down a little; it doesn't have to be today. We've got the whole of the holidays."

Josh seems to buy this. He nods dolefully and heads upstairs. As he does, I go back into the livingroom and retrieve Sam's phone from underneath a cushion on the sofa. I return to the hall and slip it into the inside pocket of Béla's stinky leather jacket. I don't feel great about this, but, on reflection, it's the only thing I can do. Béla stole the damn thing, and I don't want Helen finding it around the house. It's best that I leave Béla to dispose of it.

"Dad, what are you doing?"

I turn around suddenly and see that Josh has been spying on me from the top of the stairs. I think for a moment about retrieving the phone but then realise this is pointless. Josh rushes down the stairs and plucks the phone out of Béla's jacket.

Then he switches it on and examines it. I walk away and fetch myself another beer from the fridge. I stare out at the patio, the garden furniture, the ivy trellis, the freshly treated shed and the blue sky of summer hovering above it as I sip my beer. So Josh is going to know everything; I wanted to protect him from the pain of learning the truth about Helen's treachery, but maybe that's just naïve. Or maybe I am being a coward, failing to protect my son because of my own anger and resentment. I feel awfully tired. The damage feels somehow unstoppable now.

A few minutes later, Josh hops into the kitchen. He bobs up and down in something approaching fury as he says: "So I get it, you and Béla have been working together, haven't you?"

"Don't talk rubbish, Josh."

"You made him go through Ndlova's stuff, didn't you? You knew Mum was seeing him and you made him find the evidence, didn't you?"

This statement surprises me. It makes me think that perhaps Josh knew about Sam and Helen before I did.

"That's rubbish. Béla found the phone of his own accord. I had no idea that Mum was up to anything at all. Did you?"

"Of course I bloody well did! As you must have done! Wasn't it fucking obvious?"

"No, it wasn't. I had no idea until today."

I look him straight in the eyes. He turns away as he says: "That's the problem with you, Dad. You miss things. You are so wrapped up in yourself you just don't notice what's happening. You know what, Dad? You just don't listen. "

"Josh, you *knew* – and you didn't tell me?"

This news, now it's beginning to sink in, really stuns me. Josh pummels his fist into his palm. "The main thing is that Béla nicked the phone, isn't it? He should never have done that!"

7pm

So I'm in the shower, feeling the gorgeous stream of water flow over my body, enjoying the sensation of being in such a luxurious bathroom, when someone starts banging on the door. I try to ignore it but it doesn't let up.

"Béla, open this door now!" Josh yells.

I step out of the shower and undo the latch. Immediately he screams: "Get out, get out of my house, now!"

"Josh, what the fuck?" I say, wrapping the towel tightly around my midriff.

"That's my towel!" he says, and pulls it off me with one deft hand movement. I do my best to cover my genitals as I respond: "Josh, look, please, just tell me…"

"You nicked Ndlova's phone, didn't you? Then you showed my dad!"

I snatch up my underpants and put them on quickly, even though I'm still really wet. "Josh, you fucking framed me, you cunt!"

Josh snaps the towel at me like a matador intimidating a cowardly bull. I flinch as I pull on my trousers.

"My parents are going to get divorced now because of you!"

I start buttoning up my shirt. "I was just trying to save your dad from being sacked, but you – you tried to get me shanked!"

"I came and fucking rescued you, you cunt, although I don't know why I did!"

"Only out of guilt coz it was you who got me shanked in the first place!" I spit back.

The towel hangs limply in Josh's hand as he says: "You had no right to meddle, Béla. No right at all."

Josh is not a violent person, otherwise he would definitely try and beat me in. He drops the towel on the floor. He says: "Just go, just go away."

And then he walks away, leaving the bathroom door open, and trudges down the stairs. I sit on the edge of the bath and look down at my feet. There are tufts of black hair on my big toes. New tufts.

As I am putting on my sock, Martha pops her head around the half-opened door. "Are you all right, Béla?"

I nod grimly.

"It's all right, you know, Josh is like that to everyone."

I put on the other sock. "I thought I was doing the best for everyone."

"I'll be your friend if that's the problem."

"That's nice of you."

"If you tell me what you've done wrong."

I look up and see her bright eyes staring at me expectantly.

"I…" I trail away, aware that there's no way I can tell her how I found out her brother has been trying to get her dad sacked from his job and her mum is shagging old

Loverman. I can't tell an eight-year-old that.

"Will you still be my friend if I don't tell you?"

Martha muses a little upon this. "My mum is always saying that it's important to get something in return when you give something."

"Does being friends work like that?" I ask.

"At my school it does. You give someone some help with their homework, then they're your friends."

"I used to think that friendship worked like that. I was trying to give people help, but the trouble is sometimes people don't want your help. Sometimes they say your help is meddling. And sometimes those friends actually want to see you suffer."

"Have you got into trouble for poking your nose into other people's business?" Martha asks.

"Maybe. I've got quite a nose on me, too… "

Martha giggles. "That's another thing my mum says to be careful of."

Even Martha is starting to get on my nerves now. I button my soiled shirt, ready to go. I stand up. I need to get out of this fucking house.

7.13pm

Sam is on the doorstep again. He looks agitated in his golfing top, which is a bit sweaty now. A moist smile hovers about my lips.

"I saw him but he ran away," he says, looking beadily at me. "He was with Josh so I wonder if he's come back here."

"He's here," I whisper, letting my old friend in and shutting the front door behind him.

"Just get him for me," Sam says, putting his hands on his hips. It's difficult to decide who is having a worse day now: me or him.

I move closer to him and smile.

"You're drunk, Martin. You're drunk. Just get Béla for me."

But I can't help myself. I want to taunt him. "What are you going to do now, Sam? Resign?"

I think about asking him how his marriage is, but I don't. Clearly, Helen still hasn't apprised him of the new landscape in our lives. That's a good sign, I think. I call upstairs for Béla.

Martha comes down first, followed by Béla, who shrinks at the sight of Sam. I soothe him by saying that it's fine, nothing bad is going to happen, we just need to sort a few things out. As he descends, Josh appears behind him, watching from on high.

Sam holds out his hand before Béla. Martha gazes up at the three of us in wonder.

"Just give me the phone, Béla. And I'll go."

Béla looks at me in astonishment. "But I don't have it."

"Then why were you running away from me on the street?" Sam snaps.

"I don't have it!" Béla repeats.

"Béla, I take it you won't mind me searching your pockets, will you? This one, is it – your jacket?"

Béla shrugs. Without saying any more, Sam puts

his hands into the pockets of the leather jacket hanging on the hook in the hall. He quickly produces his phone and holds it before the dumbfounded Hungarian. Sam's look is not exactly triumphant, but he seems jolly relieved.

"But I didn't have it! Someone must have put it there. I gave it to Mr Hick!" Béla shouts out while hastily making his way to the door. "I was going to put it back. I swear, I swear, sir."

Sam looks at me in bewilderment – and then painful recognition. The thought that I might know about his adultery with my wife is clearly sizzling through him – but I manage a bemused shake of the head. It's enough to reassure him that I have never seen the phone and that Béla is lying.

Pressing his lips together, he points at the wretched boy. "Béla, I will consider my options. But I'm seriously thinking about calling the police. I really am."

Béla's hand hovers over the latch of the front door: he's clearly getting ready to run for his life. Which is perfect because it makes him look so guilty. "But sir, it really didn't happen like that," he protests hopelessly.

"It did," Josh says, now descending the stairs. "Béla had the phone all along."

"But…" Béla looks at my son in despair as he opens the front door. "Josh, you're not telling the truth."

"I'm calling the police," Sam says, his fingers hovering over the dial pad.

"You've got to believe me," shouts Béla, as he steps outside into the strange, lit-up evening. "Please, I took it but I was going to put it back. I promise. Mr Hick held onto it!"

Sam follows the Hungarian out into the street, still holding his phone in his hand. Then he puts it away. Béla relaxes a little and remains stationary.

"It's lies," Josh says, now joining me on the threshold of our house. "Total lies."

Slamming the door of his Merc dismissively, Sam drives off. Béla stares angrily at me and Josh on the doorstep. My boy has come good. Ultimately, his loyalties lie with me, not his dodgy Hungarian friend. That's very good to know.

"You, you, you…!" Béla yells and then tapers out. He wants to call us bastards, fuckers, whatever, but he can't. He's still in shock that we'd do this to him.

I close the front door and look at my son. I would like to give him a manly pat on the back, but I know this would be unwise. He's still giving me the evil eye. Tomorrow, maybe, when things have blown over.

7.20pm

Walking home through the dusty city, I feel pretty fucking sorry for myself. My clothes stink of pig shit, my damp skin itches and my head hurts.

Soon, I'll get even more shit from Loverman. My prospects of returning to school are slim but my chances of getting a criminal conviction pretty fucking high.

The last thing I want to do is go home. Checking my phone, I see Ma has phoned me five times in the last hour, leaving messages to say that I have to make the Count his supper. But I just can't face him – or her. She'll go mad when she hears about this shit. I wonder if Loverman has phoned her already and that's why she's chasing after me. I haven't even listened to the messages. I don't dare.

I walk up Virginia Road, past some boxy, grotty houses with overgrown gardens and onto Columbia Road. Sivill House towers above me as I make my way to Ravenscroft Park, past a group of chavs who are drinking beer at a metal table. They're shouting at their pit-bulls and admiring their mopeds, which are resting on the grass like sleeping children.

I sit down on the bulge of a tyre and go up and down, leaning back and looking up at the deepening blue sky.

I fly high, high into it, thinking I've made such a mess of things, wishing I could go back… It would be so great to be a kid again. I remember how Dad used to take me to the park by the Danube and I'd go on the swings then.

I think of my dad, his wry smile, and I wonder where he is, where we go when we die.

"Over here, Pongy!" a voice shouts out. I look down and see that it's the GMF: Mercy, the Bentley twins and Jakaria. In normal circumstances, I'd be terrified but, given everything that's happened, I couldn't give a shit. They could throw me into fast-moving traffic and I wouldn't particularly care. I swing up and down until the twins get hold of the chains and yank me to a halt.

They hold me by the shoulders as Mercy peers into my face. She stinks of cheap perfume and dope. Breathing her deadly breath on me, she says: "So how is my fine Pongy this evening?"

I lean back into the twins' grip. "Look if you're gonna kick the shit out of me, why don't you just get it over with?"

Mercy smiles at me. "Would you like us to?"

"You gay fuck, we're gonna fuck you up. Fucking shank you, you bastard!" the twins say in unison. They're weird like that, they kind of talk together when they're getting ready to beat someone in.

Suddenly they let me go. I fall off the swing, flopping to the spongy tarmac. I remain lying there. It's nice lying on the ground. Not being bothered to do anything. Just letting fate do its work. I shut my eyes.

Surprisingly, I don't feel any kicks or jabs.

I open my eyes. Mercy is kneeling down by me.

"Are you OK, Béla?"

"Let's fucking kick his fucking head in. He's all ready for it!" the twins chant.

"No!" Mercy shouts at them. "This ain't the Pongy we know, you mongs. Something's happened. Why don't you lot fuck off for a bit, I think I would like a little chat with him…"

There's laughter. "A chat with his cock?" one of the twins says.

"Fuck off!" I yell. And with that, Mercy leaps up and punches the offending twin in the head, then hits him again in the chest. He reels back in shock.

"Hey, hey…" he says, but trails off. He doesn't want to

piss off Mercy anymore.

"I been thinking I want a little word with Pongy here. And don't you fucking say nothing coz I'll kick the fucking shit out of you..." she says.

The twins and Jakaria retreat into the depths of the playground as Mercy lifts me to my feet.

"Let's take a walk, Béla."

7.30pm

"You did the right thing, Josh," I say, opening the fridge and fetching myself another beer.

"Dad, now you must do the right thing and say sorry to Mum."

I offer Josh a beer but he shakes his head. I shut the fridge door, peel off the tab and take a glug. I've drunk enough to be feeling quite good about things. Alcohol is great like that.

"What do you mean?"

"I mean, Dad, you're going to be in the divorce courts if you don't do something."

"What are you, Josh? My marriage counsellor?" I attempt a wry smile.

"Dad, she's going to go off with Sam if you don't do something urgently."

"How do you know that?"

Josh's teeth nibble his lips. We're still standing in the middle of the kitchen surrounded by all the accoutrements of married life: the Le Creuset pots stowed in the lower cupboards, rice and pasta in the upper ones, dirty crockery in the dishwasher, frozen peas in the freezer, the grease-smeared clock on the wall…

"I talk to her, Dad."

"I talk to her all the time too."

"You nag at each other."

I take a good glug of beer.

"Josh, you shouldn't be noticing that kind of thing."

He runs his hands through his long hair in a very similar way to his mother.

"Why don't you go to the hospital and take her some flowers or something?" he suggests, approaching me now and touching my forearm.

"Is that what she told you I should do?"

Josh takes a step away from me and shifts about on his feet. "She said you never romance her. You never make her feel special. Sam did that."

I've nearly finished my beer. God, that went fast.

"Josh, what has she been talking to you about?"

"That doesn't matter. What matters is that you don't leave all of us in the shit by making her walk off with that…"

"You don't like Sam?"

"Of course I don't! You know what he's like. He's a fucking smooth-talking git!"

I pause for a moment and think about this. I'm not sure I do know what Sam's like. At college, he used to be quite silly – mucking around, smoking spliffs, making jokes, singing songs – now he's so sober, so considered. I blame Barack Obama. He's imitated him far too much; he's got that same steely expression, that same Messianic sense of purpose.

"Has he come round here when I've been away?"

Josh shakes his head.

"Martha seems to know him quite well."

"I think he spoke to Mum after Mr Humphreys died. I think he came round here on that day. In the evening. You were at the mortuary."

The mention of the mortuary sets my heart racing – I think of Jack, his white, frozen features, still apparently in agony. "Things are beginning to make sense," I say, almost to myself.

"You should go to the hospital."

"Not now! Mum won't want me interrupting her."

Josh grips my wrist. His eyes fix on mine. "Sam's going there now."

"What?"

"Yes. I just spoke to Mum. Sam is saying he is going to leave his wife."

"He is?"

"He's obsessed by Mum, Dad. He's in love with her."

"And what about her?"

Josh lets go of me. "She likes it."

"Maybe I should go."

"Get a cab, Dad. You've drunk too much. Have some coffee. Sober up. Brush your teeth."

"What are you, Josh? My fairy godmother?"

"I see more things than you do, Dad."

I need a piss. I chuck the beer can into the recycling bin and think: God, how ordered life is. There are even separate compartments for our rubbish.

I sit on the toilet and let the urine gush out of my system. It feels good to let go. When I return, Josh hands me a steaming mug of coffee. I take it.

"I've called a cab," he says.

7.50pm

"Fuck, you live in exactly the same building as me!" I say.

It's really weird being in Mercy's flat because it's a carbon copy of ours. I recognise the layout immediately; the open-plan kitchen overlooking the livingroom area, the two adjoining boxy bedrooms and the bathroom. It's strange because it's some distance from us, much nearer Columbia Road, tucked away behind St Peter's Church in a grimy cul-de-sac.

"Totally the same?" Mercy says, grinning at me.

"It's like we've been leading parallel lives. Your flat is full of smoke too!"

This place is engulfed in smoke. I feel it agitating my lungs almost immediately.

But unlike my flat, which feels empty during the day, this place is overrun with people. There are five young children sitting around the television playing Grand Theft Auto on a PlayStation, four dodgy-looking guys sitting around a battered dining-room table smoking ganja in their vests, fiddling with their phones and playing cards, and two faded-looking women bustling

253

around in the kitchen. The noise of the jabbering TV, the gabbling children, the throaty grunts of the card players, the bleeping of the phones, the bubbling in the pans, the fuggy smoke, the smell of batter and male sweat, of mould and rancid food is quite overpowering. I find it difficult to stop myself from putting my hand over my nose.

No one looks up. It's like they're all used to Mercy bringing total strangers into the house.

"We'll go to my room," Mercy says. She nods to the men at the table and exchanges glances with the two women in the kitchen. "But before we do, you're leaving that jacket here!"

I shed my stinky jacket, leaving it on the floor outside the room, and enter. Once we're in her room, she shuts the door behind her.

"Who are all those people?" I ask.

"Just family," she says.

I look around her room. There are two beds which are separated by a make-up table which has a big mirror and is heaped with beauty products: perfume, nail varnish, eyeliner, lipstick, make-up compartments, combs, brushes, earrings, tweezers, razors. On Mercy's bed, there's a battered second-hand laptop.

The bedclothes are quite bright with lots of African patterns on them. They are by far the newest-looking things in the flat.

The room stinks of perfume. But it's a much nicer smell than next door.

"So do you share your room with someone?"

Mercy sits down on the bed and pats the bedclothes beside her, indicating that I should join her.

"Yeah, my aunt and my little sister."

"Where does your little sister sleep?"

"Sometimes on the floor, sometimes in my bed. Depends."

Mercy's tone is matter-of-fact. It's not sorry-for-itself, just that's the way things are.

"I have to share my room with my great-uncle. I hate it. He's disgusting. Always coughing and sniffing."

Mercy doesn't seem particularly interested in this. She edges closer to me on the bed. I have been carefully avoiding looking at her big breasts, poking out of her green T-shirt, but now it's impossible.

"Have you ever fucked anyone, Béla?"

This shocks me so much that I jolt away from her. She extends her powerful arm and pulls me back.

"I know you want to fuck me," she says. Her fingers entwine mine. Then tighten. It hurts but I don't complain.

"I do?" I ask.

"Of course you do. You is obsessed by my tits. I know you are. You can't stop thinking about them."

Mercy flashes her big white teeth in my eyes. Then she reaches for a small bottle on her dresser and squirts some breath freshener into her mouth. She hands me it. I hold the bottle in trembling hands for a minute and then squirt. The peppermint freshens my mouth and I can feel an erection starting to stir in my skinny jeans. But my body is jittery.

"So, what have you got for me?" she asks.

My trembling increases. It's what Mercy always asks her victims before she jacks them.

I pat my pockets. "I haven't really got any money. This is all I've got."

I pull out my trouser pockets and show her my empty wallet, my library cards, my Oyster card, my mobile phone. She takes them and puts them in her drawer. She hits me on the back of the head as soon as I do. It's quite hard, but I can tell that she's not too mad at me.

"Oww!" I exclaim.

Mercy grins. "That's for fucking taking my phone earlier, you fucking cunt. I know I should do you proper but I kinda like you, Béla. I mean, you and me, we're kinda alike. We were Macbeth and Lady Macbeth, weren't we? I feel I know about you, stuff you don't need to tell me…"

She trails her long fingernail along my arm.

"Now, tell me something bad. Something bad about your family."

"What?"

"Something real bad. Something you don't want other people to know."

"My great-uncle smells."

"Not good enough," she says. "Something badder."

"My mum smokes too much!"

Mercy grabs my neck and squeezes hard. I scream out in pain. "Something people don't wanna know. Don't worry, I won't tell anyone. I like you."

The pain is excruciating.

"My mum pretends to be disabled to get benefits!"

Thank fuck for that! Mercy lets go. She smiles at me and strokes my scalp.

"Take off your shirt."

I obey.

She folds up the shirt and puts it neatly by the bed.

"Take off your jeans."

"But Mercy…"

"Just do it!"

"These are my best skinny jeans."

"Just do it, you fucker!" she snarls.

There I was thinking that she was going to be nice to me. Possibly let me fuck her, or something. And now it's turning into this.

I give her my precious jeans.

I sit before her in my boxers. Looking afraid. What's she going to do? Pull out a knife and shank me? Fuck me to death?

"OK, what else you got for me?"

I shrug. "I've given you everything I've got. I ain't got nothing else. Except my boxers."

"Take them off!"

"But Mercy! Mercy!"

Mercy pulls out a knife from her box and points it at me. I take off my boxers and cover my genitals with my cupped hands.

"Show me your dick!" she says, waving the knife in the air.

"But Mercy…"

"Show me it!"

I take away my hands. She examines it with her hands.

My fear quickly turns into desire. It becomes hard.

"So have you fucked anyone?" she asks.

I shake my head. Mercy's hand starts to rub up and down my penis.

"You've never had a blow job?"

I shake my head.

She bends down and starts sucking my cock. My brain is telling me that I should run for my life, but I can't seem to do anything but stand there.

I'm a bit worried that she might bite it off, but she doesn't.

"Do you want to feel my tits?" she says, now standing up and taking my cock in her hands.

I nod dumbly, thinking about all of the top places I could lose my cherry:

1. On a beach in the moonlight.
2. In a blue lagoon.
3. In a Transylvanian castle.
4. On a fast-moving train.
5. In an aeroplane toilet.

Certainly not in Mercy's room. But does it matter?

I feel the huge heft of Mercy's breasts through the fabric of her T-shirt. Then I try and take her T-shirt off. It's difficult because it's so tight on her body. Now we're really not talking at all. But looking at each other. For the first time ever, it feels like we might be equals. She helps me get off her T-shirt. Then she takes off her big bra. Her amazing breasts roll deliciously before me.

"You can kiss them if you like."

I do this and find myself getting lost, drowning in them.

Mercy takes off her black hotpants and then gets a condom out of a drawer. She unrolls it expertly and puts it on my knob.

I embrace her, feeling the whole of her great magnificent body. My cock is bobbling around near her cunt. And then I'm inside her, and it feels like nothing else I've felt before. Like being clamped by a very strong oyster. Her big breasts jiggle in my face as she moves up and down on my cock. She groans a bit, but not too loudly, saying: "I'm gonna shank you real bad one of these days. Stick my fucking knife into you and watch you spurt all over the place."

I'm shit-scared, but I remain stiff. And it's not like I love her or anything, but it's like I love this moment, this moment of extreme excitement, the most extreme excitement I think I've ever felt. It's what I've always secretly dreamt of, and now it's happening.

Then it's gone with a huge rush in my head and a ginormous gush out of my cock.

8.03pm

I walk down the melancholy corridors of the hospital, sobering up. The coffee and the cab ride helped. I catch glimpses of sick people lying in beds through the portholes of the flapping doors. A big, fat black

259

man on a drip and oxygen is rushed past me by some medics. A vision of me in a few years' time?

I turn down the now-familiar corridor where Helen does most of her surgery and I'm nodded through by the receptionist, who knows me well.

With a lurch in my heart, I look through the window into Helen's office, to see Sam pacing up and down in front of her desk. I stop. Then walk straight in.

Helen isn't there.

Sam turns and looks at me. "Hello, Martin."

"What are you doing here?" I ask.

"I could ask the same of you."

"Where is she?"

Sam walks behind me, shuts the door and then gestures at the patient's chair in front of Helen's desk, indicating that I should sit down. Bloody nerve. He's acting like it's his office. I remain standing.

"She's doing some paperwork, signing some stuff off somewhere…"

"Has she nearly finished?"

Sam drills his dark eyes into me as he asks: "Why didn't you tell me that you knew already when I came round to get my phone?"

"Who says I did?"

Sam sighs impatiently. Takes a breath. Then says: "I'm leaving my wife, Martin."

"How did she take it?"

"I haven't told her yet," Sam says, solemnly.

I suddenly have the bizarre thought that the crotch of Sam's jeans looks very smooth. I turn away and examine a seaside photo of Josh and Martha on the desk. There isn't a single photograph of me here.

"I should also let you know that I told Gilda Ball that I can't work with you being at the school," he says, raising his eyes so that they meet mine.

"What did she say?" I ask with a touch of insouciance in my voice. None of his bullshit troubles me now.

"She said I should resign."

"And what did you say?" I ask, my smile growing wider.

"I told her I'm quitting."

My smile shrinks as I think this through. It's good for me professionally – I'll almost certainly become temporary Principal next term – but it has other implications.

Sam is serious about Helen. He's really serious. He's as serious about getting Helen as he was about getting the Principal's job. She's his project now.

"Does Helen know all this?" I ask with my heart thumping wildly.

Fuck, crunch time.

"Yes. I just told her."

"What did she say?"

"You'd better hear for yourself. She's coming back in a minute."

There's a tense silence. I leave the office and wait outside. I have nothing more to say to Sam. Nothing whatsoever.

After what seems like an agonisingly long time,

Helen emerges from the locker room. She doesn't seem surprised to see me. Or guilty in the slightest. I approach her.

"Please, don't rush into anything," I say.

Without responding, Helen opens the door to her office. I follow her inside. Once we're all sealed in, she and Sam turn to face me. They would be standing shoulder to shoulder if it wasn't for the fact that Helen is a little shorter than Sam. They look good together. Like a couple.

"Martin, I have to be honest, I don't think we can carry on like this."

Sam looks away.

"So you're leaving me?"

Helen wrinkles her lips and then says: "Yes."

"When?"

Helen looks at Sam. "We haven't thought about that yet."

"I'm moving out more or less straight away," Sam adds.

"And I think you should too," Helen says.

"You want me to move out?" I ask.

I look at Sam in his fucking golfing shirt and his smooth-crotched designer jeans. He looks so fake. What the fuck does she see in him? Has she gone mad? Has she completely taken leave of her senses?

"I have to know something, Helen," I say. "I have to know when this started… I have a right to know that."

Sam and Helen exchange glances. And then Sam

steps towards me. "I contacted Helen after Jack's death."

I check Helen out. "That's really the truth, is it?"

She looks at me severely – inscrutable.

Sam goes on: "I wanted to know her view on Jack's autopsy."

"Did you indeed?"

Helen corkscrews her index finger at me. "Jack was in a bad state, Martin, and you knew that, didn't you? And you did nothing to protect him…"

Sam puts his hand on Helen's arm; he seems to think she's going too far. Her words hit me in the guts. I reach for my stomach and steady myself.

"What? Is that what you think? You think that I drove Jack to his death, is that what you think?"

I turn away.

Sam approaches me tentatively. I don't look up at him as he says in a gentle voice: "The fact is, Martin, I tried to stop him getting involved in the playground fight. I did – but you just had to push him further into it. He was ill, Martin. Very sick. We all knew that."

I face him now. We are very close. I stink of coffee and booze but I don't care. I breathe all over him as I say: "And you're blaming me for getting him involved in the riot? Is that it? I was just trying to keep order, Sam. Order that you failed to impose!"

Sam is slightly taller than me and uses his height to commandeer the situation. He says in a calm, sorrowful voice: "I didn't know what to make of it. I didn't. His death really took it out of me. And it made me realise that I had to say the one thing I wished I'd said years ago to Helen. I have only one life. I just had to say it. I thought being Principal and having a wife and kids was everything, but you get there and you see that it's not right. I had to say it before I died."

There's silence as I absorb his words. I am still pretty drunk, but not aggressively so. I shut my eyes: Helen, Sam and Jack are all mixed in my thoughts like old clothes tumbling in the washing machine.

I open my eyes.

"Look, Helen, maybe we could have a talk by ourselves?" I say. I realise my voice is cracking. She is looking at me with more sympathy than she has done for years.

For once, Sam too seems to feel compassion for me. He makes his excuses and leaves the office.

I walk to the bookshelves and examine the spines of all the medical books there. On a high shelf, I can see a framed photograph of Helen and the kids standing in front of the Eiffel Tower that has fallen over. It's lying with its face up; the three of them smiling up at the ceiling of the office. I pick up the photo and place it upright.

"Helen... look, I don't know what to say... Are you coming home tonight? Is Sam leaving his wife right now?"

"He hasn't told her yet," Helen says, pulling her fingers through her hair.

"So you're coming home tonight?"

"Of course I am."

"And you want me to move out?"

Helen doesn't reply. She walks away from me to the window of the office, which overlooks the corridor.

"I think so. At least I thought so. I don't know. I'm not thinking straight, Martin. I've had such a day: getting all geared up for that op and then having to call it off. That mountain of paperwork. I just want to have a chat with Sam and then I'll come home tonight… Let's talk over the weekend."

"Helen, you know I love you, don't you? You know that, don't you? I will do anything, I promise, anything you want to save this marriage. Sam doesn't matter. It doesn't matter. But please, Helen, don't…"

I look at her with my eyes brimming. Somehow it would be easier if she returned my emotional plea with an icy stare. But she doesn't. She looks at me sorrowfully, biting her lip. And I realise she's not sure what to say because she doesn't want to hurt my feelings. It is worse than being summarily rejected by a cold-hearted bitch. A decision has been made. I can see that.

"But Helen, you brought me my memory stick."

She nods, tears nearly in her eyes now. "I know. Look, let's talk at home."

I leave the hospital without saying anything more.

8.30pm

I am lying naked on Mercy's bed, listening to her hip-hop music and eating Nachos. She's right beside me, totally naked too.

"You do realise that if you tell anyone, you is dead. Shanked. Doncha?" she says, munching Nachos and pulling me tightly into her body.

"Course," I say, my bones cracking in her embrace.

"That's good," she says, flashing me her big white teeth. It's like I've made friends with the wolf in Little Red Riding Hood. Little Béla Riding Hood.

"See, I ain't gay," I say.

Mercy punches my shoulder playfully. "I never thought you was gay."

"But you always said it. It was your cuss, innit."

"It was what the twins always said. They love to say it coz they is gay, innit."

"They is gay?"

"Course."

"How do you know?"

"They go to the gym with all these other gay-ers who think they ain't gay, but then they fuck each other, innit."

"God, I never knew."

"It's what I got on them. I got proof."

"You do?"

"But if you say anything…"

"I'm shanked," I say wearily. "Looks like I could get shanked for a lot of things."

Mercy punches me playfully and laughs. "You is funny, you know that?"

I take some more Nachos and crunch on them. I'm beginning to realise that I'm probably in a more precarious position now that I've fucked Mercy than I was before. She's going to be looking out for any sign of betrayal now. The perils of sex – that's what the Count calls it. Still, I did get the fuck of my life out of it. Well, my only one. So far.

"So why did you always pick on me and Josh if you knew we wasn't gay?" I ask.

"It was the way you and Josh always hung out. You looked so gay. You still look gay!" she says.

"I do?"

"Yeah, you two look the gayest of the gay. But look, I got an idea."

She rolls on top of me, her breasts momentarily press into my face and then she's off the bed, picking up her bra and her T-shirt. I watch her getting dressed.

"What are you doing?" I ask, pulling the covers over my body.

Mercy reaches for my hand and pulls me from the bed in one deft jerk. I bang my knee on the floor.

"Fuck!"

"You is coming with me," she says. She's got her tough-girl face on now. It's the kind of look you really don't mess with.

"What do you mean?" I ask, picking myself off the floor and grabbing at my underpants.

"Didn't you know, you have to pay?"

"What do you mean?" I say, rubbing my knee.

"Pay me, you cunt! You don't think I'd do that for free, do ya?"

"But I don't have any money. I don't have nothing. You took it all," I mumble, pulling myself off the floor and hobbling towards my clothes. I pull on my boxers. Fuck. I think I may have to make a run for it soon. She seems like she's back to being her normal psycho self.

"You're not gonna wear those gay clothes anymore," she says.

She leaves the room for a moment and returns with some grey trackie bottoms, a faded Arsenal football shirt, a hoodie.

"Put this on!" she orders.

I do as I'm told, leaving the rest of my clothes neatly folded under her bed. I am not sure that this is a good idea coz I may never see them again – but I think somehow I will. That thought both thrills and terrifies me.

"Come on, you're coming with me!" she snaps.

Once I'm trackie-bottomed and hoodied-up, she pushes me out of the bedroom and tells me to wait in the corner. No one seems to have noticed that we've emerged from her bedroom. The card players are still immersed in their game, the two bedraggled women are still cooking, the children still on the PlayStation. No one seems to have any curiosity here whatsoever. I think about the difference between my home and Mercy's. God, Ma would have been putting her ear to the door, listening to every moan and groan, but here there's this liberating nonchalance, this completely I-don't-give-a-fuck attitude amongst everyone.

Except Mercy. She approaches me carrying a chair she's got from the kitchen and a big black bag slung over her shoulder.

I follow her outside the front door. She sets down the chair on the concrete walkway that runs along her block of flats. She tells me to sit on the chair. Then she gets out some clippers from the bag, switches them on and starts to shave my hair.

"What are you doing, Mercy?"

"I'm turning you into one of the GMF," she says, laughing. The razor works its way across my scalp and my black locks tumble over my shoulders, onto my lap and onto the concrete pathway. It feels nice.

8.45pm

I know I should be going home but I can't. Since leaving the hospital, I've been wandering through the back streets of Whitechapel in the dusk. I cross Vallance Road and pass a couple of hookers standing on the street corner, dolled up in high heels, tight-fitting black skirts and bulging tops. Their faces are yellow. I glance at them and then move on towards Spitalfields Farm. The road is blocked off here. I stop for a moment, enjoying the quiet.

There are still some children in the farm feeding the rabbits. Why don't Josh and Martha do things like that?

I call Josh on the home number.

"Did you speak to Mum?" he asks.

"Have you spoken to her?" I retort.

"No. She hasn't called. Did you go to the hospital?"

"Yeah. I think everything is going to be fine," I say,

adding: "Look, can you carry on looking after Martha for a bit? Is she OK?"

"She's fine."

"Maybe you could put her to bed in half an hour or so?" I suggest. "Perhaps you could put her on?"

I smile when I hear her piping voice: "Are you fixing everything, Dad?"

"What do you mean?"

"Josh says you are fixing everything. Have you done that?"

"Yes, I have," I say. I ask for Josh again. "Thanks ,Josh, thanks for supporting me with Martha."

"It's all right, Dad… Look, I'm sorry…"

"For what?"

"For being horrible."

"That's OK. I'm going to sort things out."

"But Dad, you don't understand how horrible I've been…"

"Josh, don't beat yourself up! You're sounding neurotic. None of this is your fault."

"But it is, Dad. It is."

"It's not. Please… You're making me feel even worse."

I ring off. I've reached Brick Lane. Lots of trendy-looking students are milling up and down it, talking animatedly, laughing, happy. They are interspersed with various dossers and ne'er-do-wells. I look into the sour, bitter faces of these losers and think that I'm far more like them than the fresh students.

8.50pm

The Bentley twins and Jakaria don't recognise me. You see, being the master of disguise that I am, I put on this whole swaggering walk, this twisting hip-hop thang which is utterly unlike the mincing steps I used to take. I can see immediately how they respect me in a way they never did before.

"Who you got there, Mercy?" one of the twins asks. Wearing his sunglasses, he is draped on the bonnet of a black, turbo-powered Golf in the car park in the Virginia Estate. The other twin stands by the door of the Golf and Jakaria sits at the wheel, pretending he can drive. Music blares out from the speakers of the car. A couple of elderly residents pass by on the path that winds through the estate. They have their heads down.

An older kid, an Asian guy with a spangly shirt, smokes and speaks on his mobile by some broken bottles. He must be the driver.

Mercy high-fives him and then pushes me forward towards the sunglasses on the bonnet. The twin takes off the glasses and then sees that it's me. Amazement shatters his features. He gets off the bonnet, sniffs around me and then grips my shoulders.

"Fuck! You is Béla!"

Mercy chuckles again.

"He is Béla. And he is in the GMF!"

Jakaria nearly falls out of the car and the other twin bounds up to me. I am surrounded. A situation which, until an hour ago, would have meant definite beats.

Instead, they all pat me on the back. I am one of them now. It's a weird feeling. Belonging to a gang. Worrying and reassuring at the same time.

"Look, we gotta blood him, bluds," Mercy says. "Doncha think?"

The pats on my back turn into thumps.

"Bumps! Bumps!" the twins chant. They both pick me up and start flinging me up and down. Fuck, they are strong. I can feel Jakaria's trainers bashing against my back.

"Stop, you fuckers! Stop!" Mercy shouts.

I flop onto the litter-strewn tarmac. Thank God for that — Mercy's going to protect me. I get onto my feet as everyone turns to face her.

"Nah! We're not gonna give him bumps. He's gonna help us get even," she says. "We're gonna blud him proper."

"Whadaya mean?" the twins ask in their dopey way.

"We're gonna get him to break into Hicky's house and steal some stuff for us, I reckon," she says. "And then maybe give Hicky a good kicking in his bed."

She fixes me with glittering eyes. Her breasts look as magnificent as ever in her green T-shirt and her legs look so fine and strong in her black sweat-pants. The muscles on her arms shine in the dying evening light. She is truly a goddess.

"That's a plan."

9pm

There's a roar as soon as I enter the Royal Oak and walk straight into Burlington. Bloody hell! The whole Gilda Ball staff seems to be here.

Burlington motions for me to follow him. He's clearly on his fourth or fifth pint. Kylie is perched a little uneasily beside him. She's changed into a tight-fitting T-shirt, short red skirt, stockings and fuck-me pumps. I notice that she moves uneasily away from him when she sees it's me. The pair of them are squashed on a long bench at the end of a phalanx of teachers, all of whom cheer woozily at the sight of me.

"Mart, mate! Did I hear correctly that you got the job?" Burlington asks, slurring his words. Even though I've imbibed quite a bit, I'm not nearly as sozzled as he is.

"Is it true?" Kylie asks, jutting her T-shirt out at me.

"How do you know?" I ask them.

Burlington bursts out laughing. "We figured it out, mate, when Sadie bloody Renton came back into the staffroom after having a word with Sam. She was spitting blood, mate. You should have seen her. None of this nicey-nicey stuff any more."

"That figures. She said I should get the job. But I knew it was bullshit," I say.

I scan the assembled crowd but can't see any sign of Sadie. Kylie sneaks a smile. Since there's no room on the bench, I kneel beside her as she says: "She was very cross. She was shouting at Julia Webb, like it was her fault."

"I think she thought Julia had fixed it all up for her," Burlington interjects.

"We heard her saying, 'Now they've given that man the job there's nothing for me at this school!'"

"So I'm 'that man', am I?"

"You are mate, you are!"

I laugh along with them all. Their response to my appointment uplifts me. "Well, guys, I've got some even more interesting news for you." I open my arms expansively. "Sam has resigned."

There's a huge intake of breath and some alarmed faces. I pause for them all to absorb this information.

"And I think I'm going to be your headteacher next term."

Looks of relief diffuse the tension.

I continue: "It's only temporary in the first instance, but I think Gilda likes me. If it goes well, then it could well be permanent."

Everyone stops drinking. Jeff seems pretty stunned. A huge wave of admiration spreads through Kylie's features. Suddenly, everyone starts clapping spontaneously. As they do, I realise that now I've told them this, I might as well go the whole fucking hog. I sit down at the end of the table and wait for the applause to die down.

"Look, before you hear all the rumours, I want to tell you the truth. Mr Ndlova in his wisdom had to resign because he was shagging my missus and tried to cover it by having me suspended. I only found out myself today. I knew nothing of it before. It doesn't look like my marriage is in a great shape but I am going to do my best to fix it. Rest assured, it's not going to affect my work as headteacher. I am going to do my best for you guys. I'd quite like my privacy regarding this so I'd prefer it if you didn't ask me about it. But I felt I should tell you in case you heard any false rumours."

Everyone looks at each other in even more bewilderment.

I get up. Somehow it doesn't really feel appropriate to hang around. I'm their headteacher now, not their mate. I can feel that in my bones. Burlington and Kylie follow me to the bar.

"Fuck, Mart, that's…" Burlington says, tailing off.

"Look, as I said, I would rather not talk about it. You know the basics. That's all you need to know."

"Martin, you look after yourself, won't you?" Kylie says, looking at me in extreme concern.

I nod at her gravely and then leave the pub.

9.10pm

The brick hovers in my hand.

"Go on, go on, you tosser, fucking throw it!" Mercy shouts behind me.

I raise the brick up high, stretch my arm back and then hesitate. Hicky and Josh may have fucked me over but

275

I can't do this. Although I guess it isn't quite as bad as Mercy's first plan to break into their house and kick their heads in while they are lying in their beds. The brick-in-the-window plan is much simpler, less time-consuming and doesn't involve staying up so late.

I look at Mercy. She's standing confidently beside me, but the Bentley twins and Jakaria are getting ready to leg it at any moment.

Suddenly, I think this is too like the time when I let off the firework. Mercy more or less forced me to do it. Then I'd done it to survive, now it's more to belong. If I do this, I will be properly part of the gang. That will certainly carry its advantages: I will be able to walk the streets without fear, I will probably be able to shag Mercy again, I will probably get enough money to buy all the gadgets I want. But there are downsides: I'll basically become a drug dealer, I might get attacked by other gangs, and I'll have to keep Mercy happy.

Mercy fiddles with the gold medallion around her neck when she sees Josh standing at the window, staring at me.

"Fucking get the gay bastard! Fucking throw it! He fucking got you excluded, man, for chucking a firework that didn't go nowhere near old Humphreys! He's a fucker, man. A complete fucker!"

I continue to hesitate. The memory of that firework sizzles in my mind, feeling sharper amidst all this stress. It's shooting into the air. Nowhere near Humphreys. Is that what really happened? Mercy looms towards me.

"Look, if you don't fucking do it, I'm gonna fucking tip

off the benefits office about your scum-bag mum."

Josh eyes me with real contempt.

I chuck the brick.

9.11pm

I enter the green-fronted off-licence on Columbia Road and buy four cans of Special Brew. I know it's not the kind of thing that the new Principal of Gilda Ball should be purchasing, but I feel I deserve a little private celebration. Or is it commiseration?

With the tinnies safely ensconced under my arm, I cross the road, cut across Ravenscroft Park, past the memory-laden swings and into the estate, where I find a safe, hidden alcove to have a quick drink. Slumping down against the shadowy wall, I gulp. My phone goes off. It's home again.

"Dad, you've got to come quick! Béla's just thrown a brick at the house!" Josh yells.

"What?"

"He's with the GMF!"

I get up quickly and fling my drained can onto the ground.

"Look, I'm coming. I'll be there in a sec."

"Shall I call the police?"

"No, I'll sort this. Don't worry."

Tucking my other cans safely behind the rubbish bin where I can collect them later, I run home and find the GMF hovering outside my house. Béla is with them, garbed in a grey hoodie and with a shaven head. He looks surprisingly evil.

Crucially, all of my windows are intact. A brick lies on the pavement just underneath my sill.

"Now pick that up!" Mercy yells at Béla.

But the Hungarian stands there, saying nothing. The Bentley twins and Jakaria hoot with laughter.

"That was the gayest throw I've ever seen in the whole of my life!" Mercy yells at Béla. "The gayest of the gay. That throw was so gay you could have fucked it up the arse! That's how gay it was! Now pick that fucking brick up and fucking throw it like a fucking man, not a mong!"

Béla looks paralysed. But then he sees me.

It's like my face acts as a trigger. He rushes up to the brick, picks it up, draws it back like a slingshot and then flings it with all his might at my house. I watch in horror as it flies through the air and shatters my lovely bay window.

"Hey! Hey! What are you doing?" I scream at Béla. But he just looks at me dumbly and, seeing that he has nowhere to run to, he jumps through the smashed window into the house. It's a deft move; he manages not to snag himself on the spikes of glass that now line the outer edges of the window.

I consider following him but I know I'll come a cropper.

"Attaboy Béla! Attaboy!" Mercy hollers.

She smiles malevolently at me, stalking towards me with far too much confidence. She thinks she can frighten me but, while I may be crap at solving my marital problems, I'm really in my element now.

"You set him up to do this, didn't you?"

"You are going to get fucking killed!" she says. "I am gonna make sure you die, mate!"

"Mercy, how's that going to help anything?"

At this point, somewhat fortuitously, a siren sounds and a police car appears at the top of the road.

"Fucking filth!" the Bentley twins say in unison. They bolt immediately. Jakaria starts waddling away too.

"You're a fucking chicken, do you know that?" Mercy says, edging away from me.

"I didn't call the police, Mercy," I say. "I wanted to sort this out between ourselves."

Mercy cocks her head at me, looking like she's trying to decide if I'm telling the truth.

"How's about you and me properly sort this out, heh? Midnight, Ravenscroft. Then we will proper sort this out, innit."

"Don't be stupid, Mercy."

Jabbing her fingers at me in a silly hip-hop fashion, she says: "You need to step up and fight fair! I got a code of honour, you see."

"Don't be daft, Mercy."

But she hurries away before I can reason with her anymore, when she sees a police car approaching from the end of the road. The police car draws up before the house. A female cop gets out. "Sir, we had reports of a disturbance?"

"Yes, some youths just smashed one of my windows. One of them is still in there."

The policewoman nods to her companion in the car, who gets out. They follow me into the house, where we find Josh clasping Béla tightly by the rim of a small lake of glass. Béla isn't struggling. Josh looks quite comic clinging so tightly to him.

"Dad! I got him!"

The police draw out their truncheons. "Sir, if you could step away, we can deal with this."

I look at Béla's immobile, miserable face and feel a pang of guilt. I'm to blame for this, I'm sure. If I hadn't planted the phone in his pocket and we hadn't turned Béla out in the way we did, I am certain he wouldn't have turned to the GMF.

"It's all right," I say.

"Dad! He fucking smashed our front window!" Josh says.

"Countess Feckula made me!" Béla responds quietly.

Josh lets go of Béla.

"I don't want to press charges," I say.

"Are you sure, sir?" the policewoman says.

I look at Béla. His eyes are fixed on Josh – who is now turning away from him.

"I know this boy. He's a pupil at my school. He wouldn't have done it on purpose. Things just got a bit out of hand. A misunderstanding…"

"If that's what you want, sir, but I must warn you against wasting police time."

I escort the police to the door and apologise. As I

do so, I feel more certain than ever that I've done the right thing. The last thing I want to do is ruin Béla's life by giving him a criminal record. The boy needs all the help he can get.

Although they are clearly not fully convinced, the cops get back into the car and drive off.

I return to the front room. The two boys are examining the smashed window, not talking. Béla eyes me glumly. I know he's thinking about apologising – but realises that words are somehow inadequate.

"Why are you dressed up like that?" I ask.

"Because he's a fucking member of the GMF now, Dad!" Josh interjects.

Béla shrugs. "I'll help you clear it up."

"No, don't bother!" Josh says. "I'll do it." He disappears, leaving Béla and I looking at the broken glass. The late evening sunlight lands on the shards and makes them glimmer and glow like bits of volcanic rock.

Martha bursts into the room and blurts out: "Daddy! Béla broke our window! Then the police came! I saw everything from upstairs. I was going to come downstairs but I didn't want to get murdered!"

It's only after she's finished saying this that she sees Béla is there. She puts her hands over her mouth.

"Are you going to murder us? Is it because Josh was nasty to you?" she asks.

Josh enters the room with a dustpan and brush.

"Martha, get away from here! You haven't even got any shoes on! There's broken glass everywhere."

He starts sweeping up.

"Béla, what were you thinking?" I ask.

"It doesn't matter. I'm going to get my head kicked whatever."

"By Mercy?"

Béla nods. "I'd better get back to her," he says like an indentured slave.

"You don't have to, you know," I say. "You can stay here."

Josh stops sweeping up, shaking the dustpan as he expostulates: "No, he can't!"

"I don't think that would be such a good idea," Béla says, with his back to me as he leaves the room.

Josh resumes sweeping as soon as Béla has gone. As I watch Josh prissily attending to the floor, I can't help feeling irritated. He's such a fucking prig, my son. There are no two ways about it. Chippy and self-righteous too. You could never accuse Béla of that.

After hesitating for a bit, I leave the house and run to catch up with Béla. He is trudging up the street. I try to reassure him. "Look, I'm sorry about that phone business. I'm certain I can stop Ndlova saying anything. Certain of that."

He wraps his arms around the hand-warmers of his hoodie and says, with his chin wobbling a little: "I know you said that I chucked that firework at Mr Humphreys. Well, the truth is that I just let it off. I admit that. But it didn't go anywhere near Mr Humphreys. It really didn't!"

"Why are you bringing this up now? What has this

got to do with anything?" I reply immediately, startled by his accusatory expression.

He looks me full-square in the eyes. My hands feel sweaty.

"It's just that I don't have a chance, do I? Whatever I do, I'm fucked!" he says, pressing his palms against his eyes.

I touch him lightly on the back.

"I'm sure I can help broker some kind of truce between you and Josh."

"It doesn't matter," he says in such a mournful way that it sounds like it matters a lot.

He turns the corner and I lose sight of him.

The incident with Mercy has bucked me up; it's reminded me what I'm good at. Fire-fighting. Dealing with difficult characters. I saw her off – it was no sweat. If Helen had seen me, she'd have been proud. I am, at heart, a tough guy. I really am.

I rejoin Josh in the front room. He's done a good job of clearing up. I switch on the light and have a good look for any bits of glass he might have missed.

"You should have had him arrested."

"I couldn't do that, Josh. I know you're mad at him, but he is your friend."

"He's not my friend, he's a complete fuck-up."

"Josh, he did what he did."

Josh doesn't reply. There's a limit to what both of us can say because Martha is sitting at the far end of the room, watching us.

"Béla was nice until he broke our window. Now I think he's quite nasty. Why did he do it, Daddy?"

"I don't know."

"Did he do it because Josh was horrible to him?"

"Martha, why don't you fucking shut up!" Josh snaps.

"Daddy! Josh swore at me."

"Quiet, both of you, please! We need to figure out what to do with the window."

"Yes, that's right, Daddy. We don't have one," Martha says.

"Martha, could you go and get that cardboard box that's in the cupboard under the stairs? I think we might be able to make a temporary stop-gap."

Martha is happy to do this. It gives me a moment to ask Josh whether he's spoken to Helen. He says he has and that she's coming home soon.

"I'm working on things, Josh. I really am," I reassure him, picking up the dustpan and looking at all the shards of broken glass in it. "Who knows, all of this might bring us together as a family."

"What, a broken window?"

"Yes. It can take smaller things…"

We check to see if Martha has found the box under the stairs. She hasn't, chiefly because she wasn't able to reach the light switch. But when I turn it on we find it quickly. The three of us take it to the front room, squash it flat and spread it out. It's nearly big enough to cover the hole. Using masking tape, we manage to fix it onto the frame.

"That'll do until tomorrow at least," I say.

"Are you sure, Daddy? Won't burg-ulars be able to push through it and burgle us?" Martha asks.

"I doubt it."

There was a time when Josh would have replied with something like "Yeah, and they'll come and murder you in your bed" and scared the living daylights out of her. But he doesn't.

9.20pm

The twilight is falling fast. I think: I could have told Hicky there and then that his son was the Countess. Why didn't I? That would have been true revenge, wouldn't it?

But as much as I'm fed up with Josh, I don't hate him that much.

I don't want to see Mercy or the GMF, but I know there's no alternative: if I don't seek them out, they'll hunt me down.

I find them in the car park in the Virginia Estate, surrounded by broken bottles and crumpled beer cans. This is one of their favourite spots.

An older bloke has turned up in a black BMW and is nosing around Mercy. He is much bigger than me and covered in tattoos of pit bull terriers. The door of the Beamer is wide open and music is pumping out. I can see that quite a few people on the estate are peering down at us through their back windows, but they are obviously too frightened to protest.

Mercy is smiling and giggling as Tattoo-Dogman makes

eyes at her and pokes her lightly on the arm. Although there's a tiny, incy-wincy part of me that feels jealous, there's an even bigger part that feels thankful.

Mercy waves. "It's my Pongy boy! My main man!"

She high-fives me, congratulating me on bricking Hicky's window. Tattoo-Dogman registers this but continues trailing his nose against Mercy's cheeks. She slaps him playfully as she asks me: "So did you get nicked?"

I nod lugubriously like I did.

Tattoo-Dogman stops nuzzling Mercy and clocks me. "How come they didn't take you down the station and charge you properly then?"

I look into his eyes and see that he's got quite a few crow's feet. He's older than I thought. Very old. Maybe even Hicky's age.

"I got to go tomorrow. Report to the station then."

"Fuck, he went and had you nicked. The bastard cunt bastard," Mercy says.

She takes a swig of the beer bottle that's resting on the top of the Beamer. The Bentley twins and Jakaria hover, not doing much except looking a little cautiously at Mercy and her new bloke.

She hands me the bottle.

Then she does an unexpected thing. "Get off me, you fucking pervert," she says, pushing Tattoo-Dogman away. "I need to talk to my man here."

It's the kind of talk that I would expect would lead to him getting lairy, but he doesn't. He backs away with a laugh, takes the beer bottle and sits down in the driver's seat. The Bentley twins and Jakaria join him in the car as I am led away up the path towards Columbia Road by Mercy.

She wraps her arm around me. It's both nice and scary because I sense she likes me best of all.

"I'm gonna get him, Pongy. I'm gonna take him down."

"OK."

"You realise I gotta take him down, don't you?" she says, punching her hand into her palm.

"You do?"

"Yeah. They're laughing at me coz of what happened today."

"They are?"

"Yeah. They're saying that this fat fuck fucking beat me in."

"They're not," I say, as Mercy wraps her arm more tightly around my neck.

I can smell her spliffy breath and her pungent perfume and her body odour. She smells of sex and drugs and fear. She leans close to my ear and whispers: "I can see them dissing me with their eyes, Pongy. I can see the diss. The big long pissy diss."

"But Hicky would never fight you."

"That's where you're wrong, Béla."

Mercy smiles triumphantly like she knows something I don't.

"He ain't that sort," I say. But then it dawns on me: maybe she's got a point. Hicky likes a scrap: think about the way he flung himself into the thick of things on the day Humphreys died, how he attacked Mercy earlier in the afternoon and how he almost seemed to relish the prospect of the GMF attacking his house. "If he knew that he wasn't gonna get reported for doing it, he might," I say.

"This is about my honour," Mercy says, kissing me on the cheek. "I've got my honour to consider here. If I don't get it back, then they're gonna get me."

I look at the twins and Jakaria peering in and out of the BMW and think that they're like the scuzzy squirrels, just pawing at life, scrabbling around for survival, happy with whatever nuts and titbits come their way.

"There's no way they're gonna get you," I say.

"Look, here's what I want you to do. Call Hicky and tell him that I want a proper fight. One that will settle things. Midnight, Ravenscroft. No fucking around. Just an honour fight."

"Do you think it'll really work?"

Suddenly, Mercy grips me by my arms and pinions me against the wall. "I know he never had you arrested, Pongy. I know you're secretly his mate. I know he let you off."

"You do?"

"Yeah. I know everything about you, Pongy. I know what you do."

Her dark eyes snake into mine, insinuating their way into my mind. It feels like her brain is coiling itself around mine like a python.

"But…"

"Look, this is what you do. You get your bum-chum to meet me at Ravenscroft, midnight. Then we'll have a proper fight. That's all I want, a proper fight. One that shows everyone who's boss. I'm honest that way. I ain't gonna shank him or nothing, it'll be bare knuckles, nothing more. Coz you gotta realise, Pongy, I am a good person at bottom. Not a bastard. He's not; he ambushed me without me knowing nothing about it, but I ain't gonna do that to him. I'm gonna fight fair."

"You're a good person. Not a bastard," I repeat.

"If you don't agree, I'm gonna tell the benefits office about your mum, tell everyone you take it up the bum, and fuck over your flat with a fire-bomb."

She strokes my wrist playfully, sensually. Her eyes are widening with desire. I cough: "Since you put it like that…"

Mercy smiles. Her teeth glint in the streetlight which is flickering into life above us. She dives at my lips. Suddenly, her tongue is coiled around mine.

"And if you arrange it," she whispers in my ear once she's finished kissing me, "I'll give you the fuck of your life."

9.44pm

"Go on, Daddy! Kill him! Machine-gun him! Get him!" Martha shouts, clutching at my arm as she watches me tussle with an evil sheikh in the desert sands. I grab my machine gun and splatter him into pieces. Blood, guts and bits of brain spray everywhere. I shouldn't be playing this game in front of Martha, but she knows it's not real. She's a clever girl like that.

The three of us cackle with laughter. We haven't had so much fun in ages.

It's actually a very good video game; killing people in it requires genuine tactical skill and advance planning. It's great the way Josh explains what I should do. I am now wending my way through a blasted-out city, shooting and butchering with greater efficiency.

"That's it, Dad! That's it!" Josh says, as I slaughter a suicide bomber.

Then Josh stops and looks up. I've been so immersed in the game that I haven't noticed that Helen is home. Martha has, though. I feel her fingers claw into my upper arm.

"Martha, could you go upstairs, please?" Helen says, in her severest voice.

Uh-oh. Helen is generally very disapproving of computer games. She switches off the TV and pads towards me. I twiddle uselessly on the joystick of the console. Sitting on the sofa, I am level with her waist. I avert my eyes.

"Mum, we were just in the middle of a game," Josh wavers. He is the only person in the house who has a good enough relationship with Helen to voice complaints, secure in the knowledge that he won't be gunned down.

"Never mind. I need to talk to your father, you two," Helen says. "Maybe you could let us speak alone?"

Josh shakes his head. "Mum, I know everything.

There's no point."

Martha hasn't left the room. She stands at the door, sucking her thumb. Helen shoos her upstairs. Then she scrutinises father and son.

It seems odd to me that Helen hasn't even mentioned the broken window. As if reading her thoughts, Josh says: "It was Béla, Mum. He threw a brick through the window."

"Why?" she asks.

"I think he was forced to by the GMF. They'd shaved his hair and put him in a hoodie and everything."

I shift over on the sofa and pat the cushion next to me. Helen blanks the invitation.

"The last I heard, Josh called me saying that the house was about to be attacked by a gang of youths," Helen says, folding her arms. "Evidently, you had better things to do than keep me updated about the situation."

"You were out; we didn't want to spoil your evening," I say with a wry smile.

"Where's Béla? Where's the GMF?"

"I saw them off," I say, leaning back on the sofa and spreading my arms out.

Josh tips his eyes to the ceiling. It's quite dark in the room now; this is partly because the blocked-out window has diminished the remaining light outside.

"Josh told me that you'd already had a fight with this girl earlier in the day. Flew at her, apparently."

"I'm sure Sam confirmed the story," I say with confidence.

"As a matter of fact, he did."

"And so you came back here to have a go at me and point out yet one more of my manifold failings. Well, now you have another to consider: my inability to defend the house from flying bricks."

I get up off the sofa and switch on the lamp on the coffee table. Its light softens the room, throwing our shadows across the pine floor. I drop the blinds over the blocked-out window and the other panes.

"Josh said he called the police. What happened to them?" Helen asks.

"They weren't needed, Helen. There is no problem."

Helen paces up and down the room, full of angry energy. "There is no problem! There's no problem: I come home to find my eight-year-old daughter watching you and Josh machine-gun each other to death, the front window completely smashed in, and to learn that a psychotic gang have got a vendetta against us! 'There is no problem!' What planet are you on, Martin?"

Josh gets up off the sofa and tries to soothe his mother. "Mum, Dad did do his best."

"His best isn't good enough, I'm afraid."

"Josh, you'd better let us speak alone. I'm not sure your mother knows what she's saying."

"I'm not leaving you two here!" Josh protests. "You'll just scream at each other!"

Helen stops pacing up and down and approaches me. I hitch myself up a bit on the sofa. "Martin, your machismo behaviour is putting all of us in danger now. You just don't think, do you? You just don't!"

"Helen, I know what this is about. I can hear Sam talking here. You're using his exact words. Like it or lump it, I did the right thing. I'm going to tell you what happened, because sooner or later you'll find out. Unlike you, I don't believe in having secrets. Béla was forced to throw a brick through the window because one of the GMF has a grudge against me. I got her expelled from school and also chucked her out of the school today."

"Chucked her out? What do you mean?"

"I forcibly ejected her from the premises!"

Helen shakes her head disconsolately.

"Anyway, the police came. I think Josh had called them earlier."

"At my insistence," Helen adds.

"They asked if I wanted to press charges against Béla. I said no."

"You said no?" Helen says, looking incredulous.

"Helen, that boy's future is in our hands. He's a very clever and good boy. He's mixed up with the wrong people, but he'll come back to the Sixth Form next year and I'll get him on the right track. I really will. That's what it's all about. Giving people a second chance."

Helen sweeps her hands back through her hair,

pulling it back tightly against her scalp.

"Martin, I just can't believe it. This boy threw a brick through our window! What if it had hit Josh or Martha? What then? Jesus, Martin, you've got all your priorities wrong."

"You can't blame me for everything, Helen, you just can't!"

"So who is to blame then?" she asks, enticing me to say what she knows I am gagging to say.

"The one who's been fucking another guy behind my back!"

"Mum! Dad! Stop it! Stop it, please! I can't stand it!" Josh shouts, putting his hands over his ears and shutting his eyes. Tears dribble down his face.

"Don't you speak to me that way," Helen says in a low voice, crouching down a little as she does so. "And not in front of Josh either. You have no self-control. None. You just let it all hang out. You swear at who you want to, you booze to your heart's content, you abuse whoever you want, whenever you want. You're despicable, do you know that?"

"Speak for yourself."

Both of us look numbly at our son. He still has his hands clapped over his ears and his eyes tightly shut. His cheeks are wet but he's stopped crying. He looks like he is about to scream. Helen touches him gently on the shoulder.

"I'm sorry, Martin, but there's no alternative. You're going to have to leave," she says in a quiet voice as she puts an arm around Josh.

"You've got to be fucking joking," I spill out, conscious that my swearing has weakened my position as soon as the words are out of my mouth.

"I'm not. I can't have your abuse here. I can't bear it. And nor can Josh and Martha. We deserve some peace."

Josh opens his eyes and pulls his hands away from his head. He pleads in a dry voice: "Mum, you can't kick Dad out. Just give him a chance. He's drunk. He doesn't know what he's doing."

"Like he's drunk every night. I can't take it, Josh, I just can't. In fact, I've already called Jeff. He said he would put him up for the night."

This gives me real pause for thought. I get up off the sofa. "Oh I see, so this whole row was engineered to get me out of the house, was it?"

"No, it wasn't. I just knew it would happen, that's all."

"Don't give me this bullshit, Helen. You want me out of here so you can invite Sam over. You just want to…"

"Sam isn't coming over here tonight. Don't be so crude."

Helen turns towards our son and starts to cry. Turning on the fucking water-works. So bloody manipulative. Even though he is so distressed, Josh now finds that he is putting his arms around her, enfolding her as she sobs. It's shocking that Helen is putting him in such a difficult position. I know it's all a show. Helen doesn't generally cry. She's much tougher than that.

Nevertheless, I can't be totally certain it's an act. I have to confess, she's out-manoeuvred me.

"OK, OK, I'll go, but just you remember, Helen, it wasn't me that ruined this marriage. It wasn't me that went off with someone else, it wasn't me that walked out. I was bloody well kicked out. Just remember that!"

I leave the room and go into the hallway, where I lean against the wall, trying to steady myself. Things are starting to swim around in a soupy, dark swirl: the furniture in the house, the faces of my family, the bile in my head. The door of the sitting room opens and Josh emerges. "Dad, Dad! Why don't you just go upstairs and lie down?" he whispers conspiratorially. "I don't think you should go out like that."

I put up my hands. "Don't worry. I'll be fine. I'm always fine. I'm a survivor, Josh. If she wants me to go, I'll go."

"Dad, Dad, please don't! Please..." Josh's tears return.

I can't bear it. Helen appears in the hallway and puts her hand on his shoulder.

"I don't think this is fair!" I complain. "Josh doesn't want me to go."

But this doesn't seem to persuade Helen. Her face contorts into a rictus of hatred. "Out! Out! Out! Get out!"

She flings open the door and then grabs at my arm. She is stronger than I would have guessed. I find myself falling into the street.

9.45pm

"Pick it up with your mouth, you cunt!"

The Bentley twins seize me by the shoulders, push my face to the ground and make me eat the litter that's scattered around outside the Birdcage pub. The drunks smoking outside the pub hoot their heads off. It's not a middle-class pub.

I bite into a crisp packet and then a squashed milk carton. Fuck, this is disgusting.

"Now eat it! Fucking eat it, you cunt!"

This is the trouble with me being a junior member of the GMF. As soon as Mercy disappeared with Tattoo-Dogman, I got grabbed. Jakaria used to be their whipping boy, but now it seems I am.

I try to eat the crisp packet but find myself gagging.

Fortunately, my rescuer is at hand.

"Fucking get off him, you cunts!" I hear Mercy shouting.

She jumps out of the car and pushes the twins away, picking me up off the ground.

She has a black bag slung over her shoulder.

I spit out the litter, fall forward, choking and coughing. Mercy stoops down and rubs my shoulders.

"You fuckers, the filth will arrest you if they see you doing that in the street! Fucking idiots!" she barks. Her strong arms and legs shine under the streetlight. Her breasts point proudly towards me.

"Sorry, Mercy," the twins say in unison. I get the impression it's a phrase they say a lot.

"Look, I want to make one thing clear to you fuckers,"

she says to the twins. "Pongy here ain't to be touched.
And you want to know why? Pongy is with me. He's mine
now. You understand that?"

"What, Pongy?" one of them asks in amazement.

"Yes, fucking Pongy. Do you have a problem with
that?"

"Nah," they both say with bowed heads.

But as they turn away, I can see the twins looking
stunned. Ever out of the loop, Jakaria sidles up to them
and asks what's going on. They slap him over the head
and tell him to mind his own business. He looks shocked
when he realises that I am protected – and he's not.

The twins don't say any more, but they've got the
message. It's amazing: Mercy must really like me. It makes
me feel a bit guilty because I'm not that sure I really like
her that much. What's scarier, being Mercy's lover or her
enemy?

"Did you get hold of Hicky?" Mercy asks.

"I ain't had time," I say.

Fortunately, Mercy acknowledges this and doesn't
threaten to fire-bomb my house. She takes my hand and
we walk across the zebra crossing, away from the twins
and Jakaria, who are pretending not to notice us. Fucking
hell, she's holding my hand! I feel very uneasy about it.
What if Tattoo-Dogman sees us?

"I think it's best if I see Hicky in person," I say.

Mercy accepts this and then tells me that she wants me
to take her out tomorrow. I look at her wildly.

"To the movies, you fuck! And you're gonna dress up
and stuff. We'll go up west."

"OK," I gulp.

Once this has been established, I walk away. Easy-peasy. I just point my head in the direction of Hicky's house and stride confidently towards it.

Finally, free, I walk down Columbia Road with the GMF watching me. As soon as I am out of view, I call Ma. She's back from work. Which, for some reason I can't quite put my finger on, makes me feel more secure.

"Béla, you must come back here now. It is bad for you to be on the streets. Very bad!" Ma says.

"I'll be home soon, Ma. I am with Mr Hick so it's OK. He's going to get me my place back at school next term. Everything's all right."

I ring off and approach Hicky's house very slowly. I have no idea what I am going to do or say.

After the initial euphoria of getting away from the gang and Mercy's clutches, the truth is sinking in that I am in a bit of a situation. I realise that Mercy's request is not nearly as straightforward as it seems. She must know that there's no way I'll be able to get Hicky to turn up at midnight at Ravenscroft. It's a near-impossible task. But is that the whole point?

If he doesn't show, she can blame both me and Hicky. That way I'll have failed her and she'll have to set me another task, and Hicky will look like a chicken.

I can see now that as long as I am with Mercy, I'll always have a job to do for her. Mind you, the thought of going up west with her tomorrow night doesn't fill me with dread. It kind of warms my heart. Another real rhubarb and custard chew of feelings.

I stop for a moment and stand at the very top of Hicky's street. God, it looks so nice twinkling under the emerging starlight! If you saw it with its expensive cars, its freshly painted doors, its insulated window frames, its lovely brick walls, you'd almost think that flats like mine didn't exist.

Suddenly, Hicky's front door swings open. I duck behind a silver Audi. People are shouting. I can make out Mrs Hick's voice and Hicky himself. He tumbles out onto the street. His suit looks very crumpled. The door slams shut.

Hicky gawps up at his house for a moment, gazing at the cardboard in the front window – this makes me feel guilty – and then cranes his neck as he peers up at the upper floors.

He opens his mouth. He's thinking about shouting something at the bricks but he shuts his mouth before any words come out. He turns away and starts to walk up the street, swaying on his feet.

Naturally, I decide to follow him.

9.55pm

"Helen is a good woman," I hear you say. "She's just independent, that's all. Strong-willed. It's good to see that in a woman."

You poke a toothpick into an olive and put it to your mouth. I gasp at the vividness of the memory. It's just like you're alive. We're in the Pizza Express on St Martin's Lane and you're in your tweed suit. You've come to see me straight after work: you haven't had time to change.

We have been to see Death *of a Salesman together in the West End. I've finished my capriccioso pizza and I'm on my third glass of wine. I lean across the table as I whisper: "But Jack, I haven't had sex in over a year."*

"She's a good woman. You shouldn't let that get in the way of your relationship."

"But Jack, I'm a man..."

"Look, Martin, this is off the record, but perhaps you should get your relief... elsewhere?"

"But where? I don't want to have an affair. I mean, I probably could with Kylie, but I don't want to get involved in that. My life is complicated enough as it is."

You spear another olive, eat it and spit out the pip. "You can always see it as a commercial transaction. You need something, pay for it. I've never been prudish about the matter."

I catch my breath. I can't believe that you have said this, but you have. You've always been so respectable, so wise, so upstanding, but now you're admitting to paying for sex. The conversation unwinds from there; your wife has never been particularly "keen" and so you've come to a modus vivendi where you'll do what you want without causing any embarrassment.

"I've always been discreet. That's the important thing. Stay safe and be discreet," *you say.*

But Jack, how can I hold the affair against Helen considering what I've done?

Now I'm in Browns, a strip joint, by Shoreditch

301

Church, my head in my hands, surrounded by lots of sad fat guys like myself. A young woman with fake breasts is gyrating to loud, thumping music on the stage. She looks young enough to be one of my pupils, but her brown eyes are full of cynicism. Helen has never looked that old.

I know you'd tell me to try and keep things going with Helen at all costs. That was your way; stay married, say whatever has to be said, be forgiving.

I leave the striptease joint. I'm back on Old Street. Like a somnambulist, I'm walking towards your solution, Jack. I don't want to. It always makes me feel filthy afterwards but I can't help myself.

I climb the stairs of the block of flats and knock on number 43.

10.00pm

Crouching down low, I track Hicky. It's easy to hide from him because he's pretty pissed.

I follow him onto Hackney Road, where he joins all the clubbers. I watch him go into a strip joint. The bouncer on the door lets me go in without any hassle. My outfit clearly has some advantages.

I watch Hicky sink his head into his hands on the counter as these naked women wander around lots of gawping men, asking for them to put money in a beer glass. I pass this place all the time but it's not what I pictured at all. I imagined lots of men shouting and cheering and women slapping their thighs and singing burlesque songs. But this place is so fucked! The men look shifty and the women seem bored.

Hicky is especially depressed. It makes me think that perhaps I should talk to him. He seems so lonely with all these slags and lads pushing past him. It might be a good chance to sweet-talk him to go to Ravenscroft. Or not. Just suppose Hicky gets the shit kicked out of him?

No. No, I can't lead him to his doom. He's not that much of a bastard.

I can't.

Or can I?

He drinks up quickly, and then continues down Old Street. At the roundabout, he detours down towards the City, down to Bunhill Fields, and then turns down a side street. It's deserted. I have to be extra careful with my ducking and diving. On the odd occasion, he turns around.

Doing this makes me recover some of my old zest for detective work. It's good to know that the CIA or MI5 will want me for undercover work when I'm older.

I nearly lose him when he disappears into a block of flats near Whitecross Street. It's quite a modern block. But not that skanky.

He presses a buzzer and goes up a flight of stairs. I have to move double-quick in order to get in before the door locks shut – but I make it. He makes his way along the open-air landing on the first floor, which overlooks quite a nice garden, then he knocks on the black door of number 43 and goes in. A wrinkled woman with frizzy blond hair and lots of make-up pokes her head out onto the landing, checking to see if there's anybody else about. I duck backwards. She doesn't see me.

Who does Hicky know there?

It wasn't anyone I recognised.

10pm

"Is Christine on tonight?" I ask when I'm through the door.

"Yes, love," the croaky-voiced old madam says. "Here, I'll fetch you a beer. She'll just be a few minutes."

"Is she with someone?"

"Yes, love. Now, you're a Stella man, ain't you?"

I sit down in the bleak front room with its closed blinds and stacks of *Nuts* and *Playboy* magazines. Apart from the free beer and the porn, it's a bit like being in a doctor's waiting room. The madam brings me the beer. I lie back on the sofa and sip at it. I'm drinking myself sober now. I'm that far gone.

My phone starts to ring. It's Jeff.

"Where are you, mate? Helen said you were coming over."

"It's all right. I'm busy at the moment."

"But you will be coming over?"

"I don't think so."

"You won't be?"

"I can't."

"I really think you should come around to mine and have a proper chat with Helen in the morning."

I might feel more inclined to take his advice if he

sounded sober himself. But he doesn't. "Hey, Jeff, I got the bloody Deputy Head job when no one believed I could, and I'll sort this stuff out myself as well."

The truth is, the last thing I want to do tonight is stay in Jeff's happy marital home: I've slept over a few times after a few ragged Friday nights and it's been disgusting because he always tries to fuck his wife when he's pissed. And she doesn't seem to mind. The noise of her giggling and his grunting made me ill.

I'd probably be sick all over his carpet. I'd actually prefer to sleep rough – or chuck myself in the Thames. I really would.

Eventually, after some noises in the hallway – a deep male voice, the madam talking, the front door shutting – the old crone peeps her head around the door and says Christine is ready.

I traipse into the room. There's a medical bed, a sink, a waste-paper bin and some pictures of naked women on the wall. No Christine.

I take my clothes off quickly and lie on my back on the bed.

Christine enters. She used to ask for the money upfront but she doesn't anymore. She trusts me. It's not a trust I should be proud of.

She's a brunette, wearing a silver and black kimono, and a bikini thong underneath.

"Christine, can you hit me tonight?" I say. "Hit me hard. Can you get the whip and do it hard? Don't worry about making marks. It doesn't matter any more."

"Jack, are you all right?" she asks in her eastern European accent.

"I'm fine. I just need you to hit me, that's all. And say that I'm fucking disgusting. Say that I'm a fucking disgusting fat fuck. Oh, and call me by my full name, Jack Humphreys."

"OK, Jack Humphreys. Let me go and fetch the whip."

10.15pm

After I've done the dirty deed, I sink back on the bed for a moment. Panting.

Christine snaps on some underwear, wraps herself in her kimono and disappears. I know I should be putting on my clothes, but I feel pretty tired.

Christine enters the room again. She helps lift me off the bed. I sit upright, gazing down at my voluminous hairy stomach. Once I was a child with such a skinny chest, now I'm this great big hairy man. A brute.

"I think my son knows about me coming here," I say.

Christine snorts as she busies herself. "I didn't know you had a son."

"Yeah. I've got a son and a daughter and a wife and, well, quite an important job actually..."

Christine is silent. She's neither unsympathetic nor particularly interested.

I put on my boxer shorts and my shirt. Christine

hovers about me.

"Where are you from, Christine?"

"Latvia."

"Do you like what you do?"

She shrugs and doesn't answer. "There are worse jobs. And the money's good. It's a hundred and forty today. The whipping was extra."

I pull the cash out of my wallet. I hadn't reckoned on it being this expensive.

"Thanks," I say as I hand over the cash.

She takes the money quickly and disappears again.

Once I'm outside, I look around and see that there's no one in sight: only an empty walkway, dark stairs and the night hanging over the estate. I make my way through the block of flats and back into the City.

I'm still pretty drunk, but feel like I'm sobering up a bit.

I've been to see Christine a lot since Jack died, and I've always wanted to speak to my late friend afterwards. I've wanted him to reassure me that I shouldn't feel guilty and dirty for paying for sex. That it's the right thing for my marriage.

Tonight, I find myself talking to him again. Oh God, how I wish he was here! He was the only person I shared any of this stuff with.

But of course, he's nowhere.

Jack is dead. And I am alone on the empty, dark street.

10.18pm

I've been hanging around outside the flat for a while but no one has come out. Then I have an idea. I get out my phone, tap the mobile connection to the internet and type "escorts" into Google maps. There are quite a few in this area. I tap on the icon that's nearest to my location. No address is given but there's a phone number. I call it.

"Yes," a croaky voice answers.

"I'm wanting to fuck tonight."

"You are, love, are you?" the voice says.

"Need a fuck. A big fuck."

"It'll cost ya."

"How much?"

"Hundred for an hour. Sixty for half. That includes A and O levels."

I'm not sure what they are but I don't want to ask.

"Where are you?" I ask.

"Old Street."

"What part of Old Street?"

"Next to Whitecross street."

"You're near."

"We're in a block of flats by Whitecross Street, number 43."

"OK, thanks," I say.

Bingo!

I leave the piss-streaked telephone booth lit up with the power of a major revelation.

Things are beginning to make sense.

I don't need to stay here any longer. I need to see Josh.

10.32pm

God, I'm starting to feel horny again. I blame Old Street. It encourages unbridled lasciviousness. It's a cornucopia of high heels, black stockings, shapely bums wiggling in short skirts, tits bursting out of tight tops, slutty make-up and fuck-me eyes. In a way, my lust comes as a relief. It distracts me from thinking about Helen, my job, Jack.

Jeff calls again. I answer as I carry on walking past the nightclubs.

"Hey, Mart, where are you?" Jeff asks.

"I'm just wandering around."

"Look, I'm getting a cab back home from the Royal Oak at about 11.30. Why don't you come and join me?"

"I'm not so sure," I say.

"Mart, believe me, I think this is the best thing right now."

"Look, I might check in on Helen first."

"Is that wise, Mart?"

"Is anything wise?"

"I've spoken to Helen just now."

"Well, don't believe everything she says – she's certainly not wise."

"Look, I'll wait for you at the Royal Oak, matey."

"Don't wait up."

"Why don't you just come straight over to the Royal Oak? We can have a night-cap and head home together."

The word "home" makes me rebel against his plan.

I tell him I have to go and ring off.

I stagger past a club called Mother and think about entering it because some pretty girls are going in there ,but, for some reason, the bouncer on the door won't admit me. Cunt. However, I do find some refuge in Browns again. I have another pint there and watch a few girls gyrate and undress on the stage, writhing around their silver pole.

The thing I love about these strip joints is that the guys are so well behaved. There's never the sort of rowdiness you see in pubs or clubs. The blokes here just sit or stand and gawp. Some of them, the richer ones, talk to the girls while slipping fivers into their suspenders, but most of the punters just stare.

Like me right now. I sit splay-legged with my pint, staring at silicone-enhanced tits, and think what the fuck has happened to my life. But I feel like my thought processes are more in control here. Right now, it feels good not to have Jack hovering around, speaking to me in the back of my mind.

Still, there's no getting over the fact that this is a depressing place. I finish my pint and head home. My home. My fucking home.

What would you advise me to do, Jack?

Knowing you, you'd probably tell me to sober up and speak to her then. It's never good to have a serious discussion with your missus when you're utterly pissed. Yes, you'd definitely advise me to leave things well alone. Like Jeff.

I find myself staring at my home without even considering the prospect of entering it. The lights are on upstairs but not downstairs. Helen must be up.

You liked to compartmentalise things, didn't you Jack? Home is for sobriety and chastity, brothels are where you have sex, pubs are where you get pissed with your mates, and school is where you teach and pupils learn. That was your credo, and it's mine too. It has to be mine because I have nothing to replace it.

But I can feel the cracks... There are definitely structural problems in the container ship: holes in the walls, water leaking into the engine room, everything sinking. Because nothing really works like that, does it? Everything I've done with Christine has profoundly and unutterably changed my relationship with Helen. And with my family, and with the school, too. It's dragged me into the unutterable meaninglessness and tawdriness of it all.

I stagger on, leaving home behind me. I can't face going to the Royal Oak. It would be too much like admitting defeat. Far better to sleep rough for a night and then go back to Helen in the morning looking horribly dishevelled and pathetic.

I find myself back in the playground where I used to take Josh when he was a little boy.

I lie down on the bench where I used to watch him climb up and down the slide.

Yes, better to sleep off my woes here than end up trapped in someone else's home.

11pm

"Just let me talk to you, Josh," I plead into the mobile phone.

"Fuck off," comes the familiar reply.

I am standing outside his house, looking up at his window. Sirens whirr in the distance, but everything is peaceful in this street. I clutch my phone tightly and think: sometimes niceness just won't do. Sometimes you've got to be like Mercy.

"Josh, I think I know something you know. About your dad. Something no one else knows," I say.

There's a pause.

"What?"

"Just let me in and we can talk about it."

"You're bullshitting me."

"I'm not. I saw him go in there – just now. I called the number and everything. I know, Josh. I know the real reason why you are the Countess Feckula."

Shortly after this, Josh appears at the door. He doesn't say anything. It's dark in the hall but the streetlight comes through the fanlight, partially illuminating the big framed photograph of the family by the seaside hanging on the wall. They all look so happy.

It suddenly strikes me that part of the pleasure I derived from coming here all these years was the aching jealousy I felt. My secret desire to be part of a family like this. It was like an itch which made me come back for more.

Now I've come back for one last time to set the record

straight. "Hey, Béla, why don't we have a spliff and make up?" Josh whispers. "I mean, we've both been fuckers, haven't we?"

This surprises me, but I agree. Maybe this won't be the last time I come here. Maybe Josh and I will be proper friends again.

I tag along with him to the back of the house. He opens the patio door to the garden. We cross the concrete paving, I breathe in the scent of lavender and coriander that comes from the herb beds, watching Josh as he heads towards the shed – the place where he keeps his secret stash.

He tells me to wait in the dark gap between the high garden wall and the shed. It's the only place in the garden where you can't be seen by anyone; where we smoke spliffs together.

But instead of getting the puff, he emerges from the shed holding two spray cans.

I raise my arms in alarm. "Josh, don't! Don't! They're not my clothes!"

But it's too late.

He whooshes and squirts the aerosol paint all over Mercy's hoodie and trackie bottoms at full force, ruining it forever.

I am drenched in the fucking paint. Absolutely fucking drenched. The smell of the solvents and the shock of seeing my ruined clothes make my head feel quite giddy.

"You deserved that," Josh says, looking at me with real pride.

11.05pm

The park bench by the small swing is quite comfortable really. Lying there in my half-drowsed state, I listen to the city rumble and choke in the distance and I remember the sound of Jack's breathing as he died. The exhalations sinking, sinking, sinking. Then nothing.

"Jack, I got your job, but I don't know if I can do it, mate, I really don't," I say out loud. The desperate urge to talk to him is back again. "Things are not working out, mate. Helen wants to divorce me. And I…"

I trail off and shut my eyes. Behind my eyelids I am back in the school on the day of his death.

The last day of Year 11. Only a couple of months ago, but it seems like aeons now. I'm talking to Jack. It's early in the morning and we're meeting in his office to discuss tactics. He looks thin in his tweedy suit, but his face is pale. He's beginning to look his age. He sips his coffee and rubs his arm.

"What's the matter? Drank one too many last night?" I joke.

Jack laughs but it is a hollow laugh. "Yeah. I'm not feeling too hot today."

"Well, you're going to need all your strength: I've heard that Year 11 are preparing a right bonanza for us."

Jack and I had begged Sam to send the whole of Year 11 home the previous day so that they would start their study leave a day early and we'd thereby avoid the "normal" high jinks that goes on their last day of term. But no, Sam would have none of it: we were disrespecting the students by thinking that they would riot.

At the beginning of school, we'd seen the whole year group girded to the loins with pump-action water guns, canisters of shaving foam and an array of fireworks.

But thanks to my patrolling with Jack during the first break, the pupils had been shepherded into assembly without much hassle. Sam was able to give his leavers' speech without too many interruptions. Even though they were chucking confetti and squirting water pistols, Sam told the children how marvellous they were; how they were the new generation who were going to do great things; how the older generation had a great deal to learn from them.

Towards the end of the assembly, some of the kids at the back started chanting "Hickory Dickory Dock", which irritated me a great deal. After they were dismissed, though, the children became noticeably rowdier. I found Jack in the corridor, trying to keep order as the kids pushed past him. He was clutching his arm. I saw that he was sick. I saw that.

"This looks bad, Jack, really bad. Did you hear how they were abusing me?" I said. Jack said he hadn't. After hearing noises in the next corridor, Jack and I ran through the swing doors where we found great bits of gloopy egg yolk dripping down the walls and flour floating in the air. It was a horrifying mess.

The colour drained out of my friend's face.

"Look, I might have to lie down for a bit. Perhaps you could take my place."

"Don't be ridiculous, Jack! No one can take your place!" I said, feeling like I was encouraging him not to lose courage.

"I think you're going to have to," he said.

"Come on, Jack, we need to deal with this," I said, taking him by the arm and leading him to the scene of the worst riot. "You'll feel better when we've sorted this lot out."

Oh God, Jack, I shouldn't have done that, should I?

Once we were outside, everything happened very quickly. It seemed like the whole year group ran into the playground – all a hundred and twenty pupils. The noise was deafening. Some boys, particularly the gym-honed ones, stripped down to their "thongs", while a few girls cavorted about in their lingerie. What a bloody embarrassment!

To my annoyance, I saw Sam slinking away from the scene – he claimed later he was calling the police. After he vanished, Kylie surfaced, looking mortified. She screamed miserably above the din that someone had posted something disgusting about me and her on Facebook. She'd heard from Béla that he'd seen Mercy sneak into the staffroom while everyone was at the assembly.

Suddenly, the chant began to make sense. Kylie and I heard it properly for the first time now in the playground. Pupils pointed their fingers at us as they chanted:

Hickory dickory dock,
Rouse sucked the cock!
The clock struck one,
The cock spunked
On her tongue
Hickory dickory dock,
Rouse sucked the cock!

Of course – it had been about me and Kylie! It was all over the school and, even worse, plastered all over the internet. Mercy truly was a bastard.

I told Kylie to go indoors – some of the pupils were pawing at her clothes, clearly wanting to strip them off. Then I pushed my way through the crowd and into the centre of the playground where the real troublemakers were. Surprise, surprise, Mercy and the Bentley twins were in the thick of things. They were changing the tone of the riot. Whereas it had been high-spirited in the assembly hall, now it turned extremely vicious: Mercy was flashing a knife around and the twins were pummelling the kids near them with knuckledusters. They were going to turn the scene into an orgy of violence.

Mercy didn't try to hide the knife from me. She was clearly high on drugs.

"Give me that! Give me that now!" I said, stretching out my hand.

"I wasn't doing anything, I was only playing!" she said, looking at me like I was mad to insinuate that she might have been about to use it.

"Mercy, give me the bloody knife!" I screamed.

But just as she was lunging towards me, Jack staggered towards her, distracting her from stabbing me.

"Mercy, don't be so silly. Using a knife is not going to help anything. It's only going to hurt people," he said in a calm voice. Unlike me, Jack wasn't in an aggressive mood; his words were said much more in sorrow than anger. And they had the desired effect. Mercy put the knife back into her black bag and Jack waved his long, thin hands at her, shooing her away. She joined the Bentley twins and Béla at the frontline of the fight, where she encouraged everyone to get whatever missiles were to hand and lob them at the windows of the Academy. Both Jack and I tried to stop them but to no avail.

A hail of sticks, bricks, stones, cans and other detritus smashed against the academy's windows, shattering them with surprising alacrity. The whole façade of the school entrance collapsed in a shower of glass.

I ran back into the building, my feet crunching over broken glass, and fetched a loudspeaker from a terrified school secretary who said to me: "They're animals. Complete animals."

I screamed at her to tell all the teachers to come down to the playground immediately. Then I returned to the action.

I found Jack sitting in a crumpled heap as lots of

kids wandered past him, too high on the thrill of the moment to notice a sick teacher. They had run out of eggs and flour, and were picking up bits of glass and flinging them at anyone or anything.

I tried to encourage him to get up but he seemed in a complete daze. Suddenly, a firework spurted out of the mass of shouting, screaming faces. A firework that appeared to have been thrown by Béla.

The firework whizzed and flared in the air. Almost as soon as it exploded, Jack clutched at his chest. I watched him helplessly as he toppled over from his sitting position, with his arms wrapped around his ribs. I bellowed through the loudspeaker: "Everyone go home! Everyone go home! Now!"

I scooped Jack up in my arms and held him tight, saying: "It's going to be fine, it's going to be fine."

"You did it," Jack whispered in my ear.

The way his breathing gradually diminished and then stopped was truly terrifying.

I think he was probably dead when Kylie appeared. Her shirt was torn and her make-up smudged. When she saw that Jack was floppy in my arms, she knelt down by me and seized my arm. "Martin, Martin, I called an ambulance. He looked so ill earlier I was worried."

"I think he's gone, Kylie, I think he's gone," I said.

His hands felt cold in mine and his body was stiff. The life had left him. It just didn't seem possible. It just didn't. I thought: if I hold him long enough, he will come back. He will. He must. It can't happen like this.

"Oh Martin, Martin," Kylie said, putting her hand over her mouth.

By then a lot of the pupils had calmed down and could see that their Deputy Head was comatose on the ground. A deathly hush swept through them as they crowded around us.

I am alive. Jack isn't.

I am still here. Lying on the park bench near midnight.

11.13pm

I slide down the wall, friction burning my skin.

"These ain't my clothes, Josh," I say. "They're Mercy's. Now she's really going to kill me. Proper kill me."

"Do I look like I care?"

I lie down on the floor, trying to take stock of the situation. "Look, Josh, I know you hate me, and I'll go soon, but you haven't got any spliff by any chance, have you?"

Even though his face is in shadow, I can see that Josh's expression is hostile. Nevertheless, he gets out the puff and skins up.

"You'd better be careful lighting up near me," I say. "Otherwise I might ignite."

Josh doesn't smile. Instead, his match hovers for a moment near my top before it lights the spliff. He sucks in some smoke and then hands me the joint.

I take it in and think, God, I'm a worse fucking mess than Hicky's marriage.

"It's all right. I've got some good clothes you can have. Better than those. Clothes you'll like," Josh says.

"I suppose if I was tough, I would have a fight with you," I say, handing him back the joint. I take a puff on my inhaler to help the spliff go down.

"But you're not tough."

"No. I guess I'm not."

"You're a fucking pain in the neck. But you're not tough."

"I'm a fucking pain in the neck," I repeat.

I hand the spliff to Josh. He sits down beside me. I've always liked it in this hidden corridor between the shed and the garden wall. Leaning back, I look at the sky. The night is cloudless and I can see quite a few stars.

"Look, Josh, mate, I'm sorry," I say.

"It doesn't matter. It's all fucked anyway. There's no way my parents are going to stay together."

We watch the smoke rise up into the stars.

"I mean, when you think about it, your dad was going to find out sooner or later. I just accelerated things."

Josh doesn't say anything, so I continue. "And besides, like I said, I think you know things about your dad which don't exactly make his position very good. You know that he goes and sees hookers, don't you? That's why you're so mad at him, ain't it? I couldn't figure it out until now, but it all makes sense. You're really pissed off with him, and yet you want him and your mum to stay together, so you invented Countess Feckula and made up that allegation, so that he would get sacked from school. Then he could be more at home and be pussy-whipped by your mum."

Josh is silent for a moment. He carries on smoking the spliff. Then he says: "You think you're really clever, don't you, Béla?"

"My dad was a detective. I got his instincts. Now pass the spliff."

But Josh doesn't.

"How come you hooked up with the GMF, Béla?"

"Pass the spliff and I'll tell you."

The lighted end of the spliff hovers in the air for a moment, looking like a grim-faced fairy, and then finds itself in my hand. I lean back against the wall. It feels like Josh has got over his anger. This is good. This is very good. He really is my best friend. My only friend – in truth.

"I fucked Mercy," I say. The moment I say it, I realise it sounds much, much better than it actually was.

"You what?" Josh exclaims. He can't believe it.

"Yeah, I did. After you and your dad booted me out, she dragged me to her place. She lives in a flat just like mine, except it's full of kids and guys and women cooking stuff. It stinks. But she's got a bedroom, and she took me in there and basically fucked me."

"You make it sound like you were raped!"

"It wasn't exactly like that, but I'm not sure I had much choice. She knows what she wants."

"Fucking hell."

Josh laughs. I laugh too.

"I think she really likes me, Josh. She asked me out

tomorrow night."

"Fucking hell, I'd be worried if I was you."

"That's the thing. It feels like it's worse being her boyfriend than not. I'm kind of trapped now. It's a difficult feeling to explain, but it's both a nice and nasty feeling."

"But what about when you were fucking her? Was that good?" Josh says, snatching at the spliff.

The dope has gone to my head now and I feel quite a bit more relaxed.

"Yes. It was good. It was like I saw beyond the normal Mercy. It was like…"

"Fuck, that sounds like love!" Josh spurts out.

"I wouldn't say it was exactly that."

Then both of us laugh together. Josh gets up off the floor, saying: "I'll get you some clean clothes."

He disappears, leaving me contemplating life and love.

I could set fire to his shed and his house if I wanted to. Burn it all down to the ground. And take me with it.

But I'm not going to. I'm not going to do what Dad did. Just give in. I'm not going to do that. I feel my strength returning, my inner strength. I had lost it during the day when I felt so trapped. But now, I think: God, I can do what I want. Mercy, Josh or Ma can't tell me what to do all the time. I can act on my own.

11.20pm

You did it.

Until now, I'd interpreted Jack's last words as reassuring: that I had sorted out the problem. Now, staring up at the polluted urban sky from the bench, I have a horrible feeling that he actually didn't mean that at all.

Was he rather saying: "*You* did it"; suggesting I caused his death? If I'd listened to him earlier, if I'd told him to take some time out and sit the whole thing out in the staffroom, would he be alive today? If I hadn't been so bloody obsessed by the job?

Did I kill him? Jesus! Were those his last ever thoughts?

11.16pm

Josh returns.

"I've got you some new clothes. Good clothes," he says in a much nicer voice than before.

He dumps them on my head. The fabric feels slightly rough against my face and smells a bit of mothballs. I shake them off.

I examine the clothes beside me. It's a gentleman's suit. A really expensive tweedy suit.

"Is this your dad's suit?"

"No, it's Mr Humphreys'!"

I drop the suit immediately.

"Mr Humphreys? You want me to wear a dead man's suit?"

"My dad's been keeping it in his wardrobe. I reckon it's time we got rid of it. My dad actually talks to it!"

"He does? He talks to Mr Humphreys' suit?"

Josh nods. "He's stressed, mate. Very stressed. That's why he needs to take some time off."

This information is both consoling and upsetting. I say: "I talk to my dad, you know. I still talk to him. Maybe it's like that between your dad and Mr Humphreys."

"Or maybe he's just nuts – and you are too!"

"You know, you should take more time to understand him. I mean, he has his faults, but don't we all?"

Josh contemplates this.

The news that Hicky talks to this suit lifts my spirits. There may be no point to anything in the universe, but there's still a mystery. Somehow the dead and living mingle all the time. Ghosts are all around us.

I take off the paint-spattered hoodie and then put on the shirt. "Is this Mr Humphreys' too?"

"Yeah! It's the one he died in!"

"You're fucking with me, right?"

"No, man."

I think Josh is expecting me to freak out, but I don't. I feel some sort of resurrection happening. I can feel it rising.

11.20pm

I'm lying on the bench when I hear a female voice calling out my name: "Martin! Martin!"

It feels like Helen's voice calling from all those years ago on the Uist beach. I stagger to my feet.

"Helen?"

It's dark in the playground. I can see the outline of the swings and the playground, and not much else. A woman's silhouette appears in the streetlight in the distance, near where the Royal Oak is.

"Helen?"

The silhouette is curvy. Its top spangles. Naked Helen on the beach morphs into Kylie. She's joined by a much bigger form: the unmistakeable pot-bellied outline of Jeff.

"Martin! Where are you?" he says.

Although I love Jeff dearly, I don't want to see him now. I slump back into the shadowy recess of my "memory" bench.

"Martin, mate! Are you there?"

Jeff seems to have spotted me and is kicking aside the litter of the playground, his form bobbling behind the latticed structure of the climbing frame. Kylie follows him. They sit down beside me. Jeff slaps a hand on my back and Kylie's knee touches mine.

"Oh Mart, mate, we can't have you staying here! We can't! You're going to have to come home with me, mate."

My head gyroscopes on my neck. I feel quite sick.

"I can't go home with you, Jeff."

A cab stops with its lights blinking on the kerb nearest us.

"There's our cab, Mart baby, we're going!"

Jeff pulls at my hand, trying to lift me off the bench. I wobble a bit but I remain glued to it, next to Kylie. "I'm not going, Jeff. I couldn't listen to you fuck your wife again!"

Kylie suppresses a tipsy giggle.

"What are you talking about?" Jeff asks, getting up off the bench, clearly offended.

"I can hear everything, Jeff. I couldn't do that to-night. I couldn't listen to you pump, pump, pumping away again!"

Jeff looks at Kylie in a very disgruntled fashion. "He's not coming, is he?"

"I'll stay with him," Kylie says, patting the tops of my hands.

"You can't do that, he's pissed out of his head!"

"Go, Jeff! Fuck off home to your rumpy-pumpy wife!" I shout.

"Martin, if you weren't drunk, I'd smack you in the mouth!"

With that, Jeff stomps off to the taxi. As soon as he's gone, Kylie and I look at each other. This should be our moment. And, as if on cue, she begins to rub my arm soothingly. I'm just about to kiss her when my phone rings. It's Josh, who goes mad when I joke that I'm going to have a show-down with the Countess Feckula. He's so hysterical I don't understand him. Is he saying he's the Countess? No, it's not possible!

I put the phone down and look at Kylie. I hiccough and say: "That was my son. He sounded worried about me."

"Of course, he must be – we all are."

"I think he might even love me, you know," I say. "Not that I deserve it."

Kylie hooks her arm under mine, nuzzling my neck with her hair. "Of course you deserve it."

11.21pm

I put on the suit. It fits me fine. It's weird to think that me and Mr Humphreys were quite similar physically.

"How do I look?" I say, standing up.

"Better than you did in that hoodie!"

Josh makes another spliff and we smoke it. I am careful not to let the hash drop onto my suit and cause pinhole burns. The suit is beginning to grow on me.

"Do you think anyone will notice it's Humphreys' suit?"

"Nah. Only my dad, and, trust me, after tonight, I don't think he's gonna complain about much."

"Why do you have so little sympathy for him, Josh?"

"Look, Béla, he's been fucking these prostitutes, and yet he gets all holy and mighty with Mum about how she's not a good enough wife and everything. He's a total and utter hypocrite!"

"But maybe she don't give him enough," I suggest. "After all, men are men. Well, some are."

Josh shakes his head. "I don't buy into that bullshit. He's a fucking disgrace!"

"When did you find out?"

"On the day Humphreys died. He was acting quite weirdly, and so I followed him. Then I saw him go into the flat, and then checked it out on the internet and found out what goes on there."

"You're a detective too, ain't you, Josh?"

Josh sighs and then gets out his mobile. "I'd better see how the old git is." He calls his dad. I watch his face flicker with concern.

"No, Dad, you can't spend the night in fucking Ravenscroft Park! Come home now," he says.

I put my hand to my mouth as a very deep and grave realisation creeps upon me. I say: "Oh fuck, Mercy!"

"What?" Josh says, putting his hand over the receiver.

"Mercy, the GMF! That's where they are intending to fight him tonight. I was supposed to lure him there. But he seems to have gone of his own accord!"

"Shit!"

"Tell him to get the fuck out of there!" I shriek.

Josh responds immediately, shouting down the phone: "She's going to kill you! Get out of there... No, no, no, Dad, she's not the Countess Feckula!" he shouts into his mobile phone.

"Josh, you're going to have to tell him," I say, gripping his arm tightly.

Josh stares at my tightening hand and then blurts out loudly: "Dad, you have to get out of there! Mercy is not the Countess! I was the fucking Countess. She wasn't, OK?"

There's a pause. "Dad, I'm sorry, I truly am. But that fucking teaching job is killing you. I thought I was doing you a favour. Dad, you don't have time for this!"

Josh shakes his head, clearly dismissing his father's drunken ravings. Then he says: "Look, just stay there. Don't move. We'll come and get you."

He shovels his phone into his pocket, looking like a popped balloon.

"He's just lying on a bench in the playground, saying he's gonna kill Mercy even though he knows she isn't –" he says with his whole body shaking. "We'd better get the fuck over there before he gets mashed."

He runs into the house. I follow him indoors into the darkened kitchen, watching him as he pulls off two knives from the rack on the counter. Their blades glint in the dark.

Memories of fucking Mercy flash through my mind.

"What are you waiting for, you pussy?" Josh spits at me.

I bunch my hands into fists as I say: "We shouldn't take these."

Josh's face is cauterised by the yellow light outside and the shadows of the kitchen.

"Béla, this is the GMF we're talking about. We can't reason with them."

"They'll kill us if we have knives."

"We're not gonna use them, we're just gonna call their bluff, that's all. Béla, fucking Mercy has fucked your head. She was only using you. Look, we've got to fucking go." He takes a rucksack off a coat hook and puts the knives carefully in the front pocket.

Then I say: "You know what else would be good? The aerosol cans. They'd make good flame-throwers. That would be more likely to scare them off than knives."

"That's a plan," Josh agrees, pumping his arms up and down in the air in an unconvincing fashion. Does he seriously think he can take on the GMF? Is he on a suicide mission?

Josh goes back to the garden, gets the cans he left on the wall and puts them in his rucksack. I take some matches by the oven.

When we're in the hallway, Josh grabs a balaclava from a hook and chucks it at me.

I catch it and put it on. "She'll know it's me," I say.

"Come on, you bender, let's go!" Josh says, charging out of the house. The cans make clicking and clanking noises as Josh runs with the rucksack on his back.

I lag behind him. The balaclava makes my face itch. At the top of the road, underneath the streetlight, I pull it off, put my hands behind my head and slow down to a heavy trudge. "Oh fuck, I can't go there. Mercy will kill me. I can't, Josh. You're better off calling the police."

"Béla, the cops won't come in time. We've both got to go."

I shake my head vigorously.

"But I'll die, Josh, you don't understand. She'll kill me. She thinks I'm on her side!"

"Oh, you fucking coward! I saved you this morning, didn't I? Who was it who came and pulled you out of that rubbish bin? If you put your balaclava back on, she won't know it's you."

"But it's more than that, Josh. This is wrong. It's not the right way to go about this."

Josh sneers at me in disgust and then rushes off, leaving me standing underneath the streetlight. I shout after him, telling him that he shouldn't do it, but he either ignores me or doesn't hear me.

There's no way I'm going to Ravenscroft.

11.27pm

Remember, there are always second chances, I think, as Kylie and I kiss. Her tongue enters my mouth and then, remembering that it was my son who was the Countess Feckula, I suddenly feel violently ill. Vomit surges up from my stomach. I jerk away, roll off the bench and start chucking up.

As I'm doing this, Kylie screams.

"It's all right, I'm only being sick!" I say, feeling quite a bit better for having deposited most of my evening's calorific intake on the grass.

But the screaming continues. "No, no, no! Please no!"

I straighten up and feel a horrible tasting rag being shoved into my mouth.

"Oi, fucker, what you got for us?"

The big, sweaty hand muzzling my mouth has long fingernails. I look up at their owner mutely. Two other figures flank the muzzler. Although I can't really see their faces, I recognise the fingernails immediately: it's Mercy. And behind her, the Bentley twins.

Mercy takes out a knife and trails it down my shirt, jagging at the buttons, and popping them off. I can feel she's broken the skin. I'm bleeding.

Kylie is screaming desperately. "Get off him, you

bastards! Get off him!"

"Your sugar daddy is going to die," Mercy says.

Kylie screams even more vociferously when she sees what's happened to my chest. Blood is now dribbling down my belly.

"I'm calling the police!" she shouts. "You'll get put in jail for this, Mercy. You will."

Mercy gives a hollow laugh. "Don't talk shit. We're only having a bit of fun."

She and the twins take me by the armpits, lift me up and then push me onto a nearby swing, rolling me over it like a piece of dough. My buttocks are now in the air and my bloody belly is squashed against the swing.

A knife rips through the material of my trousers. There are jeers and more laughter as one of the gang pulls down my trousers. Another gang member feels my jacket for stuff and takes my wallet from my inside breast pocket.

I try to spit out the rag but I can't. Just as I try and pull it out, someone ties my hands behind my back and pushes the rag deeper into my throat. Almost immediately, I start choking. I can't see Kylie, but I can hear lots of screaming and shouting mingling together.

Despite my drunkenness, I feel degradation seep into my skin.

"This time, Hicky, I did it. I well and truly beat you, man, and I want everyone to see that," Mercy proclaims.

Suddenly, I look up and I see two jet sprays of fire. To my utter amazement, I see a heavenly figure walking through the fiery fountains. I can't believe what I'm seeing.

It's Jack! It's his suit and his body. And yet he has no face. Just darkness. And he seems to be talking calmly to Mercy. Not fighting. Not shouting. Just chatting calmly with her. Someone has released my hands. I pull out the cloth from my mouth and fall off the swing. Pain throbs through my chest and arms. I scream: "I'm sorry. I'm sorry, I'm sorry! Jack, I'm sorry. I should have never have made you do it. Jack, I'm sorry."

And then I rest my head on the ground, screaming out in pain.

11.28pm

I break into a run when I realise that I can't leave Josh to fight the GMF by himself.

Once I reach the shuttered-up council office, the one-stop shop, I have a good perspective on the playground. I can see the GMF have grabbed Hicky and are pushing him towards the swings. For some reason, Miss Rouse is there. I don't get that at all: she's all tarted up like a prozzer.

Hicky looks like he's got all this horrible stuff coming out of his mouth, but when I run closer, I see it's just a rag.

As I expected, Josh is standing uselessly on the edge

of the action. He hasn't pulled out his knife. When he sees it's me, he looks at me pathetically. It's obvious he feels completely powerless as the gang push his father onto a swing and rip away his trousers with their knives, slashing at the cloth around his bum.

Josh's lower lip starts to tremble as the Bentley twins rifle through Hicky's jacket for his stuff and Mercy takes some photos of his hairy, gashed bum on her phone.

They're all carousing and laughing, and Miss Rouse is yelling her lungs out. Without thinking anymore, I run up to Hicky. Since I'm wearing a balaclava, Mercy doesn't clock it's me. She's also a bit distracted by kicking the shit out of Hicky.

She yanks him off the ground like a floppy doll, pushes him back on the swing, rips down his trousers and stuffs the rag down his gullet. The twins flank him as he lies uselessly on the swing.

Both Josh and Miss Rouse are wimpering now. I have to do something, otherwise he's going to die.

"Miss Rouse, call an ambulance. Josh, squirt some stuff at them, and I'll get your dad!" I shout out.

My command makes Rouse reach for her phone and galvanises Josh into action: he grabs the aerosols from the bag and lights one. It flames out at the twins and, dazed by the spurting fire, they back off. I run towards Mercy.

"Béla, is that you?" she asks in alarm, not sure what she's looking at.

I can see that the combination of my balaclava and Mr Humphreys' suit have unnerved her.

I pull off the balaclava.

"Yes, it's me."

She looks at me in shock. "What are you doing?"

"You beat him, Mercy. Why don't you just leave it now?" I say calmly and then add in a low whisper so that no one can hear: "I will never speak to you again if you don't."

We both look at each other. A strange moment of understanding occurs between us. I don't have to say anything more. Mercy steps away from Hicky and turns to the Bentley twins.

"We're done here," she says with a sweep of her hand. "And give back his wallet and stuff."

"But…" the twins protest.

"Give it back!"

Reluctantly, the twins throw Hicky's wallet and keys back onto the ground underneath the swing. Hicky's so out of it, he don't notice anything, but Josh does. He rushes up and collects his father's things.

The GMF walk away. Mercy doesn't look at me as she leaves the playground. But nor does she call me a treacherous cunt, or similar.

Hicky falls off the swing and lies on the floor moaning and crying.

Josh kneels by his dad.

"Dad, Dad, I'm sorry!" (A bit late for that now!)

Kylie comes over and crouches beside Hicky, too.

I would like to stay but I realise that I'm done here.

11.50pm

"Dad, Dad, are you awake? Can you hear me?"

"He seems to have blacked out."

"Dad, can you hear me?"

I open my eyes.

"Jack, Jack, are you there?" I ask. In the darkness, I can make out concerned faces examining me like I might be ill or something.

There's no sign of Jack. I feel he's completely gone.

"It's all right. I've called an ambulance," a female voice says. I recognise it now, it's Kylie's.

I sit up and find Josh's arm around me. "Dad, can you hear me now?"

I rub my eyes and look down at my chest. It's still bleeding. "Jack, where's Jack?"

"He's not here now," Josh says.

"Here, drink this," Kylie says. She crouches down beside me. I take the bottle she offers me and sip at some water. It tastes good.

*　*　*

The next thing I know, I'm in an ambulance, hurtling through the city. Josh is sitting beside me, holding my hand.

"It's all right, Dad. It's going to be all right."

*　*　*

I'm in another bed now, a hospital bed. I'm being wheeled through a corridor with bright lights overhead.

Helen is running beside me. She is holding my hand. "Martin, Martin, can you hear me?"

I feel very, very weak but I manage to articulate the words: "I can."

"You've had a heart attack. You're going to go into surgery in a few minutes. I will be there with you. We're going to be all right, Martin. It's going to be fine."

I try my best to squeeze her hand. "I saw Jack, Helen, I saw him finally again."

"Try your best to conserve your energy, Martin."

"Helen, you brought back my memory stick."

"Your memory stick?"

"Don't you remember? This morning. I dropped it in the car, and you brought it back. The memory stick that had my presentation on."

Helen gulps as one of her tears drops onto my face. "I did, Martin. I did."

11.50pm

"Béla, Béla, I need you to get my ciggies first thing tomorrow morning," Ma barks at me the moment I come in the door.

It's like nothing has happened at all today. She doesn't even comment on the suit I'm wearing. She'll get around to it eventually, but she clearly feels I don't deserve that kind of attention right now.

She's sitting at the table in a cloud of smoke in front of her Rolodex of contacts with her glasses on.

I can tell she's mad at me by the way she's flicking through the contacts as if looking for a missing person: the good obedient comrade that used to be me. My great-uncle is sitting in the armchair in his silk dressing gown, smiling at me, covered by a blanket.

"What are you smiling at?" I say to the Count.

"Ah, yes, that is a question indeed! Perhaps the frivolity of youth! Perhaps, my memory of seeing *Bluebeard's Castle* for the first time at the Budapest Opera House. My mind is so fluid these days that I seem to think so many things. I was also smiling at the thought of the delicious cup of cocoa that my Béla is going to make for me!"

His talk of Bluebeard's castle reminds me of something he said earlier on in the day. Feeling his and my mother's eyes upon me, I go to the cupboard underneath the sink and get a screwdriver. I head for Ma's room.

"What are you doing?" Ma asks.

"I need to check something out," I say.

"What?"

I open the door to her room. She gets up from the table and follows me.

"Béla, I didn't say you could go there!"

"I won't go any further if you tell me what you do during the day!"

"Béla, I work in human resources."

I ignore her and go in. After switching on the light, I take the screwdriver and slide its narrow head in between

339

the doors of the cupboard.

"Are you going to tell me?" I ask Ma.

"Béla, get out of my room this instant!"

I wrench open the door with the screwdriver, and see what's really there.

Instead of finding the S&M gear I expected, I discover a mop and a cleaner's uniform.

Ma sees that I see it but doesn't say anything.

I leave her room and sit down at the kitchen table.

"You're a cleaner!" I say.

"That *is* human resources."

"It's cleaning, Ma."

There's silence. I look at my great-uncle who is doing his best not to smile sarcastically.

Then Ma tries to recover her dignity.

"Béla, did you hear what I said? First thing, you're down Shitty Street Post Office, getting my fags. At seven sharp. Do you understand?"

I should nod but I don't. Something in my neck freezes.

The Count peers up at me, pulling his blanket more tightly over his chest.

"Are you not going to ask what happened to me tonight? Not going to ask about why I'm wearing this suit?" I ask.

"Well, why are you? I'm sure that you've been up to no good so perhaps it's better not to hear," Ma replies. "Now the main thing is tomorrow and your chores. The first of which is getting my fags from the post office."

"I'll think about it," I say.

Ma takes off her glasses and puffs out some smoke.

"Excuse me, but did you say you'll think about it?"

She gets up and stands over me, angling her cigarette at my head like she might stab it onto my face. I don't flinch.

"Yes, I'll think about it," I say, fixing my stare at her black eyes.

"And I am surmising that you'll think about making my cocoa as well," the Count adds.

"He won't! He will make your cocoa right now!"

"I surmise he will think about things while making my cocoa," the Count comments.

I think about this proposition: should I make the Count's cocoa or not?

My life would be much easier if I made it.

Ma edges away from her interrogation position, puffs on the very last bit of her cigarette and then crushes it in the ashtray. "What's going on, Béla?"

"Ma, you can get your own cigarettes tomorrow. I'm not getting them. I don't think you should smoke them. They're not good for you, or me, or him!" I shout out, my finger trembling as I point at the Count, who, as if on cue, begins to cough.

Ma peers down at her Rolodex, not looking me in the face. Then she lights another cigarette.

"I said cigarettes are not good for you," I say.

"I heard you the first time," she replies.

For a moment, I think about going up to her and grabbing the cigarette out of her hand and crushing it in the ashtray, but I don't move. I glance at the Count, who is looking at me for the first time ever with

341

something like respect.

I step towards my mother with my hands outstretched and say: "Ma, that's the last cigarette you're going to smoke in this flat, do you understand that? From now on, you're going to think about me and the Count and smoke outside. You're going to think about yourself. Do you understand that?"

Ma doesn't look at me – and doesn't answer. She sucks very, very deeply on her cigarette and then blows the smoke luxuriously out in the air.

My fingers curl over her cigarette packet. Even though the cardboard is hard to crush, I savour the sensation of it scrunching in my palm.

Acknowledgements

Thanks to Jane Harris, Lawrence Norfolk, Tom Shankland, Ceri Swanpoel, Erica Wagner, Michael Whyte and everyone involved at Short Books for giving this novel so much time and consideration. Any faults or shortcomings are entirely mine.

The settings, events and characters in the book are entirely fictional and purely products of my imagination.

Nothing in this book bears any relation to things I've encountered in my own life.

Francis Gilbert has taught in a variety of comprehensive schools in London and currently teaches English part-time. His previous books have included I'm A Teacher, Get Me Out of Here (Short Books, 2004), Teacher on the Run (Short Books, 2005), Yob Nation (2006) and Working the System (Short Books, 2009). He lives in east London with his wife and son.